A CASE OF HABEAS CORPUS

Mr. James Winter was elderly; tall and thin and dry-as-dust in manner, as though he had spent years in perfecting his role of family solicitor; but with a certain humor in his disposition that was apt to gleam through even in his most serious moments. If compelled to sum him up in one word, however, that word must infallibly be "respectable"; the last man in the world, one would have said, to come violently to his death in the midst of his everyday avocations. Yet there he sat at his desk near the window, with a knife in his back; and most certainly he was dead.

SARA WOODS' MYSTERIES FEATURING ANTONY MAITLAND

"The best of barrister dramas."
ALA Booklist

Avon Books are available at special quantity discounts for bulk purchases for sales promotions, premiums, fund raising or educational use. Special books, or book excerpts, can also be created to fit specific needs.

For details write or telephone the office of the Director of Special Markets, Avon Books, Dept. FP, 1790 Broadway, New York, New York 10019, 212-399-1357.

BLOODY INSTRUCTIONS

Sara Woods

AVON
PUBLISHERS OF BARD, CAMELOT, DISCUS AND FLARE BOOKS

AVON BOOKS
A division of
The Hearst Corporation
1790 Broadway
New York, New York 10019

Copyright © 1962 by Sara Woods
Published by arrangement with the author
Library of Congress Catalog Card Number: 62-20130
ISBN: 0-380-69858-7

First Avon Printing, February 1986

AVON TRADEMARK REG. U. S. PAT. OFF. AND IN
OTHER COUNTRIES, MARCA REGISTRADA, HECHO EN
U. S. A.

Printed in the U. S. A.

WFH 10 9 8 7 6 5 4 3 2 1

> *But in these cases*
> *We still have judgment here, that we but teach*
> *Bloody instructions, which, being taught, return*
> *To plague th' inventor. This even-handed justice*
> *Commends th' ingredience of our poison'd chalice*
> *To our own lips.*

MACBETH, ACT I, Scene VII

BLOODY INSTRUCTIONS

CHAPTER 1

SIR NICHOLAS HARDING was in chambers, and his study of
the brief before him had reached what his nephew was accustomed to call the "snarling" stage. This meant that the
never-noisy activity around him was still further muted: old
Mr. Mallory went about his business in a subdued bustle—a
performance perfected over many years, and carefully calculated to be both unostentatious and impressive; even the
most junior of the clerks was awed into silence, conversing
when necessary in a penetrating whisper, to the extreme ag-
gravation of all who heard him; the very typewriters (aged
machines, with wide, heavy carriages) seemed to racket
along, if not by any stretch of imagination quietly, at least
with a sort of respect; and Antony Maitland, uncomfortably
placed near the heart of the storm, eyed the topmost of the
papers on his desk with every appearance of diligence, and
let his thoughts dwell lovingly on the Long Vacation.

This was unwise, even though the case he was concerned
with was not due to come up for several days. Sir Nicholas
was never inclined to suffer fools—or folly—gladly, and in
this instance the argument was unusually complicated. Antony sighed, and ran a hand through already disordered hair.
It seemed to him that the activities of Mr. Isaacs were dubi-
ous at best, and he for one would view with little concern
their temporary curtailment. However . . .

At this point in his musings there was an explosion in the
next room, an inarticulate roar which he had no difficulty in
recognizing as a summons. This was surprising—Uncle
Nick was evidently running ahead of schedule. Antony rose
and crossed to the open door that connected his bare little

room with Sir Nicholas's more elegant sanctum. His uncle peered at him in a distraught way from behind a barricade of books and documents. "What the devil," he demanded aggressively, "does Prentiss think he's doing?"

Antony took his life in his hands and went over to the desk. "Charles is on holiday. What's up?"

"Holiday!" said Sir Nicholas. "Holiday! Why? Do *I* take holidays in the middle of the Trinity Term?"

"No," said Antony. "You don't!" And his tone was regretful.

"He knows perfectly well that no one else in that benighted firm can prepare a brief properly." Sir Nicholas was not yet ready to be diverted from his grievance. "Look at this! 'Enclosure 3: affidavit by Edward Cliff, bookseller.' " He brought his hand down with a bang upon the desk, and three long blue documents slithered to the floor. "But do they enclose it? Oh, no! That would be too simple, too straightforward. That would make matters much too easy. They send me—the addlepated nincompoops—a rambling and irrelevant statement by a domestic servant, marked clearly 'Settled out of Court.' Winter's past it, that's what it is."

"Well, he doesn't bother much with the court stuff these days," said Antony, unimpressed. "I expect you can get on just as well without it—there's sure to be a summary somewhere or other."

This rash remark had the expected effect of diverting Sir Nicholas's exasperation. He spoke at length, and with some heat, on the wrongheadedness of the younger generation, who did not realize the immense and overriding importance of verifying their references. This gave Antony a chance to sort through the papers on and under the desk, and—discovering that the affidavit in question was indeed missing—to fetch his hat. His uncle broke off in midsentence and inquired suspiciously, "Where are you going?"

"Round to Winter's. With your permission, sir."

"Well, don't be all day about it. Take this with you." Sir Nicholas threw the offending statement at him violently. "Might be of interest to the Sunday press. None to me. And tell Winter to fire his junior clerk."

"Good lord, why?"

But learned counsel had already resumed his reading. He said vaguely, "Error in office. Case of doubt—always fire junior." He looked up again to glare at his nephew. "Well, don't keep me talking all day, boy. I'm busy."

Antony withdrew.

The offices of Messrs. Ling, Curtis, Winter and Winter (that old-established firm of solicitors, of which the last-named Winter was now the senior partner) were situated in Bread Court, not more than five minutes' walk from the Inner Temple. Antony was glad to get out into the June sunshine, and had no intention of hurrying. He had at least an hour, he considered, before Sir Nicholas would have finished arranging his case; this happy consummation would be the signal for another and more terrible outburst, in the course of which the barrister would anathematize his client, the solicitors responsible for sending him the brief, the judge, and the opposing counsel, not to mention any members of his own staff who were unwary enough to be at hand. At this stage, also, he would demand his nephew's presence, and Antony had every intention of being back before this happened. If his uncle then wished to verify his references, that would be time enough. Meanwhile, Miss Harris would most likely give him some tea, and any gossip there might be. And, undeniably, he had been finding the affairs of Mr. Isaacs rather heavy going.

Miss Harris was thin, and efficient, and forty-five. She received him with pleasure, and some surprise.

"Why, Mr. Maitland! You know Mr. Prentiss is away, don't you?"

"Hallo, Miss Harris. Yes, I knew that. I've come on business."

"Well, I hope you have time for a cup of tea. Now let me see—I know just how you like it. No, it isn't any trouble. Mr. Winter has got his, and there's plenty in the pot."

Antony settled himself as comfortably as he could on a tall stool. He had known this dusty room nearly all his life, and in all that time there had been little change in it other than the small annual variation of the calendar that hung above the telephone. Even Miss Harris, whom he could imagine in no other setting, had changed imperceptibly; merely growing a little thinner, a little more efficient and nearer forty-five with every passing year. Sometimes she was typing at the low desk under the window, sometimes she was writing at the tall desk along the left-hand wall, sometimes she was wrestling with the enormous, outmoded copying press, and sometimes she had disappeared headfirst into the stationery cupboard beside the door; but always there had been the same pleased, flustered welcome, the same orderly disorder. He stirred his tea, and grinned. "I believe this is the same cake you fed me on twenty years ago, when Dad used to leave me to plague you while he talked business. It even has the same fruit in—three sultanas and half a cherry. What do you suppose would happen if you took Mr. Winter a doughnut instead, or a cream bun?"

Miss Harris smiled. "I really *cannot* think." She had, as usual, the air of one who enjoyed small pleasantries without in the least understanding them.

"Probably an earthquake. Or bears might emerge from the strongroom and devour you—would that be a suitable penalty for outraging tradition? Which reminds me, you'd better take care anyway. Uncle Nick has put a most comprehensive curse on this office, I don't think even you escaped. So I should think anything might happen."

"Oh, dear, what is it this time?"

"A missing affidavit. The Connor brief. And this in its place." Antony handed over the offending statement. "It's all right, there's no hurry."

Miss Harris had risen, but subsided again. "That boy!" she said, grimly.

"Young Willett?"

"No, Dowling. Really, I despair of him! And his finals only a few months off."

"Now, I'd have said if ever a chap was cut out for the law—"

"Oh, he *tries*," said Miss Harris, scornfully.

"I see. That's dreadful, of course."

Miss Harris gave him a look. Antony picked up his plate, and bit into the slab of cake. He said, with his mouth full, "You know, now I look at you, you're not your usual calm self. Anything up?"

"Nothing really wrong, Mr. Maitland. But you're quite right, it has been a busy afternoon; upsetting, too . . . in a way."

Antony drank tea, and grunted encouragingly.

"It began straight after lunch with Mr. Stanley's will. There was really no excuse, the draft was clearly marked urgent, but Miss Bell said she'd never even seen it."

"I don't suppose she had. Uncle Nick says it's a rule of the firm that anything marked urgent shall be put in the safe for at least three weeks, to mature."

"Sir Nicholas will have his joke." Miss Harris's tone was indulgent. Then she looked rather sharply at her companion, and went on in a tone of surprise. "In fact, it was found at the back of the safe, I don't know how it happened; so there was poor Miss Bell typing as fast as she could while Willett waited about to take each sheet to Mr. Winter as soon as it was ready. Luckily, it was fairly simple, but by the time it was signed and witnessed we were all feeling in rather a fuss. Then the next man stayed a very long time, I can't imagine what Mr. Winter was thinking of; and that held up a completion, and after that there was Mr. Dowling." Miss Harris stopped, rather abruptly, and Antony looked inquiring.

"Dennis? Oh, you mean his father?"

"Yes, Mr. Joseph Dowling. Our Mr. Dowling was out, but it was Mr. Winter he wanted." She paused again, looking rather at a loss, and then said firmly, "It was very awkward, just when I wanted to make the tea," and looked severely at Antony, as though daring him to question this statement. Then she got up in a determined way. "I'll find you Mr. Cliff's affidavit, I expect it's in the main office."

Before she reached the door it was opened by a small, dark girl in a green overall many sizes too large for her. "Oh, Miss Harris, do you know if anyone is with Mr. Winter? I want to take in his letters."

"He's alone now. Bring out his cup when you come, will you?"

They went together into the corridor. Antony finished his tea, put the saucer neatly onto his plate, and carried both across to the tray. As he put them down a door banged in the passage, and somebody screamed.

In spite of being at the far side of the room from the door, Antony reached the corridor some seconds before the occupants of the general office opposite. He turned right, past the strongroom, whose grille was slightly ajar, and was aware as he went that the light was on and somebody inside—in his haste a mere, unidentified shadow. The door of Mr. Winter's room, beyond, was open, and a shaft of dusty sunlight slanted across the passage. He collided with Miss Bell in the doorway, was aware of a commotion of footsteps behind him, pushed by her gently but without ceremony, and was brought up short halfway across the room as the full realization of what had happened hit him.

Mr. James Winter was elderly; tall and thin and dry-as-dust in manner, as though he had spent years in perfecting his role of family solicitor; but with a certain humor in his disposition that was apt to gleam through even in his most serious moments. If compelled to sum him up in one word, however, that word must infallibly be "respectable"; the last man in the world, one would have said, to come violently to his death in the midst of his everyday avocations. Yet there he sat at his desk near the window, with a knife in his back; and most certainly he was dead.

CHAPTER 2

JENNY MAITLAND inspected the contents of the oven gloomily, and sighed as she shut the door again. It certainly smelled good, but what was the use of that if it were to be burnt out of all recognition before Antony got home.

They had been married during the war, and Jenny had moved into the previously bachelor establishment, gone on with her ambulance driving, and found Sir Nicholas Harding's company both sane and comforting while Antony was away. When the war was over they managed, in face of many difficulties, to turn the two top floors of the Kempenfeldt Square house into a separate dwelling; most of the work they had done themselves, and Jenny sometimes felt she could still smell the paint. But the arrangement had worked well, the only objector being Gibbs, Sir Nicholas's butler—an old man of deceptively saintly appearance—who was outraged at having to move downstairs into one of the "best" bedrooms, and had not even yet become reconciled to this dreadful fate. Mrs. Stokes, who was cook and housekeeper, was only too glad to have her part of the house reduced to manageable proportions.

As Jenny came out of the kitchen she heard footsteps on the stairs, and ran to open the door. To her surprise it was not her husband who stood on the landing.

"Come in, Uncle Nick. You are late tonight. Will Antony be long?"

"Not very, I think." Sir Nicholas followed her into the big, comfortable living room, and looked at her with affection. "I thought I'd better let you know. He went round to

7

Winter's office for some papers, and while he was there they found Winter dead, so of course he was delayed."

"What a horrid thing to happen. Poor Mr. Winter, he was such a dear. Had he a bad heart?"

"It wasn't that. Something rather nasty, Jenny. He was murdered."

"I don't understand." Jenny looked at him blankly. "Who—?"

"I don't know any more than the bare fact yet. Antony will be in any moment, he'll tell us what he knows." He took her arm and shook her gently. "Don't look so stricken, child. It's unpleasant, of course, but no direct concern of ours."

"No, it isn't, is it?" Jenny sounded doubtful.

"Prentiss is away, and everything was in a muddle, so somebody had to cope. And after the police had gone Antony rang up to say he was taking Miss Harris home. It'll be a great loss to her, as well as a shock. She has worked there a very long time."

"I'm glad he was there then, to help her. You'd better stay to supper, Uncle Nick, then you can talk at leisure."

This time it was Sir Nicholas who looked alarmed. "But I didn't tell them downstairs—" Jenny laughed at him.

"It's quite all right, you know you always have something cold on Tuesday when Mrs. Stokes is out." She went to the door. "Get yourself a drink. I'll run down and tell Gibbs you're staying."

"Good girl," said Sir Nicholas with gratitude, and turned to look for the sherry.

As Jenny crossed the hall again after completing her errand she heard the scrape of a key, the front door opened, and Antony came in. He was looking tired, she thought, but he brightened when he saw her. "Hallo, love. Supper ready?"

"Burnt to a cinder, most likely," said Jenny, severely.

"Has Uncle Nick got in? Have you seen him?"

"Yes, he told me. How beastly, Antony."

"It is, rather. I'd better have a word with him before we go up, or he'll probably burst with suppressed curiosity."

"That's all right, he's upstairs. I just came down to tell Gibbs he was having supper with us."

"Good." They went together up the broad staircase, and Antony put his left arm round her shoulders. "I might tell you, I'm famished. There's something about a crisis that seems to stimulate my appetite."

The living room was large and cheerful with evening sunshine. It was perhaps, at first glance, an odd room, the furnishings representing as they did a selection from unwanted items at Jenny's home in the country and what was left over when Sir Nicholas had finished compressing his household into two floors. Dinner was laid on a round mahogany table near one of the long windows, and, as there were only three for the meal, the china and cutlery did not present too varied an array. For the rest, they had a walnut writing desk, a handsome oak bookcase, two venerable wing chairs with faded covers, which retained, none the less, a certain air of elegance, and an unbelievably ugly Victorian sofa, with nothing to recommend it except an unexpected comfort. This last had been introduced, in the face of Jenny's bitter opposition, by a considerable display of guile on Sir Nicholas's part; but somehow, though the years had passed and there were now without question more things in the shops to choose from, the room remained unaltered.

They found Sir Nicholas rummaging in a handsome, bow-fronted tallboy for another table mat. Antony said, in passing, "Aren't you glad I married a wife who'd be kind to my aged relatives?" and went away to remove a reasonable quantity of the day's grime.

They ate, for the most part, in silence, being each preoccupied by what had happened and at the same time vaguely unwilling to embark on a discussion. Finally, however, they were grouped with their coffee cups around the empty hearth, and Sir Nicholas said, "Well, Antony?" and sat back expectantly.

Jenny, too, looked across at her husband. She thought again that he looked tired, and moved stiffly, as though his arm were paining him. That was one of the things she had arranged with herself never to mention: the circumstances of his wartime injuries were not a pleasant memory for either of them. If Jenny had been looking at a stranger, she would have seen a tall young man, with dark hair and a thin, intelligent face; as it was she saw only that the events of the day had been unpleasant and that he disliked the thought of the tale he had to tell. She sat back in her chair and turned her head so that she could see Sir Nicholas. He was stretched out at ease in a corner of the sofa, but his eyes were alert and his tone had been demanding.

"Miss Bell found him," said Antony. "That was about fifteen minutes after I got there. She let out a yell that brought us all running. He'd been stabbed in the back, the doctor said he'd died as near instantly as makes no matter. I knew that, anyway. When we worked it out afterwards, Miss Harris took in his tea at eight minutes past four, and nobody saw him after that till Miss Bell went in at exactly half-past. He hadn't drunk the tea."

"And they don't know who did it?"

"Not unless they were being extremely cagey. I ask you, Uncle Nick, can you think of any earthly reason for anyone to kill Mr. Winter? I can't help feeling—"

"Your feelings can wait." Sir Nicholas had produced a cigar, and he waved it in a questioning way at Jenny, but without taking his eyes from his nephew's face. "Confine yourself to the facts," he demanded.

Antony grimaced. "Very well, sir. Fact number one, the other door of the office was open—the one that leads onto the private staircase down to the street. Miss Harris says it's usually kept latched. Fact number two—" He hesitated, and Sir Nicholas again interrupted him.

"Start with the people in the office. You were there, and Miss Harris—"

"Charles is away, I told you that, didn't I? That's funny, though. Miss Meadows says she saw him about four o'clock, but no one else did, and there's no sign in his office that he'd been there—"

"Is this your idea of a connected narrative?" his uncle inquired. "Marshal your facts, boy, marshal your facts!"

"Well!" said Antony. He did not sound repentant, and there was something very like amusement in his voice as he went on. "Miss Harris and I were having tea in her room"— Sir Nicholas growled something under his breath—"then she went across to the main office to find that affidavit, and at the same time Miss Bell went down the corridor to Mr. Winter's room with his letters to sign. A moment later we heard her call out. I got there first; he was obviously dead, so in Charles's absence I thought I'd better organize a bit. Miss Harris looked after Miss Bell; Miss Meadows phoned for the police; young Willett went along to the front door to lock it and stand by to let them in; and Dennis Dowling and I went out by the private entrance, without seeing anything more suspicious than the open door, and secured the door at the bottom. The other door at the top, giving on to the corridor, was already latched."

This time it was Jenny who interrupted. "Uncle Nick asked you to explain the people," she protested. "I know Miss Harris, of course."

"Miss Bell and Miss Meadows are the typists. Miss Bell is little and dark, looks rather shy; she's the senior of the two. Miss Meadows is more glamorous, a willowy female, very fair. Dennis—I must have told you about Dennis."

"No," said Jenny firmly. "Not that I remember."

"He's Joe Dowling's son. You can't say you haven't heard of him."

"That's different. But I didn't know he had a son; and if I had known I'd have expected him to be an actor too."

"Not Dennis. His spiritual home is definitely in a deed box." Antony was talking more readily now, and his earlier reluctance seemed to have left him. "He's been with them since just after the war, very near his finals now. The only other employee is young Willett; he runs errands and generally makes himself useful. All clear?"

"I think so," said Jenny. Sir Nicholas cleared his throat, but made no comment. Antony continued:

"To go back to what happened, the first person to arrive was a solitary policeman; then the doctor; then the divisional fellows, quite a crowd of them. We were all herded into the general office, and the police installed themselves in Miss Harris's room after some preliminary skirmishing; Charles's room might have been more suitable, but it's a mile away down the passage . . . that's another thing, Jenny, I'd better tell you the layout."

"Go on with your story," said Sir Nicholas. "I'll draw her a plan while you talk." Jenny moved across to the sofa so that she could look over his shoulder.

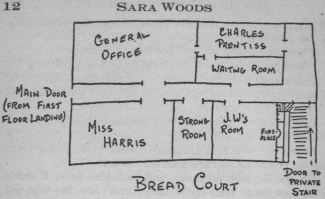

SIR NICHOLAS HARDING'S PLAN

"It was some time, of course, before they got round to talking to us. Miss Bell made some more tea; she had recovered by this time, and Miss Harris was the one who showed she was upset. I got the feeling she'd have liked to talk to me, but of course there wasn't any chance for a private conference.

"The others were all talking nineteen to the dozen. That's when I heard that Miss Meadows thought she had seen Charles, around four o'clock. She and Dennis had just come in, they'd been round at one of the building societies preparing an abstract. When the others said they hadn't seen him she decided she wasn't sure, it was just a glimpse of his back going round the corner, which made everything just about as clear as mud. Nobody could think of any reason for his having come in while he was supposed to be on holiday; and if he had come to fetch something it was difficult to see why he shouldn't at least have said 'hello' to somebody, even if he was in a tearing hurry."

Sir Nicholas finished his sketch, and handed it to Jenny. He looked across at his nephew. "Do these interesting speculations lead to any conclusion, or are they merely included in the interests of general mystification?"

Antony grinned. "The latter, I'm afraid. No conclusion, anyway. I thought you wanted all the details."

"What I want are facts. Though I'm beginning to despair of ever getting them."

"Anything to oblige. Bare bones, and no embroidery. But

if you're hoping we shall finish off with a nice clear-cut solution you're in for a disappointment.''

"So you already told us. But I can't believe—"

"Well, I don't know what the police are thinking—" ("Can't you even guess?" Sir Nicholas interpolated; and Antony looked at him reproachfully) "—but I'm pretty sure they're still at the baffled stage."

Jenny had been frowning over the plan, and taking no notice of this exchange. "Well, it's all quite clear to me," she announced. "Someone lurked in Charles's room until it was safe to come out and kill poor Mr. Winter."

"Someone with no sense, and incredible luck, if that's what happened. Your crystal ball doesn't also say who did it, I suppose?"

"I don't know *that,*" said Jenny. "Aren't you going to tell us?"

Antony raised his eyes despairingly heavenward.

Sir Nicholas said, "Your husband has just informed us, child, at some length, that he doubts if even the police—"

"I don't like mysteries." Jenny's tone was plaintive.

Antony said lightly, "They'll soon clear it up."

"But meanwhile," said Sir Nicholas, "I'm still waiting for the facts. If any."

"What a depressing thing a single-track mind is, to be sure. You can thank Miss Harris that I've as much information as I have. The inspector asked for her first, very sensibly, and she (bless her) went all feminine, and insisted on having me to hold her hand. Frazer—that's the D.D.I., a ramrod of a chap with a bleak eye—wasn't any too pleased, but there wasn't really much he could do about it, so he gave in with a fairly good grace.

"First he asked her all the usual things—personal particulars, I mean—then the things I've already told you, about the people in the office, and so on." Antony leaned back in his chair, wriggled a little to a more comfortable position, and fixed his mind firmly on the interview he was describing. "Then he got on to the events of the afternoon . . ."

Miss Harris was flustered to a most unusual, most unaccountable degree. In fact, she dithered. "I lunch at twelve, Mr. Frazer, so I was back in the office just before one o'clock. Miss Bell and Willett got back at the same time, or a very little later, and Mr. Dowling and Miss Meadows went out to get theirs. They had to go on to examine some deeds, and make an Abstract of Title, and I heard Mr. Dowling arrange to meet her outside the Building Society at two o'clock.

"Mr. Winter had gone out to his lunch some time before; I think you will find he went to Babcock's, just round the corner, as that was his habit when he had no engagement. He came in at five to two, and rang for me immediately. He had an appointment for two o'clock, Mr. Stanley Prentiss was coming to sign his will; and then we found that the draft was in the safe, and no engrossment made!" Miss Harris paused, apparently still overwhelmed by this dreadful blunder, and Inspector Frazer took the opportunity to interrupt her.

"This client now—"

"Not exactly a *client*, Inspector. Mr. Stanley is our Mr. Prentiss's cousin. I'll get you a list of all the callers, and their addresses from the ledger, before you go." Miss Harris was shaken, but still retained some remnant of her customary efficiency.

"That will be excellent. And now, what time did Mr. Stanley Prentiss arrive?"

"A little late," said Miss Harris, with disapproval. "Five or six minutes past, I should think. By then, of course, we had found the draft—Mr. Prentiss had initialed it, I can't think how it came to be mislaid after that—and Miss Bell was typing as fast as she could. It took a little time, of course, and Mr. Stanley left just before the half-hour.

"There was already somebody in the waiting room, a Mr. Green, whose appointment was for two-thirty. Mr. Winter said he would see him straightaway, so Willett went to show him in. Miss Bell was busy by then with the letters Mr. Winter had dictated this morning, so—"

"Just a moment. Can you tell me a little more about Mr.—Green, did you say?"

"I wrote to him earlier in the month, asking him to make an appointment, and he phoned the next day to do so. I remember he seemed surprised that Mr. Winter should want to see him; I think it was something to do with renewing his lease—he is the tenant of some property belonging to a trust Mr. Winter administers. He hadn't been here before, and I asked Mr. Winter if he would speak to him on the telephone, but he was most insistent that there must be an interview.''

"And Mr. Green agreed?"

"He grumbled a bit, and then said he supposed he'd better come in, and we arranged it for two-thirty today. As it happened, he was a little early—and then he stayed till a quarter past three, with Mrs. Carey, who is an old and most valued client, and Mr. Armstrong from Hill's, waiting to complete a conveyance! However, he did go at last, and fortunately Mrs. Carey is a most reasonable lady, their business was soon finished, in fact Mr. Armstrong left just after the half-hour. But Mrs. Carey stayed on chatting with Mr. Winter until ten to four.''

"That's very clear, thank you, Miss Harris. Now, was Mrs. Carey the last person from outside the office to see Mr. Winter this afternoon?"

For the first time she hesitated. She looked down at her hands, she looked across at Antony, she looked fixedly out of the window as though inspiration might be found on the wall of the office across the narrow court. What she was boggling at, apparently, was the mention of Joseph Dowling; her motive was obscure, but it was unlikely to help matters, Antony considered, if she tried to stall.

He said, helpfully, "Was that when Mr. Dowling came, Miss Harris? I think you said he had been in," and earned a reproachful look from the lady, and one equally cold from her interrogator.

"I said 'outside the office,' Mr. Maitland. I *meant* other than the staff."

"It is Mr. Dennis Dowling who is articled here, Mr. Frazer. Mr. Joseph Dowling is his father, and it was he who came to see Mr. Winter." Miss Harris had evidently decided that frankness would serve her purpose at least as well as any other course. Antony sat back and awaited developments.

"Joseph Dowling? The actor?"

Miss Harris nodded.

"What time did he come?"

"A little after half-past three. He had no appointment, but

Mr. Winter saw him when Mrs. Carey left. He stayed until seven minutes past four—I noticed the time exactly, because I was waiting to take in Mr. Winter's tea. I went in as soon as Mr. Dowling had gone, and—and that was the last time I saw him.''

"I see. And Mr. Dowling's business here—what would that be?''

"I imagine,'' Miss Harris said with some evidence of distaste, "that it would concern his divorce.''

"Mr. Winter was acting for him?''

"Oh, no, Mrs. Dowling is our client. It was most unusual for Mr. Winter to act in such a matter, Mr. Frazer''—Antony was rapidly coming to the conclusion that Miss Harris had a genius for nonessentials—''but Mrs. Dowling was the daughter of an old friend of his, and when he was convinced—but this is hardly our concern.''

"I should like, however, to hear a little more about the matter. Was it not a little strange that Mr. Dowling should call on his wife's solicitor while a divorce was pending?''

"It was—unusual, perhaps.''

"I take it that your client was filing suit.''

"That is so.''

"And was Mr. Dowling agreeable to her action?''

"No, Mr. Frazer, he was not.''

"Then he could hardly have visited Mr. Winter in—shall we say—a friendly spirit? Was their talk amicable?''

"I was not present. I know nothing of what happened.''

"Nothing, Miss Harris?'' He was pressing her now, but Antony felt this was only to be expected, in view of her obvious reluctance. "Did Mr. Winter say nothing to you afterwards?''

"I took his tea, he was writing at his desk. He thanked me for it, but he seemed preoccupied.''

"Well, now, Miss Harris, I must ask you whether you noticed anything strange in his manner recently.''

"That is a very difficult question, but I think there was nothing. He was a little put out when Mr. Stanley was here, and inclined to blame our Mr. Prentiss for the mistake that had been made; otherwise . . . I think there was nothing out of the ordinary.''

"Very well.'' The Inspector made the simple phrase

sound ominous. "I take it you have an intimate knowledge of Mr. Winter's concerns."

"Of his business concerns, that is true."

"Please think carefully, Miss Harris. Have you any idea, however farfetched it may seem to you, that might help us find the motive?"

"Nothing, nothing." She was now in no doubt about her answer. "I know of no one who could have wished to harm him."

"Very well, " he said again. "I shall be glad if you will stay until I have seen your colleagues, Miss Harris. Then I must ask you to place all the firm's books in the strongroom, which we will seal, until we have opportunity to examine them tomorrow. The partner should be present—Mr. Charles Prentiss, isn't it? Can you get in touch with him?"

Miss Harris got up. "He is on holiday, but I believe not away from home. I will telephone him now. And—there is Mr. Winter's cousin, who kept house for him. And his niece—"

"Thank you, they have already been advised."

She went to the door, and Antony started to follow. The inspector stopped him. "Just a moment, Mr. Maitland. There are a few questions—"

"That part wasn't very interesting," said Antony. "Miss Harris had said I arrived at twelve minutes past four, which was more than I could have told him, and—apart from the information about the private door—that was all I had to say. It was just as I was leaving that you rang up, Uncle Nick."

"Well," said Sir Nicholas, with an apologetic look at Jenny, "I couldn't know—"

Jenny looked from one to the other of them, and began to laugh. "Never mind, Uncle Nick. I can guess."

"Oh, no, you can't." Antony seemed to have talked himself out of his former depression. "All I could hear was a sort of Donald Duck noise; Frazer did his best to explain when he found out who was speaking (have you ever met him in court, Uncle Nick?); he also said it was impossible for me to leave immediately. When he finally hung up he turned to me with the first lightening of expression I had so far seen in him, and remarked, 'You have an affectionate relative, Mr. Maitland. He informed me, among other things, that he had no interest in your whereabouts; I could keep you as long as I liked, arrest you, hang you with his good will. What *he* wanted was the affidavit you had set out hours ago to fetch!' ''

Jenny was outraged. ''Really, Uncle Nick, that's too bad!''

''What intrigues me,'' said Antony thoughtfully, ''is the phrase 'among other things.' What else did you say, Uncle Nick?''

''At the moment I cannot recall. No doubt it will come back to me later—under the influence of suitable inspiration.''

''No doubt,'' Antony agreed.

''But all this is beside the point.'' Sir Nicholas was complacent. ''The point was, I got my affidavit; Frazer sent a man round with it.''

''That's most unfair.'' Jenny was still indignant.

''You'd better forgive him, love. After all, I have come back to tell the tale.''

''Which you have not yet completed. If you would concentrate for a moment—''

''But that's the lot,'' protested Antony, with intent to annoy.

''Nonsense! First, about this Dowling business. I gather you asked Miss Harris for further information when you got her alone?''

''Of course I did. She was definitely cagey, but I think I got it straightened out pretty well at last. I needn't tell you about Joseph, he's been news for a long time now. His wife's a bit younger than he is, in her early forties. She married young, according to Miss Harris, and Dennis arrived about a year later. No other offspring. Of course, I don't know how they've been going along all these years, but a few months back Mrs. Dowling came to see Mr. Winter in great distress, wanting his help in getting a divorce. He'd known her all her life, and did his best to dissuade her; next thing was, she'd removed herself to a hotel. That convinced him she was serious about it, and he agreed (still unwillingly) to act for her. Her story was her husband had neglected her for years, and now was involved in an affair with his current leading lady.''

"No!" said Jenny. "Not Lady Macbeth?" Sir Nicholas began to laugh. (Grossman's production of *Macbeth*, then running at the Cornmarket Theatre, was notable for its two main actors: Joseph Dowling, for many years acknowledged as a leading Shakespearian; and a new Lady Macbeth, Margaret Hamilton, a young Scottish actress, who portrayed that unamiable character with unexpected power and venom. The papers made something of a mystery of her, as she was fresh to London, and rarely appeared in public.)

"That's right. Joseph, however, denies it with some vigor. His relations with the lady have been purely business. In fact he's very annoyed about the whole matter, and has been saying so, very loud and clear, ever since he realized what was in the wind. His visit today wasn't the first, by any means, but apparently the most violent. I gather he blames Mr. Winter for persuading his wife into the steps she has taken, and said so at the top of his voice. You can imagine it was impossible to avoid knowing what was going on—nobody ever complained they couldn't hear him at the back of the gallery.''

"And is this supposed to constitute a motive?" inquired Sir Nicholas.

"Well, Miss Harris, perhaps naturally, felt a certain delicacy about mentioning it to the police—because of Dennis, I mean. Of course, as I pointed out to her, she'd just made Inspector Frazer bristle with suspicion; and he was bound to get the full story out of someone the moment he started to make inquiries. And you know, sir, I've heard far more unlikely motives adduced in court.''

"True enough.''

"Well, what I want to know," said Jenny, "is—what does poor Dennis think about it?"

"It's a pretty rotten situation for him. Naturally, nobody has talked to him about it. He's still living with his father, but in the circumstances there's not much else he could do. Miss Harris says he's been depressed, which is not really surprising; I gathered an impression that he's been sitting, unhappily and uneasily, on the fence.''

"Then the position, so far, is this." Sir Nicholas paused a

moment to consider. "Mr. Winter spent a normal afternoon, interviewing clients, the last of whom, Mr. Joseph Dowling—" ("In the interests of accuracy, not a client," Antony interrupted. His uncle gave him a look) "—Joseph Dowling left at seven minutes past four. Miss Harris went in a minute later with a cup of tea—did she change her story of how he seemed when you saw her alone? Was he agitated by the interview?"

"No. She still used the word preoccupied."

"After that nobody saw him, as far as has been ascertained, until Miss Bell found him dead at 4:30. Now, of the people in the office, who could have gone to his room during that time?"

"Miss Bell was typing, she didn't leave the general office. Nor did Willett. Miss Meadows went into Charles's room, by the door that connects directly with it; she still couldn't quite believe she hadn't seen him. She says she only went just inside the door, looked around, and came straight out. The others were busy, and just didn't notice. It might have been as she said, or she might have been gone several minutes. Certainly, she hadn't got very far with the abstract she'd been taking down during the afternoon (I had a look at her typewriter), but I don't know how quick a worker she is—anyway, they're a bit tricky to set out, I should think. Dennis was in the strongroom, looking for something. I saw him there—at least, I saw somebody was there—as I ran past after Miss Bell screamed. That's all, isn't it? Though, to round off matters nicely, I should add there was nothing to stop Miss Harris doing it, as she is the last person known to have seen him alive."

"Nonsense," said Jenny, firmly. "Miss Harris wouldn't—"

"I didn't say she would, my love. I said she *could* have done it." Jenny made a face at him.

Sir Nicholas, however, approved. "Very proper. Now, access from the outside, as I understand it, would be most easily effected through the door that leads from Mr. Winter's room onto the private staircase to the street—either by the person concerned being admitted by Winter himself, or through the door being left unlatched. Any other possibilities?"

"I think we can rule out access through the main door and along the passage. When Dennis and Miss Meadows came in at about four o'clock, the performance was in full swing, and fully audible. Dennis went straight to the strongroom, I imagine to keep out of the way; he'd be bound to feel awkward. But he had the door open, he saw his father leave, he saw Miss Harris go in and out, he saw Miss Bell go along with the letters. I think he's probably right when he says he'd have seen anyone who went past."

"The only other possibility, then, would have been someone in Prentiss's room—lurking was your word, wasn't it, Jenny?—but that is ruled out by Miss Meadows's inspection."

"Well, they could have been in the waiting room, or even round the corner of the passage, out of sight. I think that is very unlikely, though. Even a person who knew the office and its routine very well couldn't possibly have been sure nobody would see them. No, it seems fairly safe to concentrate on someone who came by the private door—as an alternative to the staff, of course—particularly as it was open when it should have been closed."

"If somebody in the office did it, they could have opened it as a blind," said Jenny. She consulted the plan. "If Miss Meadows went into Charles's room she could have easily come through the waiting room, and straight across the corridor to Mr. Winter's door, without being seen by anyone."

"And why should a respectable shorthand-typist murder her employer?" (Jenny, he thought, seemed to have got over her professed dislike of mysteries.)

"You didn't say she was respectable," Jenny pointed out. "You said she was glamorous."

"Well, she'd still need a motive."

"I don't see why. Uncle Nick always says that motive doesn't matter!"

"I've said it shouldn't matter, in court, if juries had a true appreciation of the laws of evidence. That's rather different. You had some comments to make about the door, Antony, hadn't you?"

"Willett is certain it was locked at two o'clock. It's an ordinary Yale latch, by the way. While they were looking for the draft will Mr. Winter told him to see if it was in the cupboard in his room; the two doors are side by side, and the knobs are near together. He got hold of the wrong one, because he was looking over his shoulder at Mr. Winter while he tried it; when it wouldn't open, he found it was the outside door he was rattling. That's one point. The other is that Miss Harris swears that never, under any circumstances, would Mr. Winter have let anybody in by that door. He did, occasionally, let himself in and out that way, but it was a rule of his that nobody else should use it. It's reasonable, really; he wouldn't want the chance of someone butting in at the wrong moment. And you know what he was like if he once got an idea in his head.''

"I know." Sir Nicholas spoke reflectively. "In that case—"

"It's pretty obvious what line the police will take."

"Precisely."

This infuriated Jenny. "What do you mean? It isn't obvious at all."

"You pointed out one possible theory yourself, that he was killed by one of the staff. Failing that, they'll concentrate on the people he saw that afternoon, any of whom might be considered to have had the opportunity of fixing the latch so that they could return at will."

"Oh," said Jenny. "Yes, I see."

"Then that gives us some more names for our list. Let me see—"

Antony counted them off on his fingers. "Stan Prentiss, re last will and testament—and I can't imagine what he has to leave; Green, business about lease that took an unexpectedly long time; Mrs. Carey, completing the sale of some property, and at the same time (or part of it) a clerk from Hill's whose name is Armstrong, who attended with the cash presumably, and the deed signed by the purchaser. After them, the aforementioned Joseph Dowling."

"Considered as suspects, not very promising," said his uncle. "The next thing is, the weapon."

"It looked from what I could see to be very like a commando dagger, I'd guess at a broad, two-edged blade. As for the blow, there's no telling, it was a neat bit of work, but whether by good luck or good judgment—you pays your money and you takes your choice!''

"Hm," said Sir Nicholas. "No doubt the police will be wiser when they've been through the firm's papers."

"You'd expect the motive to be apparent, certainly." He grinned reflectively, and added, "Poor old Charles, how he'll hate it," with no great excess of sympathy in his tone.

Jenny said, "Poor Charles," and sighed a little.

Sir Nicholas looked from one to the other with sudden amusement, but did not voice his thoughts. And presently the talk drifted to other things.

CHAPTER 3

THE NEXT DAY was a hot one, too hot for June. Antony sweated it out in court, and returned to chambers for a conference with a sad little man whose melancholy refrain "to think they think I'd do a thing like that!" wasn't really helpful. He left for home at last in a reflective frame of mind.

Since reading the paper that morning he had given no thought to James Winter's death. Now he wondered how the police were making out, and whether Charles Prentiss had managed to keep his generally unruly temper in the face of official questioning. But his own small part in the affair was temporarily in the back of his mind when he let himself into the house in Kempenfeldt Square. To his dismay Gibbs was in the hall. He looked to be in one of his more disagreeable moods, and was obviously waiting to deliver a message.

"A person called to see you, Mr. Maitland . . . a person from Scotland Yard, as I understood him," said Gibbs with obvious distaste. "I informed him you had not yet returned, and he asked that you would telephone him to make an appointment. Detective-Inspector Sykes . . . I have the number written down." His manner conveyed to a nicety that he disapproved of Antony (which was true), and that he would regard him as personally responsible for any scandal arising from the household's association with the police. Antony went upstairs halfway between amusement and irritation.

That, however, was not destined to be the end of the evening's activities. He got upstairs to find Jenny hovering. She said, without preamble, "Charles rang up. I promised you'd meet him at nine o'clock."

Antony said, "Oh, hell!"

"Wasn't that right, darling? He seemed dreadfully upset. He said he'd *got* to talk to you."

"Yes, of course it was right. I was only cursing at the idea of going out again, Did he say anything else?"

"No, just that. I asked him to come here, of course, but he didn't seem to think it would be a good idea."

"Where have I to meet him?"

"At Marble Arch. He said near the entrance to the underground—he said you'd know."

"All right. Will you talk to Scotland Yard for me, while I bathe? Detective-Inspector Sykes . . . tell him I'm tied up pretty well tomorrow, but if the evening would suit him—"

Time was getting on, and the bath had to be a very hurried affair. Nor was there time to linger over supper, and Antony was feeling distinctly ruffled and nearly as hot as ever by the time he reached Marble Arch.

Charles Prentiss was a sandy-haired, youngish man, in general aspect not unlike a badly groomed Airedale terrier. When Antony first observed him, however, he was prowling up and down outside the entrance to the tube station, to the inconvenience of passers-by, and wearing the look of an animal less domestic and a good deal more dangerous. Antony caught him up, and spoke over his shoulder, and he turned with something like a snarl.

"Got here at last, have you? I thought you were never coming."

Antony, already irritated by the disruption of his evening, very nearly replied in kind. He remembered in time, however, that the other might be regarded as having some excuse for a display of temper, and answered mildly, "Three minutes late. Not so bad, really," and was glad of his moderation when he looked more closely at his friend. Charles was never a particularly even-tempered individual, but now he had a look of strain about him that explained, and even excused in part, his present lack of cordiality.

His tone was a little less sullen when he replied, "Well, anyway—what I want is a drink." He looked about him vaguely, as though expecting some oasis to materialize within a few feet of him.

Antony took his arm. "What you want is a quiet stroll in

the park, where nobody can overhear us. You said you wanted to talk."

"So I do, but . . . oh, very well!" This was said with very bad grace, but Antony was already piloting him towards a suitable crossing place. By the time they reached the park they had come near to annihilation on no more than three occasions, upon which he congratulated himself. Charles was shortsighted, and in any case too preoccupied this evening to take much note of obstacles. He allowed himself to be steered in a direction that promised comparative privacy, when Antony at last relaxed his grip, slowed his pace, and said, "Now, then," encouragingly.

Charles took a deep breath, and grinned suddenly. "Sorry to be surly. It's been a hell of a day."

"That's all right. I didn't expect to find you singing and dancing, and strewing roses out of your hat. What can I do?"

"Well, I'd like your advice, I suppose."

Which being translated, Antony reflected, means he wants someone to talk to. "You've seen the police? How much do you know of what's happening?"

"I saw the divisional chap, Frazer, yesterday. He wanted information, and wasn't giving anything away."

"I thought perhaps you might have got some idea—"

"No ideas at all. In fact, I hoped *you'd* be able to tell *me*—"

Prentiss hesitated, casting a sidelong, appraising glance at his companion, before he said abruptly, "They think I did it."

"Do they, indeed? That's quick work. And—did you?"

"Don't be a fool, Antony. Why should I murder J.W.?"

"Suppose you tell me."

"But—but—"

"It's quite reasonable. You say the police think you've committed murder; if you're right, they also think they know why."

"Oh—well! It's pretty much of a mess, isn't it?"

"There I agree with you."

"Girls have no sense." He paused to disentangle himself from a dachshund that had run to them across the grass, its lead trailing; but he did so in a preoccupied way, and with no show of impatience. "If Eve had a grain of sense she'd never have started that business about seeing me in the office yesterday."

"Eve being—?"

"Our Miss Meadows. A nice girl, mind you, but no tact."

"She was, however, very certain that she saw you."

"Of course she saw me!"

"Did she now?" Antony sounded meditative.

"I'd better tell you what happened." Charles did not seem to find the necessity pleasant. "I was a bit bothered about taking a holiday. Winter was getting on, and he didn't seem to be able to keep track of things any more. Well, it isn't done to check up on your senior partner, but there were some papers I simply had to see, so I thought the best thing would be to go in quietly, by the private stairs, and have a look at them." Again Antony noticed the appraising look his companion gave him.

"Wouldn't it have been simpler to have gone in openly—to fetch a book, or a pipe, or something?"

"Simpler, yes. But I couldn't think of any errand that would plausibly give me half an hour or so, alone. The strongbox in question was in my room when I left, so I took a chance it hadn't been moved, and sure enough, it was still there."

"Just a minute. What time did you get to the office?"

"About half-past three, I should think. A bit earlier, perhaps."

Antony was annoyed by this vagueness, and allowed the fact to show. "Haven't you given any thought to the matter? Accuracy may be important . . . or hadn't that occurred to you?"

"Of course I've thought about it! What the hell do you think I've been doing ever since Miss Harris rang up yesterday evening? I just didn't notice the time. Why should I?"

"Never mind. By the way, did you leave the door at the top of the stairs unlatched? The one to the corridor I mean, of course."

"No, I didn't!"

"All right. Go on."

"I found what I wanted, and spent some time looking it

over. I was just going out the way I came when Eve Meadows and young Dowling came in at the main door. I waited
until they had gone into the general office, and then left.
When Miss Harris phoned I felt a bit awkward about
admitting I'd been in on the quiet like that, and as I'd seen
nothing I didn't think it would matter. I heard Joe Dowling
carrying on, of course, but so did the others, I expect.''

"My good idiot, the very fact that you saw nothing might
matter.''

Prentiss scowled. "Well, I didn't think—''

"Obviously," said Antony.

"It's all very well for you, young Maitland," retorted
Charles with some heat. "You might not sound quite so
clever if you were involved.''

"Perhaps not," said Antony, pacifically. "Anyway, you
told the police—?''

"They were waiting for me at the office this morning—
Frazer and Sykes, he's the C.I.D. chap. I told them I'd been
walking on Wimbledon Common. Then we spent hours
going through J.W.'s affairs. It wasn't till much later I heard
that Eve had seen me.''

"Well, that takes care of opportunity. What about
motive—I asked you about that before?''

"I had no motive. . . of course I hadn't.''

"Put it another way, then: can you think of anything the
police might construe as one?''

"No I can't!''

"Then I think you're wrong about their suspecting you.
Sykes may have a good idea you are lying about where you
were, in which case he'll very naturally do his best to get at
the truth. Confess your sins, and you'll have nothing more
to worry about.''

"That's easily said.''

"And fairly easily done. Seriously, Charles—''

"Oh, very well. I'll think it over.''

"Meanwhile, go on with your story. I gather you were
overrun with policemen all day. What transpired?''

"They poked about, and asked questions. I couldn't tell
them anything.''

"No ideas at all . . . even off the record?''

"No.''

"No trouble at the office?"

"Only the Dowling business. That's made things pretty awkward, but no trouble among the staff, if that's what you mean."

"Then what about Dowling? Could he have done it?"

"Not if he's sane. But who's to know?" Charles was speaking abruptly, but suddenly he changed his tactics and began to talk more freely. "What happened was that about three months ago Mrs. Dowling was in to see J.W. I met her in the corridor, and she looked as if she'd been crying. Next thing was Joe, in a temper. I happened to be in Winter's room when he came, and he asked me to stay. Joe was very high and mighty: loving wife had left him, snake in the grass, all J.W.'s fault. That sort of thing. Poor old boy was pretty shaken. He became very stiff and correct, you know his way—pointed out the impropriety of Joe's behavior in making personal contact with his wife's solicitor—got rid of him as quick as he could. That didn't stop him coming back, though. I think Winter had some idea it made things easier for Dennis if he didn't refuse to see him. Can't say I see it myself."

"From the sound of things, nothing would make things much better for Dennis at the moment. However—what about Mr. Winter's other visitors that afternoon?"

Charles was puzzled. "The police asked me that. Can't see why they should be specially involved."

"It seems to me," remarked Antony coldly, "that your brain has ceased to function altogether. Tell me about them, anyway. Why was the draft of your cousin's will mislaid? Who was the mysterious Mr. Green, whose ostensibly simple business could not be transacted in the course of a half-hour interview, and who was so reluctant to come to Bread Court in the first place? And is Mrs. Carey the sort of woman to carry a dagger in her garter?"

Prentiss laughed; an unmirthful sound, rather more like a bark. "Lord, no! Mrs. Carey, I mean. She's a most respectable old body, with a respectable income, and a comfortable home in a respectable suburb. I don't know anything about her affairs really, J.W. always dealt with them. The business on Tuesday was quite straightforward—completion of a conveyance. As for Armstrong—he's Thomas Hill's clerk, who attended for the purchaser—I know him, of course, and I expect Winter did, too. He comes in to swear sometimes, their office is just across the court. But there was no personal contact, I'm as sure as can be about that.''

''Then . . . the others?''

''What did you . . . oh, yes, Stan. Well, the draft being mislaid was just one of those things. I'm sure I gave it to Eve to type, but I expect she's equally certain I didn't. Anyway, what the hell?''

''What, indeed?''

''You know Stan, don't you?'' Charles asked, with one of his sudden changes of mood.

''I haven't seen him since before the war. He'd have been about fifteen, I expect. He went into the army, didn't he?'' Antony's tone was reserved, and the other man looked at him curiously.

''You're not getting ideas into your head, are you? I mean, he had no reason—''

''I never,'' said Antony, virtuously but untruthfully, ''theorize ahead of my data.''

''Don't you though?''

''But I was wondering,'' he went on more honestly, ''why the will? I always thought of him as pretty impecunious.''

''Oh, that was his grandmother . . . my great-aunt Amelia. She died not long since. Up to then he was just rubbing along, some sort of fancy-goods business, not very exciting. J.W. thought it a pretty poor show as a matter of fact . . . not dignified, *you* know.''

''But grandmother didn't agree?''

Charles grinned, momentarily diverted. ''Well, as to that, he'd not have touched a penny if she hadn't died intestate. J.W. just echoed her opinion; he didn't know Stan all that well, but Aunt Amelia was an old client. She was one of those severe old girls, rigid ideas. But there you are, she didn't get down to making a will, so he scooped the packet.''

''And very nice, too.''

''Have you met his wife? Rather a weird female, name of Muriel. They live in Putney.''

''I don't remember her.'' They went on in silence for sev-

eral minutes. Charles's stream of information seemed to
have run dry, and after a while Antony prompted him,
"That leaves the chap called Green."

"Look here, what is all this? The Inquisition?"

"You wanted to see me, you know. I suppose you wanted
to talk."

"Well—yes. But what has all this got to do with what
happened to J.W.?"

"I haven't the faintest idea." Antony sounded bland.
"Do you know why he was killed?"

"No. No, I don't. I've already told you—"

"Then how can you say what's relevant?"

"Well, I can't, I suppose. Anyway, I know nothing of
this Green. Only what Miss Harris told me. And as I hear
you escorted her home yesterday evening I imagine," added
Charles, not without malice, "you know as much as she
does."

"Yes, that's fair enough." Antony was amused. "I'm
sorry answering questions seems to affect you like a visit to
the dentist."

"Damn it all, I've been doing nothing else all day."

"Well, I shouldn't worry. Tell Sykes what you were
really doing, ten to one that'll be the last you'll hear of it."

"Make me look a bit of a fool, though."

"Does that matter so much? After all—"

"I know, I know. Don't rub it in. Look here, where have
we got to? I'll have to think about getting home." Charles
quickened his pace, all at once anxious to be gone.

"Don't worry, we aren't lost. You can get the tube at
Hyde Park Corner in a few minutes if we turn down here.
And don't rush so, there's a good chap. It's far too hot."

It had crossed Antony's mind that Jenny was most likely
with Sir Nicholas: a hostage to ensure that the older man's
curiosity was assuaged as soon as his nephew returned.
When he reached the square some twenty minutes later,
however, he saw there was a light upstairs in their living
room. But he was less tired now than he had been earlier in
the evening, and decided it would be an unnecessary cruelty
to leave his uncle without a word.

The study door was shut, and no murmur of voices came

to him as he let himself into the hall. He knocked lightly and went in. Sir Nicholas was sitting with legs outstretched to the empty grate, looking extremely comfortable and slightly somnolent. The room was fragrant with cigar smoke.

"Come in, Antony. Like a nightcap?"

"Thank you, sir, I don't think so." He crossed the room to take the other armchair. "I've been talking to Charles," he added, after a moment.

"So Jenny told me."

"He's in a stew, all right."

"She told me that, too."

"She didn't know the half of it. Lord knows what he's really been up to. He *was* in the office on Tuesday afternoon, as Eve Meadows said. Like an ass he denied it, and said he was out walking. He says Mr. Winter was losing his grip, and he went in to check up on something and then felt awkward about admitting it."

"Could that be true?" Sir Nicholas wondered.

"It could, I suppose. I don't believe it, though."

"And what did Charles want you to do about it?"

"He *said* he wanted my advice, so I gave it to him. I doubt if he'll take it. He just wanted to let off steam; but that was queer, really. The moment I started taking an interest and asking a few questions, he sheered off and was quite eager to be rid of me."

"You can't have been very tactful."

"As a matter of fact, I was oozing tact at every pore. He couldn't expect me not to be interested! Especially as he started off by telling me that the police thought he had murdered Mr. Winter. I pointed out what he must have known himself, that the police wouldn't have come to that conclusion unless they thought he had some sort of motive. He swore there was none, but I'm pretty sure that was what was making him so jittery."

"Do you think he did it?"

"No, I don't." said Antony promptly. "But that's not reason, Uncle Nick, just a hunch." He got up. "I suppose we've got to get down to that Isaacs business tomorrow," he added reluctantly. "What time do you want me?"

"As soon as you're through in court."

"Right, sir, I'll see you then."

CHAPTER 4

CONTRARY to his expectations, the case Antony was just then concerned with was not over by lunchtime, but dragged on well into the afternoon; so that it was nearly five o'clock when he got back to chambers, to be greeted by old Mr. Mallory, the clerk, with a subtle air of reproach and the information that Sir Nicholas had been inquiring where he was. Antony opened his brief case, removed a bar of chocolate and an apple, and handed what remained to the clerk.

"I have marked the brief. Thank goodness that's over. And a satisfactory verdict."

"Ah, yes, sir. Sir Nicholas anticipated such an outcome. If I may remind you, Mr. Maitland—"

Antony muttered something under his breath, and made for the door. Mr. Mallory coughed. "I nearly forgot to mention it, a Mr. Sykes rang up. He asked if you would telephone him—when you were at liberty," he added firmly. Antony grinned.

"First things first," he agreed, and opened the door of his uncle's room.

Sir Nicholas's desk was as usual covered with a disorder of papers. He looked at the newcomer blankly at first, then said without preamble, "Isaacs will be in court on Monday. Got that argument clear?"

Antony put down the bar of chocolate on the mantelpiece, polished the apple on his sleeve, and took a bite. "I had, I think—but that was two days ago."

"That means you didn't understand it," said his uncle, accusingly. "Pull up a chair and we'll go through it now."

He stopped, and added in a pained tone, "Must you make that crunching noise?"

"I had no tea. And it was thirsty work listening to old Alwyn—I thought he'd talk forever. Er—in case you're interested—we got the verdict."

"So I should hope." ("Crushed again," murmured Antony.) "Now, the first thing to remember is that we shall be before Lovejoy, so you'll have to make your points with a sledgehammer, or he won't take them in. And if *he* doesn't put our case to the jury, we haven't a hope."

"I think I've got our side of it fairly clear. But what about this Carmichael woman? As far as I can see she has changed her story twice already—"

The telephone rang. Sir Nicholas eyed it with suspicious mildness, picked up the receiver and spoke gently. "Yes . . . yes . . . no, he can't . . . what's that, Sykes? . . . hold on a minute." He turned to his nephew. "Detective-Inspector Sykes wanting you." Antony stretched out a hand for the telephone. "All right, all right, but don't waste my time gossiping."

The voice at the other end of the line was pleasant, and no more than comfortably broad-spoken. "I'm sorry to disturb you, Mr. Maitland, but could you possibly put our appointment forward?"

"Well, I . . . yes, I suppose so."

"Something came up to change my plans. I have to go to North London, so if I can take you in on the way—"

"When, Inspector?"

"About five minutes from now, Mr. Maitland?"

Antony laughed. "Have it your own way," he said. He replaced the receiver, and assumed, for his uncle's benefit, a look of apology.

"Come hell or high water," said Sir Nicholas gently, "I want at least three hours of your valuable time tomorrow. Understand?" Antony got up quietly, and retrieved his chocolate. "Heavens, boy, eating again?"

"It is essential," said Antony, with his mouth full, "that I maintain my strength. Shall I take him to my room, sir? I don't suppose—"

"If we must be overrun by policemen," said Sir Nicholas disagreeably, "it may as well be here."

When the detective arrived he waved aside his apologies with the same deceptive air of calm. "Not at all, Inspector. We *were* discussing a most complex case . . . merely our bread and butter . . . any time will do for that."

Sykes was a square-built man, with a pleasant face rather heavy about the jowl. Perhaps his tweeds might have been considered more suitable for country wear, but they were of good material, and well cut. He maintained his calm in the face of Sir Nicholas's greeting, and, though his words were apologetic, his manner held no trace of embarrassment. His voice was less broad than it had sounded on the telephone, but there was no mistaking his north-country origin.

"Well, now, Mr. Maitland, you'll be in no doubt why I want to see you. It's this bad business of Mr. Winter. The district people passed it on to us, and, though I've got Inspector Frazer's report, of course, I still want to go through the statements myself. Perhaps you can tell me, in a little more detail—"

Antony obliged. He confined himself to facts, which didn't take long. When he had finished Sykes put down the notebook in which he seemed to have been checking off points, and looked up and smiled. "Yes, that's all very pretty, very correct. Just what you know 'of your own knowledge,' no more, no less. I'd like a little more, if you don't mind. You should be unprejudiced. I'm sure you are reasonably observant. And you know much more about the people concerned than I do."

"It was the best butter," said Antony, with an answering grin.

"Now, sir!"

"Well, what can I tell you?"

"You had known Mr. Winter a long time, I gather."

"Long as I remember. He was my father's solicitor. But I only knew him as an outsider, Inspector. Miss Harris must know much more about his private affairs than I do."

"Oh, yes, I dare say she does."

"But still you want my version? Well, there was another partner when first I used to go to Bread Court—old Mr. Curtis. He'd been junior partner of Mr. Winter's father and still handled the court work; that's why Mr. Winter dealt with the domestic stuff. Sometime or other there had been a Mr.

Ling, too. I don't know anything about him, except that he was dead. Charles Prentiss—you'll have met him, I expect—was articled with them, and qualified about a year before the war. The idea was that he should take over gradually from Mr. Curtis, who was about a hundred and eighty by that time, but he wanted to join up, and soon after that Mr. Curtis died, and they had a managing clerk to handle things until Charles was demobbed. I've forgotten his name—something like Wotherspoon—and he comes in sometimes to chat with Miss Harris, because I've bumped into him there. A long, thin chap, with a stoop, and a moustache I'm sure he must be proud of."

"Mr. Murphy," said Sykes, nodding, and exchanged a sedate smile with Sir Nicholas.

"Well, I don't suppose he's relevant. But you've been through J.W.'s papers, Inspector. Didn't they help you?"

"Not to any marked extent." Sykes sounded guarded.

"You must forgive my nephew, Inspector," Sir Nicholas put in, his voice amused. "Remember, we make our living to a great extent by asking questions."

Antony frowned at his uncle, and went on. "About his private affairs, I really know nothing. Except what you must know yourself by this time—even if the knowledge isn't helpful. He lived at Purley, with an elderly cousin to keep house for him. I think there's a niece, too, who is there off and on, but I've never met her."

"And what about his relations with his partner, and the staff?"

"Nothing out of the ordinary. He liked to grumble gently about young people. Things weren't what they were in Curtis's time, that sort of thing, but he and Charles got on well enough. As for the others, I think he was a good man to work for; certainly I never heard any worse complaints than the usual 'can't get in to get the letters signed'; or 'started dictating at five o'clock'; or 'asked for the file *immediately,* seemed to think I'd have it up my sleeve.' You know the sort of thing."

Sykes nodded. "And what was the reaction of all these people when they realized what had happened?"

"Surprise, first of all. Then . . . well, shock I suppose."

"And did you share their emotions?"

"Yes, I did. Afterwards I had time to be sorry—he was a nice old boy, you know—and then I think what I felt most was anger."

"And what about before the discovery? Was everything normal at the office when you got there?"

"I only saw Miss Harris, you know. She'd had a hectic afternoon, and was a bit ruffled, nothing out of the ordinary."

"You may spare your efforts to be tactful," remarked Sykes drily. "I know all about Joseph Dowling's visit, and the scene he made."

"Well, if you've seen him on the stage you won't be a bit surprised at his going about breathing fire. After all, it must be second nature to him."

" 'appen it is," said Sykes, with some disapproval manifest in his tone. "Do you know Mr. Dowling?"

"Only by sight, and I've seen him act, of course. I know his son fairly well, but I don't know anything *about* him. He's anything but an extrovert."

"Well, have you any ideas about the matter yourself? I'm thinking mainly of the question of motive."

"No," said Antony. "No, I haven't." He reflected with annoyance that he was telling the simple truth, and making it sound like a lie. His talk with Charles must have been more on his mind than he had supposed; but the trend of Sykes's questions didn't suggest that his mind was running that way.

The detective glanced at him sharply, and said, "Hm," in a noncommittal sort of way. Antony had sufficient self-control to resist the temptation to elaborate, and after a moment's expectant silence the other man went on, "Perhaps, after all, it would be rather too much to expect—" and paused again, dangling the unfinished sentence enticingly before his companion. When this gambit also proved ineffective, he sat back in his chair again and changed the subject.

"Miss Meadows, now. Do you know aught of her?"

Antony grinned, thinking of Jenny's strictures. "She is beautiful, and blonde—which you must have seen for yourself. She has been with them about a year, and I have an idea that Dennis is rather taken with her. And that's all I know of her."

Sykes said "Hm" again, but this time in a ruminative, rather than an interrogatory way. "Your friend Mr. Prentiss—do you think he was at his office yesterday afternoon?"

"Surely you know the answer to that, Inspector. Haven't you asked him?"

The detective looked at him with an air of disappointment. "That's a singularly guileless remark, Mr. Maitland. I have seen Mr. Prentiss. According to his own statement, he was not in town yesterday."

"Well, then!"

"It seems Miss Meadows was at first quite sure she had seen him."

"That was certainly her first impression."

"I see," said Sykes. And left it at that. He got out the notes he had made of Antony's original statement, read them through slowly, and on being assured their content was correct stowed away the book again and got to his feet. "I must thank you for your patience, Sir Nicholas. I won't intrude on your time any further."

Sir Nicholas smiled at him, and got up in his turn. He said, "I'm afraid you've wasted your time, Inspector. I suppose your work is rather like ours. A great deal of effort, and very little return." Something in his tone made his nephew glance at him sharply, but he was now exchanging conventional farewells with the detective and ignored the look.

Antony went to the door. Sykes followed him into the hall, but stopped as soon as the door was shut and said: "Perhaps you would have preferred to see me alone, Mr. Maitland?"

"No, Inspector."

"I thought you might have been more open with me—"

"I've told you all I know."

"Have you, indeed?" said Sykes, bluntly.

"My life is an open book, Inspector."

"That's as may be," said Sykes, somewhat sourly, "but that wasn't what I asked you." He paused only a moment, having by now reached the conclusion that his companion was not the man to be lured into unwary speech by the bait of silence. "My coat's behind you, Mr. Maitland. May I get it?"

"Antony turned, and reached up his left hand to take it from the peg. Sykes asked idly, "Are you ambidextrous, Mr. Maitland?"

The younger man looked round at him, and smiled. "Don't tell me you're looking for a left-handed murderer? That would be too literary by half."

"No, it was merely idle curiosity, I'm afraid."

"Well, here's your coat."

It was a light raincoat, and Sykes took it over his arm. He said, in the most placid of tones, as though they were discussing the weather, or the political situation in Bulgaria, "You've given me a very straightforward statement, Mr. Maitland. Only I had hoped . . . you knowing the people, and all—"

"I would if I could, but I can't," said Antony. "And I cannot conceive," he added, with a faint, unconscious mimicry of his uncle's manner, "that my opinions would be of any benefit to you at all."

CHAPTER 5

NINE O'CLOCK the following morning found Inspector Sykes already at his desk. He was writing his report, a task which he always found distasteful, and he broke off with relief when one of his colleagues came into the room they shared, his arms full of files, so that he had to push the door ajar with his shoulder and then let it slam behind him. He grinned apologetically at Sykes.

"Sorry for the row." He dropped the files on to his desk. "This is what comes of consulting records. They've given me about a week's work here. What a life!"

"You look like being busy." He picked up his pen, reflected a moment, and then laid it down again. "Well, you've properly broken up my train of thought, Wakefield. May as well fill a pipe."

Wakefield was spreading out the files, and muttering to himself like a litany. "Fair hair and complexion . . . five foot ten . . . one hundred and seventy pounds . . . old raincoat . . ."

"That doesn't sound very informative."

"That'd be too much to hope for. I only hope it's accurate. Most likely I ought to be looking for a dwarf in evening dress with dark hair and a beard."

"Anything interesting?"

"Post office job. All the rage now, aren't they?"

"By the way, Wakefield,"—Sykes rammed down the last shreds of tobacco, and reached for the matches. "Did you ever come across a chap called Maitland in court? He's Harding's nephew, and in his chambers."

Wakefield looked up, his interest caught from his work.

"Yes, I have, as a matter of fact," he said. "And I encountered him once during the war. Why?"

"He's one of the witnesses in that Bread Court murder. I went to see him yesterday afternoon, and got the idea there's more to him than meets the eye."

His colleague grinned. "I should say so. You know he was in Intelligence during the war?" Sykes nodded. "Well, I met him up in Harrogate . . . Raymond Foster, he called himself. Well, I didn't know then but what it might be his real name. And a proper turn he was, and no mistake."

"How was that?"

"A poet, he called himself; and he'd prove it, too, by spouting the stuff at you by the yard, if you didn't head him off in time. You know the kind of thing, all death and despair. According to the way he talked he was pulling strings to get a job in the M.O.I., and keep out of the army that way. And some very odd company he used to keep, no question about that. We kept an eye on him, as you can imagine." He paused, and smiled at his thoughts. "Then I saw him in action one night, and there was nothing languid or affected about him then, I can tell you. Spent the night in the cells, till we got it straightened out next morning, and you should have heard him playing off his airs for the D.D.I.—as good as a play, that was."

"Hm," said Sykes, reflectively. "You're sure it was the same chap?"

"Oh, yes, not a doubt. I saw him in court one day. Tuppence ha'penny affair—bag-snatching, or some such. Couldn't believe my eyes at first, but I recognized him when he got up to talk, for all he was acting as innocent as you please."

Sykes said, "Hm," again. And added, doubtfully, "Sounds a proper caution."

"What's he been up to now?"

"Nothing at all. He was present when Winter was found dead. Perfectly legitimate business in the office, everything quite in order."

"Well, then!"

"I said I was curious. Besides, Briggs thinks—"

"Has the super got his knife into him?"

"That's a highly improper suggestion, Mr. Wakefield," said Sykes, primly. "To do Briggs justice—"

"I know, I know. And you know what I mean."

"Aye, I do, at that. No, they've never met. But I got the impression Maitland knew something more than he told me. Something came up last night that suggests it's something pretty important. Briggs wants to know, he's got a hunch it might help his case."

"Can't say I blame him. He's got a case, has he?"

"The makings of one."

"Against Maitland?"

"Nothing like that. I said, I think he knows something; but as for killing Winter (which doesn't arise, actually) I'm pretty sure he couldn't have done it."

"An alibi? I thought you said he was there."

"So he was. No, I mean, he's physically incapable. There's something wrong with his right arm. It's not very obvious, but he never raises it very far, and I'm pretty sure he wouldn't have had the strength for the blow that killed Winter."

"Still," said Wakefield, with the air of one determined to make the best of what he has, "you think he was hiding something?"

"Yes, I do. And I expect he'll look me in the eye when I bring it up and say he forgot all about it. And that'll be that!"

"Well," said Wakefield, "I'll be interested to know what happens."

Sykes smiled, and picked up his pen. "For that matter," he remarked, "so shall I."

Mrs. Carey had already breakfasted and was writing at her desk in the window. The room caught the morning sun, but somehow, nowadays, it could never be too warm for her. Her bank statement was propped up before her against the old-fashioned inkwell, and her checkbook lay ready open to her hand. Such a pretty color the checks were, she reflected; *eau de nil* they used to call it. She would try to get some material that color to make a party frock for Betty. Taffetas, perhaps, or a really good satin. The child was just the age to enjoy nice clothes, and with her hair . . .

Meanwhile, there was the check for Paul. Now that the Station Road house was sold she could well afford to send him what he needed. Perhaps this time things would work out just as he planned. It wasn't as if she needed the income from the property, though Mr. Winter had looked so disapproving when she told him she wanted to sell, it had made her feel quite guilty. Poor Mr. Winter, it was strange to think he wouldn't be there to consult when she needed him. She spared a sigh from her busy, homely thoughts for her old friend; but lately she had found the idea of death had lost its strangeness, it had become the expected, the inevitable. Even the manner of his death had made small impression on her. It was all very shocking, she supposed, very shocking, and when she was young people would have looked askance at a visit from the police in what was still a most select neighborhood.

But now there was the check to make out, and a letter to write to Paul to make sure he realized that there was no difficulty about sending the money, no difficulty at all.

Stanley Prentiss was on a bus, crossing Waterloo Bridge. He had been lucky to get a seat, but it was on the sunny side and he was beginning to perspire. To his further discomfort he was by now certain that his breakfast had not agreed with him; his own fault, he had been late, and everything overdone and unappetizing. Sometimes he wished he hadn't encouraged Muriel to go on with her own career, but it had seemed a good idea at the time. Neither of them need work now, but money was money, and the shop would have to be nursed along until a purchaser appeared; just as he was doing with the business, but that would take even more time, he supposed.

The bus stopped again, and he craned forward to see round the driver's shoulder. Looked like another traffic jam. He was filled suddenly with impatience. These delays were maddening. And he had a pile of orders to catch up with, after having to attend the inquest yesterday, and then they hadn't needed him after all. Stood to reason they wouldn't. It was a pity about the old boy, of course (his mind made a perfunctory concession to convention), but it couldn't be helped now, and the police were only enjoying their own importance, wasting people's time.

They were moving again now, about time, too. The bus was like an oven. He mopped his forehead, conscious that he was not as fit as he had been a few years back. Putting on weight, too, ridiculous at thirty-six, that was what city life did for you. He'd be early tomorrow, make time to walk from Waterloo; perhaps if he did that regularly it would help.

John Proctor Armstrong was already at work. He was sorting Thomas Hill & Son's morning mail with practiced speed. There was sunshine on the pavement outside, but it would not reach the window until later in the morning. Meanwhile the room was cool, and surprisingly neat. Even some bundles of documents were dragooned into precarious order; the typist's outdoor things, including her bag and gloves, were banished to a cupboard; the office boy had not yet arrived.

That was something else for Mr. Armstrong to do, watch the clock and note the time. Three times late in one week! Not that Mr. Hill would notice. "A growing boy, Armstrong, needs his sleep." That was all very well, but it didn't get the work done, and the deliveries made at a reasonable hour. Much Mr. Hill cared about that. A clever man, of course, a good employer, he admitted that. But Not a Good Example. Get in about ten, he could, perhaps even later. Affable as you please, but no good complaining to him. And there was Mr. Winter, one of the old school he was, as far as you could tell about anyone and giving him the benefit of the doubt, murdered in his own office. Seemed a shame, a respectable gentleman like that, but there had been a reason for it, of course, only they hadn't found it yet.

Mr. Armstrong turned from the high desk with a little pile of papers in his hand. "These only want acknowledging, Miss Seymour. And here is the draft of the Walworth Conveyance, which has been approved. It should be engrossed without too much delay, if you please."

Arthur Green was still in bed. He had just turned over, muttering, as the sun reached his pillow. Then, finding that he was irrevocably awake, he rolled onto his back and blinked reproachfully at the ceiling. Might as well get up, he supposed, not that there was anything to hurry for, and he was very comfortable. There'd be nothing doing until tonight, unless Fred phoned in during the afternoon. He'd take it easy, fix up some toast and coffee, and then wander out for a decent lunch. There was nothing to worry about now, and a good bundle of cash coming in during the next day or two, to keep the wolf from the door.

Nothing to worry about, not even the lease, though that could have been awkward. The old boy had only been doing his job, and good luck to him, but he hadn't seen his way to meeting the situation, not at first. And this place was convenient, no denying that. However, everything had settled itself nicely, no need to bother about it any more. There'd be no trouble with the junior partner, no reason why there should be. He'd taken the trouble to look him over yesterday, full of his own worries, poor chap, or looked it.

And the inquest safely over . . . adjourned, of course, but that needn't concern him. Good thing there was Jennings in the background, an alibi was always a useful thing to have. He rubbed his chin with his hand, and let his mind play idly with the important question, whether he should shave before or after he had breakfasted.

Joseph Dowling, too, had just awakened; awakened to the uncomfortable consciousness, which now greeted him each morning, that he was alone. It was not a consideration, however, to which he allowed any indulgence. He mumbled thanks to his servant, who had just deposited a tray on the bedside table, then roused himself sufficiently to say, "No, leave the curtain," and to hoist himself onto one elbow. One of the side mirrors of the old-fashioned dressing table was pushed back, so that he found himself glaring at his reflection. He opened his mouth to call his valet back, but the door was already closed, and he had not the energy for a bellow. He consoled himself with tea, and ignored the tiresome fellow in the mirror.

Last night had been a bad show, literally. He was allowing himself to get rattled. True, the police were unpleasantly persistent, but they'd get tired of asking questions after a while, and things would settle down again. As for Meg, she was a little wretch; he had given her her chance, and now she told him to his face that he was playing badly.

Unfortunately for his righteous indignation, it happened to be true!

He set down the empty cup, and again caught his own eye in the mirror. This time he allowed his reflection a little grudging amiability. It was, after all, an old friend. It was not Macbeth who looked back at him across the room, but a man of middle age, with an undeniably egg-shaped head and not very much hair. Macbeth was a man at his full energy, brisk, as befitted a soldier, and rough, as befitted a barbarian, a Scot. (Joseph Dowling had been somewhat soured by Meg Hamilton's forthright words.) Tonight London should see Macbeth played as he should be played; as only Joseph Dowling could play him! His grandiloquence collapsed with the reflection: it's wonderful what make-up can do. Not to mention false hair.

CHAPTER 6

As IT HAPPENED, Sir Nicholas had a conference that morning. Antony, breakfasting late, was torn between the obvious need to have another look at the Isaacs brief, and a strong inclination towards visiting the office in Bread Court. "It isn't that I'm unduly inquisitive," he explained carefully, "but I am beginning to feel I should like to know what Charles is up to."

"I can understand your being curious," said Jenny (answering with wifely tactlessness the spirit rather than the letter of what he said). "I am myself. But I do wish," she added, "it wasn't people we knew." There seemed to be no answer to this, and her husband did not attempt one.

It was midmorning before he reached the office, and he found Miss Harris sitting at the high desk and staring fixedly at a ledger. But her pen was lying idle beside her, and she greeted his arrival with evident relief.

"Uncle Nick sent his sympathy, Miss Harris, and wants to know how you are now."

"How kind of Sir Nicholas; and of you to come, Mr. Maitland." Antony realized he hadn't needed any excuse. "I'm quite all right, you know, only I still can't believe it really happened."

"That's understandable. I feel rather that way myself. Are you busy, am I interrupting?"

"Oh, no! Everything is in such confusion, but there isn't much any of us can do unless Mr. Prentiss is here. And he just phoned to say he won't be in this morning. As a matter of fact, Mr. Maitland"—she lowered her voice confidentially—"I think the police may have wanted to see him again.

47

There have been so many questions, though I must say *I* have found them most polite and considerate.''

"I gather Charles didn't?''

"He seemed a little impatient. But, of course, he's upset by Mr. Winter's death. It seems so awful when you think of it, that he's dead, and in that dreadful way.'' To Antony's horror her eyes filled with tears, but she turned away from him, shutting the ledger firmly, and concentrating for a moment on placing it with exact symmetry in the center of the desk. When she spoke again her voice was composed. "Of course, I can't expect the others to feel it quite as I do. They're young, and I'd known him so long. What about you, Mr. Maitland? I hope the police inquiries haven't inconvenienced you. I didn't see you at the inquest.''

"No, they didn't call me. Just as well, we're pretty busy. I must admit to being curious, though. Has anything emerged?''

"Not to my knowledge. Not, I think, from any talk they have had with me. It is my impression that they are concentrating their inquiries on Mr. Joseph Dowling, but I may be wrong.'' Miss Harris's tone implied that this was of all things most unlikely.

"What gives you that idea?'' Antony, whose mind was still firmly fixed on Charles and his evasions, was inclined to be skeptical.

"It is difficult to say. The trend of their questions, the fact that our Mr. Dowling seems unduly silent and nervous. I can't give you any definite reason, I'm afraid. But it does seem that they are making rather too much of Mr. Dowling's loss of temper.''

"They dearly love a motive, perhaps that's the nearest they can get to one. Miss Harris, now you've had a chance to think about it, can't you suggest anything at all, any reason for someone wanting Mr. Winter dead?''

"That makes it so much worse, that there seems to have been no reason. You know, Mr. Maitland, you know as well as I do, he wasn't that sort of man; not the sort someone might want to kill.''

"Hate isn't the only motive. What about his will, does that help at all?'' Miss Harris, he knew, would normally have bristled at so indiscreet a question; but by now, surely,

Mr. Winter's dispositions must be fairly common knowledge.

"There were a few comparatively small bequests. £1,000 to his cousin, the one who kept house for him. He left me £500," she added with rather a pale smile. "Would you consider that a motive, Mr. Maitland?"

"In the circumstances, no."

"Well, there were several charities, all very respectable, the ones he used to recommend to clients if they asked his advice. After that, he left everything to his niece; Mr. Prentiss is to have the option of buying her interest in the firm over a period of years."

"Well, now. That's something, isn't it? Do you know the niece?"

"Really, Mr. Maitland," Miss Harris protested. "Mary Winter is a *nice* girl."

"Then, what about her boy friend, if she's got one?"

Miss Harris gasped, and gazed at him in wide-eyed consternation. "But he wouldn't . . . oh, no, that's sheer nonsense."

"What's nonsense?" said Antony, nettled. "It's jolly good sense. Profit motive, most convincing of all for a jury. Ask Uncle Nick."

"How can you say such things?" She was now really annoyed.

"Look here, who are we talking about? You mean, it's someone you know?"

Miss Harris recovered her poise, and eyed him with dignity. "It would be most improper for me to discuss a matter about which I have no firsthand information," she said, stiffly.

Before Antony had time to try to retrieve the position, the door burst open after the most perfunctory of knocks, and John Willett, the office boy, appeared. He was a stocky youth, with mousy hair and an engaging smile, and it was by now legendary in the office that he never walked anywhere. He was usually out of breath, but this might have been due either to the rate at which he talked or to his rate of progress.

"Coffee, Miss Harris," he announced. "Oh, hello, Mr. Maitland. I say, Mr. Maitland, we all had to go to the inquest yesterday. I thought it might be exciting, but it was

frightfully dull. Would you like some coffee? I expect
there's plenty.''

"You may bring mine in here, Willett,'' said Miss Harris, frigidly. "I have work to do.''

Antony took the hint, muttered something about seeing
her later, and went into the corridor. As the door closed
Willett grinned at him. "What's up with her?''

"Put my foot in it. All my fault. She'd known Mr. Winter
a long time, you know, and his death has upset her pretty
badly.''

"Well, so it has me. I liked him frightfully. Only, I can't
think about it all the time.'' Willett's face clouded. "Do you
think I'm very callous?''

"Don't worry. I think that's quite as it should be. What
about that coffee?''

"Oh, yes.'' Willett erupted through the opposite door
into the general office, and Antony followed more sedately.
"Here's Mr. Maitland, will there be enough for him? And
can I have Miss Harris's cup, she's busy?''

Miss Meadows, who seemed to be superintending the
brew, nodded at them both amiably. She was looking rather
flushed, probably due to bending over the electric heater
which was lying on its back nursing a large blue enamel pan.
The heat in the room was stifling, but neither Miss Bell nor
Dennis Dowling, who were calling a document at the far
side of the room, seemed inconvenienced by it.

". . . thesaidpartiestothesepresentshaveherehuntosettheir
handsandsealsthedayandyearfirstabovewritten. Et cetera,''
concluded Miss Bell triumphantly. "Good morning, Mr.
Maitland. I hope you aren't looking for Mr. Prentiss, he
isn't in this morning.''

"No, I've been chatting to Miss Harris, but Willett lured
me away with talk of coffee. Morning, Dowling,'' as Dennis finished perusing and laid aside the document.

"Good morning, Maitland. Don't forget to initial that,
Miss Bell.''

"I won't, I'd hate to have to go through it again. We none
of us saw you yesterday,'' she added, to Antony. "Didn't
you go to the inquest?''

"Luckily for me, they didn't want me. Willett says it was
dull.''

"Daisy didn't find it so." Eve Meadows was pouring coffee, and handed the first cup to Willett with the admonition, "don't spill it." She smiled at Miss Bell, and went on, "We all had to attend, but she was the only one they called, because of finding Mr. Winter. And Mr. Prentiss. And that was all."

"It was quite enough for me," said Miss Bell firmly, taking her cup. "I didn't like it at all."

Dennis said suddenly, violently, "Can't we talk about anything else?" He walked across to Eve Meadows's side; she handed him coffee, which he took without seeming to be aware of it, but stood eyeing her with a rather uncomfortable intensity. She returned his gaze, and said lightly, "What else is there to talk about just now?"

"I—" He thought better of whatever he had been going to say, and turned back to the corner he had just vacated, where he perched himself on a high stool and surveyed his companions moodily. Miss Bell looked distressed, and exchanged a look with Miss Meadows, who displayed a fixed smile that might have indicated either embarrassment or unconcern.

At this point Willett re-entered. "Are you talking about the murder? You might wait for me." He grabbed a cup of coffee, looked around, swept across to Antony with it and returned to Miss Meadows's side. "Is there plenty? Oh, thanks awfully." He turned again to their visitor. "Has our Miss Bell told you about her *ordeal*?"

Antony glanced at the young lady referred to with some sympathy. "I'd be interested to know what happened, if it's not too boring going over it all again." He reflected wryly that he was doing well, so far; last night he had put Charles's back up, this morning he had got on the wrong side of Miss Harris; now, he supposed, it would be Dennis's turn to be aggravated, if that was a strong enough word. He had the look of one who had come almost to the limit of endurance.

"Well—interested?" said Miss Bell, doubtfully. "I don't think I'd call it interesting, exactly. We all thought we'd hear a lot of evidence, and perhaps get some idea what it was all about; because, really, it is the most extraordinary thing, Mr. Maitland—"

Dennis Dowling interrupted her without apology. "We were all subpoenaed, I expect they hadn't decided how much evidence to take. All they did was call Prentiss to identify him, and then Miss Bell here. She told them why she went in, and what the time was, and that was really all." He got up, and put down his coffee cup. Antony noticed that it was empty, and wondered how he had managed to get through it so quickly; his was still scalding hot. "I'm going to draft Mr. Hardaker's conveyance. I'll be in Prentiss's room if anyone wants me," he added abruptly, and went out.

Miss Bell said, "Poor Mr. Dowling," and sighed. Antony could not read Eve Meadows's expression; he had a sudden impression that she was unhappy and trying desperately not to show it. Willett was merely concerned to get back to the subject on hand.

"Well, that was all of that," he admitted. "Only Miss Bell didn't like it at all; of course, there were rather a lot of people, I bet they were all disappointed. I thought they'd call Miss Harris, because of being the last one to see him. I told her all the books say that's very suspicious, they might think she'd done it; but she didn't seem to take it in. I don't think she can have much imagination," said Willett regretfully.

Antony eyed him with amusement. Miss Bell said energetically, "What a horrible boy you are! How would you like it if someone suggested you might have done it?"

"Well, I couldn't have." It was definitely a disappointment to him to have to say so. "Any more than you could, we were both in here all the time. Unless you did it when you went in with the letters," he added with sudden inspiration, and a sidelong glance at Antony to see how he liked this improvisation.

"No time," replied Antony promptly. "Unless she's an expert knife thrower—did you ever work in a circus, Miss Bell?" She looked at him with speechless indignation. "Seriously, though," he added, in as soothing a tone as he thought would sound convincing, "what time did you last see Mr. Winter?"

"Just before lunch, when I finished taking down his letters. I heard him go by when he came in from his lunch, but I didn't see him again."

"What about you Willett?"

"Oh, I was in and out all the afternoon. The last time'd be when Miss Harris told me to show Mr. Dowling in."

"Did you notice any difference in his manner, then or earlier?"

"He was just the same as usual. He was always the same." Willett was not yet old enough to realize that anyone over thirty could be human enough to have feelings, to which their actions might give a clue. "Did you see him, Miss Meadows, after you came in?"

"That was four o'clock, wasn't it? When you saw Prentiss?"

Eve Meadows looked up quickly, definitcly startled. "When I thought I saw him," she corrected, after a moment. "No, I didn't see Mr. Winter again." Antony thought she had steered rather neatly away from a subject she disliked, but it appeared she couldn't bring herself to leave well alone. "It was a silly mistake to make, wasn't it? Thinking I saw Mr. Prentiss, I mean."

Antony smiled at her, but said nothing. He hoped he looked enigmatic. Miss Bell remarked, with more acid in her tone than he would have expected from her, "So silly, Eve dear, that I very much doubt if it was a mistake."

"Of course it was. You heard him say he wasn't here. Anyway, why should he have been?"

"Why, indeed? The police think it's funny. I'm sure that's why they're asking him so many questions."

"But I told them I'd made a mistake. And even if he was here, that wouldn't make them think he'd done it. Would it, Mr. Maitland?"

"Any lack of candor would certainly rouse their interest," he replied carefully. "But you mustn't make too much of routine inquiries; after all, Mr. Prentiss was very closely connected with Mr. Winter, and who should be better able to tell the police about his affairs? Besides, unless there was a very clear motive, the police would surely be unlikely to suspect him."

Miss Bell shrugged her shoulders, and began to drink her coffee. Eve Meadows, far from being reassured, directed towards Antony a look which seemed to him positively venomous. Then she turned away, said casually, "You see, Daisy," and was to all appearances as calm as ever. "More coffee, anyone? Mr. Maitland?" He was quite surprised to find he wasn't being offered a cup of hemlock.

Soon after that he left and went into the other room for a word with Dennis Dowling; but such was that young man's air of preoccupation that it was useless to persist in conversation in the face of it. At the door, however, Dowling's voice stopped him.

"I go to lunch about twelve, Maitland. Would you care to join me?"

Antony turned. Something in the other's manner both puzzled him and caught his interest. He said, "I'd like that," and Dennis, who was fidgeting with his spectacles, looked faintly relieved. They fixed time and place for meeting, and Antony withdrew. The briefest of good-byes sufficed for Miss Harris, who had evidently not yet forgiven him. He made his way back to the Inner Temple, and found his uncle just seeing a visitor out of his room. Mr. Bellerby was a solicitor, a stout man and over-jovial, but acute enough in his own line. Antony bore his geniality with what patience he might muster.

When they were alone, Sir Nicholas turned to his nephew and remarked, not without malice, "Prepare yourself for a shock. Miss Carmichael has now changed her story a third time. Also, Bellerby informs me she is subject to violent attacks of hysteria unless carefully handled."

"I don't think I can bear it," said Antony. "But after all, she isn't our witness."

"She Must Not Be Upset," said Sir Nicholas firmly. "If you hadn't got your mind fixed on quite irrelevant murders, you'd realize that it would be the Worst Thing Possible."

Antony sank into a chair, and closed his eys. "One harsh word," he said, with as much pathos as he could command, "and I shall probably burst into tears. I am now regarded with loathing and opprobrium by such old friends as Charles and Miss Harris; not to mention Miss Meadows."

"The glamour girl?" queried Sir Nicholas, interested. "What have you been doing to her?"

"Nothing, I wouldn't dare. I'd better tell you about it,"

he added, soberly. "I can't say I much like the implications—"

"Facts first, implications afterwards," said his uncle.

"Well, bear in mind she seems a bit gone on Charles." Sir Nicholas closed his eyes, and appeared to be praying. "She was bickering with Miss Bell about whether he really was in the office on Tuesday afternoon; she maintaining she'd made a mistake, Miss Bell pretty sure she hadn't, and also sure the police were interested in Charles's activities. I said they wouldn't suspect someone who had no motive, and instead of being soothed she gave me a dirty look."

"And added to your impressions when you talked to Charles—yes, I see."

"That's not all. I had a talk with Miss Harris, and the only thing she had to tell me of interest was about Mr. Winter's will. The residue goes to his niece . . . according to Miss Harris, a 'nice girl.' I asked about a possible young man, naturally enough I think, and she went off pop. Said I was talking nonsense, how could I say such a thing? and anyway she had no firsthand information; and generally froze me out. Now it seems to me only too likely that our Charles, having first trifled with Miss Meadows's affections, has turned his attentions to Miss Winter. Which has the makings of an uncomfortable situation."

"Some day," said Sir Nicholas, eyeing him meditatively, "you will forget yourself, and come out in court with some vile phrase, such as 'went off pop' or 'a bit gone on.' I only hope I may live to see it."

"Yes, sir. But about Charles—"

"Your surmise is reasonable; it seems to be highly unlikely, however, that he took the further step of murdering his partner."

"That's what I feel. All the same—"

"Winter is dead, and the reason for his killing is not yet apparent. In considering the matter, it would be a mistake to ignore so obvious a motive."

"I suppose so. Poor old Charles!"

"Has anything else come to light?" (After Sykes had left them the evening before, Sir Nicholas had expressed himself with some freedom on the subject of his nephew's equivocal attitude and had declared roundly that he would

not countenance any meddling. Antony, though unmoved
by his strictures, was nevertheless amused to see that the
older man was not proof against the fascination of a mystery.)

"Not so far as I can gather. Dennis has asked me to
lunch, though . . . I'm meeting him in a few minutes. He's
in a more pronounced state of dither even than Charles, so I
don't imagine it's a mere desire for my company. It's all
very odd."

"Well, if you're lunching early, so will I." Sir Nicholas
picked up a few papers from his littered desk, eyed them
vaguely with some idea of tidying them, and then, losing
heart, dropped them back where they had been before.
"Half-past one, my lad, not a second later."

Dennis Dowling was a thin young man whose customary
solemnity of manner, combined with the fact that he wore
glasses, gave him an air of wisdom beyond his years. Antony knew him as an interesting, though not exhilarating,
companion; but he had always been struck by his reserve,
particularly on personal matters. Family affairs, of course,
had not come within the scope of their discussions; but small
matters of taste are usually spoken of openly enough, and on
these, too, Dennis had given no clue to his feelings. So it
was with some surprise that Antony, led firmly by his host
to a restaurant noted both for the excellence of its cuisine
and the elegance of its clientele, heard him direct the waiter
in a most detailed manner as to their proposed repast. It
seemed he had a facility in such matters which he had not
previously chosen to display.

The waiter dismissed for the moment, the younger man
turned to his guest. "I hope that suits you. Do you know this
place at all? It's quiet, my father likes it."

"I've been a few times." Antony was puzzled, but fell in
willingly enough with his companion's apparent desire for
small talk. "As to the meal, it sounds altogether too good.
I've a sticky case to consider this afternoon, but I should
think I'm more likely to go to sleep."

"I hope it won't be as bad as that."

"Well, as we are likely to be in court on Monday, so do
I."

"Is it one of Sir Nicholas Harding's cases?"

"Yes, he's leading."

"I've heard," said Dennis, elaborately casual, "that he's one of the really great counsels."

Antony smiled. "I'm prejudiced, of course. But I'm pretty sure there's nobody better."

Dennis seemed to be giving his guest's words more attention than their author felt they deserved. After a moment he asked, leaving the subject abruptly, "Have you seen Joe's present play?"

"No, we've had no chance yet. Jenny's mad to go, but you can't get in at a moment's notice, and we've been too busy to be able to book anything weeks ahead."

"You could use our box, if you'd care to."

"Are you sure we wouldn't be in the way? Perhaps your father—"

"That's all right. What about this evening, if you're free, and Mrs. Maitland would like it?"

"She'd like it, and so should I." As for being free, he'd fix Uncle Nick somehow. "I'm really most grateful—"

The waiter brought soup, and for a moment Dennis gave that his attention. When he decided they had not been fobbed off with any inferior product, he returned to the matter in hand.

"Actually, I think, you'll enjoy it. Macbeth is one of Joe's favorite parts, he really is good; and as for Meg Hamilton, she has to be seen to be believed."

"So I understand." Antony reflected that at this moment his companion was definitely Joe Dowling's son, who seemed to be quite a distinct person from Mr. Winter's articled clerk.

"That's settled then." The thought seemed to give Dennis some obscure cause for satisfaction. Antony applied himself to his lunch, and meditated on the probable reason for the invitation, which he did not believe entirely disinterested. However, he was well pleased with the turn of events, and inclined to like Dennis more and more as the meal progressed.

It was not until they had worked their way through to coffee, and the waiter had finally withdrawn, that their conversation turned to the subject uppermost in both their minds.

Dennis said, with something of his former manner, "I was a bit abrupt at the office this morning. Tell you the truth, I'm sick of hearing those girls chatter."

"Naturally enough. I'm interested, of course, I was fond of Mr. Winter, but I don't have to live with it."

"No, that's the trouble. Jabber, jabber, jabber, the same things over and over again. And then, they're sorry for me. All except Eve; she's a good kid, but she doesn't think of anything but Prentiss."

"Sorry for you?" said Antony, vaguely.

"The divorce." Dennis sounded impatient. "You must have heard about it. Joe's made enough shout, goodness knows. Damn' fool thing to do, of course. And now the police, well I don't know what they think, but I'm sure they don't realize he loses his temper like that at least seven times a week."

"Well, I had heard something," Antony admitted. "I hoped it might blow over, though."

"So it should have done by now." Dennis was exasperated, and sounded strangely like a middle-aged gentleman discussing the follies of youth. "I told Mother in the first place, but she wouldn't listen. And after the fuss Joe's made, I don't blame her for staying away. I'll have to do something about it sooner or later, they're both perfectly miserable. But at the moment, well—quite frankly, Maitland, what I'm worried about is the police."

If frankness was to be the order of the day, Antony saw no reason why he should not encourage it. "Have you any reasons for that, other than the obvious one, that your father quarrelled with Mr. Winter?"

"Well, that's bad enough. Joe quarrels with everybody if you don't keep an eye on him, but I can't expect other people to understand that. But there's something more than that behind their questions. I don't know what it is, and I don't believe Joe does either. Then, they wouldn't be human if he didn't put their backs up. It's like the supper scene, with Banquo's ghost: 'question enrages him.' " Dennis looked up with a sudden smile which took Antony, who had previously observed no sign of humor in him, completely by surprise.

"I shouldn't have thought," he said reflectively, "that

the police would have made the mistake of expecting an artist of your father's quality to be quite as other men."

"You might as well say 'to act in a reasonable way,' and have done with it; I'm sure that's what you're thinking." ("Well—" said Antony.) "But it's just no good expecting Joe to be reasonable. He never was, and never will be, so far as I can see. As to what the police think of him, I simply can't imagine. I suppose anything out of the ordinary seems suspicious to them."

"Now, I'd have put Inspector Sykes down as an intelligent chap."

"Oh, Sykes! It isn't him I'm bothered about. To tell you the truth," and again there was that unexpected look of humor, "I think he found Joe pretty good value. And summed him up fairly enough, too. But yesterday evening they asked him to go round to Scotland Yard; and a fine fuss we were all in at the theater, he was only just in time to change. I heard what had happened during the first interval: he'd seen Superintendent Briggs, and I gathered they did *not* get along. Joe says he would persist in taking it for granted that he had gone back again up the private stair, after leaving through the main office; and you know as well as I do, having regard to the time element, that's tantamount to accusing him of the murder. And that's why I'm worried."

"My uncle knows Briggs. He told me he's Sykes's superior officer. He says he's capable, but apt to ride his theories." Dennis did not seem to find this cheering, and Antony added briskly, "However, theory is a far way from proof."

"There can't be any proof. Joe wouldn't murder anybody."

"That," remarked Antony, sadly, "is the sort of statement calculated to drive any barrister mad."

"I suppose so. But really, Maitland, consider the amount of steam Joe lets off in the course of one evening's performance."

"To submit that argument in court you'd have to translate it into psychological terms, and that doesn't go well with a jury."

"I thought psychology was all the rage now."

"Up to a point. But it opens the way for opposing counsel to do an 'all boys together' stunt: 'my learned friend has

gone to some trouble to explain to you this rather complicated matter' . . . then he'd quote a few of the more
unlikely-sounding bits of jargon, making nonsense of them;
'but we, members of the jury, are plain men, and plain facts
are good enough for us.' Something like that. Worked on, it
could be deadly.''

''I see.'' Dennis's tone was flat.

Antony went on quickly, ''That isn't to say I don't think
you're probably right about your father. Only you said you
were worried about the police: well, if the police think they
have a case they'll put it up to the Public Prosecutor's office,
and that's the sort of thing *they* think of. To be more cheerful, they also consider the weak points of the case; there
must be many of those.''

''Yes. Yes, of course. I must admit, though,'' he added,
with an attempt at a smile, ''I find all this extremely depressing.''

''That's no wonder. It's difficult to know what to think in
view of Briggs's attitude; from what you say, that's quite inexplicable.'' It was almost impossible, Antony reflected, to
attempt to reassure his companion in any but the most general terms; better to say nothing, taking it all in all, than utter
a string of platitudes.

Dennis shrugged. ''Ah, well. Who lives may learn.'' He
seemed to regard the prospect without pleasure.

''I know you're sick of the subject, but I'd be interested to
know what you were able to tell the police.''

For some reason this question seemed to startle Dennis.
He regarded his companion in silence for a moment, but
when he spoke his voice was as calm as ever. ''Not very
much, I'm afraid. You know I was out until four o'clock.
Eve Meadows said something about seeing Prentiss, but I
didn't take much notice. I could hear Joe's voice as soon as
we got in. That was partly why I went into the strongroom,
though there really were some papers I needed. They asked
me, of course, exactly what I was doing there . . . I will
say, they're thorough.''

''And you told them—?'' Antony seemed absorbed in
stirring his coffee, and did not meet Dennis's suddenly worried look.

''I told them I was looking in old Mrs. Prentiss's strongbox for the deeds of her house, which is being sold. That wouldn't have taken long, but I couldn't find the schedule.''

"I see." He looked up, and grinned at his companion. "Could you hear anything of what was going on in Mr. Winter's room?'' he added; and rather expected the question to be an added irritant. Unexpectedly, it seemed to have a tonic effect.

"Much less than in the corridor. I could hear voices, of course, but if I hadn't known already I couldn't have told it was Joe doing most of the talking.'' He paused to lift the coffeepot and give it a questioning shake. "Have we time to order more, do you think?''

"Not for me. I must be back at half-past one. But while we're on the subject, what happened next?''

"Oh, well, I'd been in the strongroom about five minutes when Joe left. I'd left the grille open, and was facing the door, and I wasn't too occupied to notice the people who went by. As soon as he'd gone Miss Harris whisked into Mr. Winter's room with a cup of tea, and came back almost at once. After that I heard you arrive, at least I knew some-one had come. I thought of going back to the general office and getting some tea, but it seemed better to give them a bit longer to get their discussion of my affairs over, so I stayed where I was. Then there was some movement, opening and shutting of doors, and after a moment Miss Bell came down and went into Mr. Winter's room. You know the rest: I wasn't very quick off the mark when she called out, I'm afraid. I saw you rush past, and reached the door just behind you.''

"I was wondering whether you had heard any sound from Mr. Winter's office, after Miss Harris had been in, when he should have been alone.''

"No, I didn't. I wouldn't have done anyway. You could only hear Joe because he can't help pitching his voice to carry; ordinary speech might be audible if you were lis-tening hard, but not otherwise, and the same goes for other sounds, of moving about the room, for instance.''

"And, whoever it was would naturally be concerned to be silent.'' Antony found this thought unpleasant, and got to his feet. "I don't want to rush away, but I really must get back—''

"Just a moment." Dennis produced a card, and wrote on it. "That'll get you to our box tonight. I'll see you there, that is if Mrs. Maitland won't object to company."

"She'll be delighted to meet you." Antony made appropriate farewells and thanks, and hurried away. He reached Sir Nicholas's room at one minute past the half-hour; and was thereupon plunged, without delay, into all the more unsavory aspects of the affairs of their client, Mr. Isaacs.

CHAPTER 7

As the curtain slid smoothly into place and the theater lights came on, Jenny relaxed her grip on her husband's arm and leaned back with a sigh of contentment. "It's wonderful, isn't it? I never dreamed it would be so good."

"Wonderful," agreed Antony, rubbing his arm and making a mental note to move his chair a little before the interval was over; if Jenny had got so worked up already, anything might happen when the play really got going. "What do you think of Lady Macbeth?"

"Oh, she's awful," said Jenny with enthusiasm. "I remember when they opened, the papers said she's very young, twenty-two or three; but she manages to be quite perfect. I wonder what she's really like."

"Well—not like Lady Macbeth, I expect. It's Joe Dowling who impresses me most, though." He turned as there was a tap on the door of the box, and Dennis came in quietly. He was carrying a spray of roses, and when Antony had performed the introductions, which he did with due ceremony, he handed them to Jenny.

"My father sent these, Mrs. Maitland, with his compliments." He smiled at her obvious delight. "I provided the safety pin."

"How very thoughtful!"

Antony looked puzzled, and while Jenny was temporarily preoccupied with the arrangement of the flowers asked quietly, "Where did he get them, in the middle of a performance?"

"He pinched them," said Dennis, speaking out of the corner of his mouth in a way that filled his companion with

63

admiration, "from a bouquet some fellow sent Meg Hamilton." Jenny looked up and smiled at him.

"They're really beautiful, Mr. Dowling. I hope you'll thank your father for me."

"Well, as to that, no need at all, but you can do it yourself if you like. I was to ask if you'd care to come round after the show, he'd very much like to meet you both." He saw Jenny glance uncertainly at her husband, and added, with an understanding of which Antony had not considered him capable, "Not a party, Mrs. Maitland; Joe doesn't like crowds. But I do hope you'll come."

"Of course we will. We'd love to."

Antony, standing to one side, observed them as they spoke together. It was a good thing, after all, that he'd told Jenny to change: Dennis's evening attire was perfectly cut, if carelessly worn, though his lanky figure must be the despair of his tailor. Anyway, it did Jenny good to have an occasion to dress up to. He looked at her more searchingly for a moment, trying to see her as a stranger might, her slim figure silhouetted against the red velvet hangings of the box, and her brown curls shining. Her eyes were probably her best feature: gray eyes, with a quality of steadfastness. For the rest . . . but what a soulless thing was a mere catalogue: she was Jenny, he reflected with a sudden surge of affection, and the most beautiful thing in the world. He smiled to himself, to think how she herself would have greeted such an extravagance. And Jenny looked round with an answering smile, as though she had known his thought, and the moment of detachment was gone.

Dennis was making his apologies. "I'd better get back, Joe may need me. Let them know if you want anything, Maitland. I'll be here by the final curtain, see you then."

He disappeared as quietly as he had come. Jenny stood looking after him for a moment, and then turned an inquiring eye on her husband. "He seems nice, I think. But he's . . . strange, isn't he?"

"Biggest conundrum in years, so far as I'm concerned."

"I mean, you told me he was very shy, rather awkward in his manner. He didn't strike me like that at all."

"There's more than one side to our Dennis, I only discovered that today. Mr. Winter's articled clerk is a diffident youth, interested in his work, but rather muddle-headed. Joe Dowling's son appears to be quietly self-confident; and I rather gather he runs his parents into the bargain. I have no data to theorize on possible further aspects of his character.''

"Well, I don't know Mr. Winter's clerk, but Joe Dowling's son is kind, I like him. I think you'd better help him, Antony; that's what he wants, isn't it?"

"Bless you, love, it's not me he wants. He's getting in on the ground floor with Uncle Nick, just in case."

"Oh, I see. Anyway, it's quite sensible. But it doesn't seem, from what you've told me, that the police can have a case against Mr. Dowling.''

"Dennis says there's something more than he knows, more than his father knows . . . that's what he *says*. I just can't theorize, yet."

"We shall see, I expect. Antony," she hesitated a moment, "do you think Margaret Hamilton will be very frightening?"

"Why should she be? She's very young."

"That makes it worse," said Jenny tragically. "I'm sure she'll be very elegant, and self-assured, and—"

Antony, who well knew by now his wife's reluctance to meet strangers (despite the fact that it was rarely indeed that she then passed adverse judgment on them) laughed at her gently, and took her hand. "Don't be sillier than you can help, my love. I expect, you know, we'll both survive the evening."

Jenny gave a small grimace, and as the house lights again began to dim she settled herself contentedly to give her full attention to *The Tragedy of Macbeth*.

Dennis returned as promised, to conduct them through a narrow confusion of scenery and busy hurrying people, to his father's dressing room. Jenny walked beside him in a daze, not having yet shaken off the certainty that Macbeth was dead, and that she was about to be shown his mortal remains; Antony, following, was quite prepared for her to greet their eminent host with an expression of surprise, but saw no way of stopping her. In the event, she was stricken momentarily dumb by the sight of Joseph Dowling, helmetless and wigless, his face, pink and a little greasy still from the rapid removal of make-up, softer and more indeterminate than Macbeth's. Her share of the introductory conversation was, on this account, confined to a smile, which was, however, of sufficient radiance to convince her husband that she found Mr. Dowling more to her taste than the Thane of Glamis would have been, though, come to think of it, to be able to listen in to a conversation between Jenny and Macbeth would have been definitely a rewarding experience.

At the moment Dowling seemed a trifle deflated, which was perhaps not surprising after the energy he had expended during the past three hours. After some moments' quiet conversation with Jenny he handed her over to Dennis, who took his cue neatly and led her across the room to examine Macbeth's trappings. The actor then subjected Antony to a piercing stare, said "Humph" in a tone of some satisfaction, ruminated for a moment, and then remarked:

"Not a fool, Maitland, I can see that. Don't mistake me, I'm glad to know you, and your wife—charming creature, refreshing. All the same you can guess why I made a point of meeting you, just now."

"You mean, sir, that the present is not the time you would have chosen for making purely social contacts?"

Dowling gave a bark of amusement. "Prettily put, but I'll be plainer. Meaning, I want to pick your brains, make use of your specialized knowledge—and that's probably only a beginning."

Antony grinned. "You're very welcome to such knowledge as I possess. I fancy, however, since we're being frank, that my uncle's the man you want."

"Very possibly. For the moment, I'd welcome your opinion of this police business. Dennis tells me he has put you in the picture."

"To some extent. As I understand it, your anxiety is caused by your interview with Superintendent Briggs, which took place yesterday?"

"That is so."

"The superintendent was of the opinion that you had seen Mr. Winter twice on the afternoon of his death, on the second occasion entering his office by the private stair; but you did not, in fact, do so."

"I did not." Dowling seemed to be again on the brink of vehemence, and schooled his tone to mildness with something of an effort. "I left the office in the usual way, turned from Bread Court into Fleet Street, crossed over, and went down to walk on the embankment." He cleared his throat, and went on with a trace of awkwardness, "Hasty, you know. Got to admit it. Went there to cool off a bit."

"Well, on the face of it, sir, on the facts as I have them, there's no question of the police having a case. You can see that for yourself."

"All the same, I must admit to being uneasy."

An understatement, reflected Antony; and wondered that so accomplished an actor should make such a bad show of hiding what he felt. "He may have been trying deliberately to alarm you," he suggested.

"Maybe. But I don't think so, I think he knew something, or thought he did. His manner was extremely confident."

"I see. Have you heard anything from the police since that interview?"

"No, nothing. But if I should, if they should take any— well, drastic action, I'd like to feel that Sir Nicholas Harding would be willing to interest himself in my affairs."

"I can't answer for him, of course—"

"But it *is* his kind of case?"

"Exactly. But you realize that any approach would have to be made through your solicitors?"

"Of course." Dowling's tone was definitely testy now. "I'll do everything by the book. Great believer in personal contacts, though."

"Well, we must hope you have no real cause for alarm." Antony thought he had concealed his own feelings pretty well; he wished the other man nothing but good . . . but if he had to stand his trial then undoubtedly the brief would be of interest to Sir Nicholas, and not merely from a financial point of view. "I've heard that Briggs is an awkward man to deal with," he went on, "so I think it very possible—"

"As to that," said Dowling, with a certain grim satisfaction, "I *can* be awkward, myself."

Antony suppressed a smile, and was saved the necessity of commenting on this all-too-true remark by a sudden banging on the door, and a voice from the corridor, calling, "Can I come in yet?"

Dennis pulled the door open, and Meg Hamilton came in. She was a small girl, and looked barely twenty now, with her dark hair in a long plait that was twisted round her head, and her face innocent of make-up. She looked a little startled: "I'm sorry, I didn't know—" and would have backed out again had not Dennis shut the door with decision and given her a push into the room, saying:

"Come and be introduced."

Jospeh Dowling was scowling down at her. "And what do you mean, my girl, disgracing us all by appearing in a coat like that?" He himself might be bald, and pink, and shining, but sartorially he was resplendent in a dressing gown of scarlet silk.

Meg was not abashed. "It's a fine coat, and I'll not be getting another till I've had some wear from this." The offending garment was navy blue, a little short for the fashion, and trimmed with a piece of undeniable rabbit, but she wore it with an air.

"Children, children," Dennis sounded weary. He performed introductions firmly, while his father simmered and broke in at the first opportunity:

"And now, Miss Margaret Hamilton, you'd some hard things to say to me last night. How did you find Macbeth today?"

"Not . . . bad." She burst out laughing at his expression, and said quickly, "You were magnificent, and you know it; you don't need me to tell you."

"I think Joe's right for once, Meg," said Dennis. "He knew he was bad last night, but that didn't stop you—"

"That's quite enough of that." Dowling's tone was sharp, and Dennis grinned. "What do you think Mrs. Maitland, would you recognize Lady Macbeth?"

"No, I wouldn't." She looked at Meg, smiling. "You're more impressive on the stage, but much prettier at close quarters."

The other girl frowned a little, considering the compliment, then shook her head. "Not pretty. I haven't the time. I hope I won't need to be." She looked, suddenly, uncertain, and glanced across at Dennis; but seeing that he had joined the other two men in conversation she moved a little closer to Jenny, and said in a low voice, "As for the coat, would you be spending good money on a new one, Mrs. Maitland, when this is perfectly good?"

"It all depends," said Jenny, incurably truthful. "But Mr. Dowling's only teasing you, you know."

Meg brightened. "That's what Dennis says. It's hard to tell, sometimes, things are so different here. At home, people say what they mean, and wouldn't be so rude as to discuss a lady's clothes." For a moment she was on her dignity; then she grinned, impishly, and looked even younger than before. "Of course, Mr. Dowling has a perfect right to be rude to me if he wants. I'd have got nowhere without him, but it would be very bad for him to let him know it." She glanced again towards the group of men, hesitated a moment, and then asked, "Your husband, Mrs. Maitland—Dennis was talking about him last night. Is he going to help Mr. Dowling?"

Jenny was a little taken aback by this directness. "I don't know. If he can. It may not be necessary."

"It will be," said Meg, with decision.

"But Antony said—"

"He only knows what they've told him. But I know one of the things the police have against Mr. Dowling."

"But—" began Jenny again, and again Meg interrupted her.

"Oh, I haven't said anything." Once more she looked around, and appeared reassured by the sight of the three men in close conversation. "I didn't want to worry him—to worry either of them, I mean. But I thought if I told you, you could tell Mr. Maitland, and that might be a good thing." Her voice trailed off, in obvious doubt as to the wisdom of her conclusion.

Jenny smiled reassuringly. "I can't tell, of course. But it certainly won't do any harm." She added, inconsequently, "Do you know, I was really frightened tonight at the prospect of meeting you?"

"Frightened? Of me? What fun!" For a moment Meg's smile was brilliant, but she sobered instantly. "But this is important, Mrs. Maitland, really it is."

"I'm sorry. Tell me about it."

"Well, the police came round, asking questions—"

"Here? To the theater?"

"That's right. Yesterday morning. I came in to rehearse with Hewitt's understudy, because it looked as though he'd be playing, and he said he couldn't get his reactions right without me. The sleepwalking scene, you know. It was a sergeant, I think, the policeman I mean; and he didn't want us—only to apologize for getting on stage because he had lost his way. He asked for the stage manager, and we told him where he might be, and when I went off about five minutes later I found he'd got hold of young Billy. So, of course, I listened."

"Of course," agreed Jenny, fascinated. "Do go on. I can't imagine—"

"Nor could I," Meg Hamilton's voice, already low-pitched, sank still farther, so that for a moment the merest glimmer of Lady Macbeth appeared. "It was the dagger."

"I don't understand."

"There's one missing. Not a property dagger." She sounded impatient. "A real one that someone gave Mr. Dowling for a souvenir. Adams—that's the stage manager—wasn't around, but I asked him today and he said they'd seen him later, and shown him the dagger that was used. He couldn't remember positively, but it was like the one that was missing; and he couldn't say different, not for anybody."

"Oh, dear."

"It doesn't mean anything, anyone might have borrowed it, or it might easily be lost. But I don't know if the police would understand that very well."

"I daresay they wouldn't."

"Dennis says—" But this time her glance across the room revealed that they were about to be interrupted, and she left her sentence unfinished. A moment later Dennis joined them.

"Time for me to take you home, my pet. What are you two doing, anyway, with your heads together? Plotting something?"

Jenny resisted the temptation to reply "A deed without a name!" and made some other, less facetious rejoinder.

"Well, I'm sorry to interrupt, but it's time this child was in bed."

Meg drew herself up, and gave him a look whose hauteur would have excited comment if displayed by a duchess. She relaxed a moment to grin at Jenny. "Good night, Mrs. Maitland, I hope I'll see you again," and then wrapped her somewhat skimpy coat around her with an air and stalked away.

Dennis took Jenny's hand. "I'm glad you came. Thank you." He turned away before she could reply, detached Meg with dexterity from his father and Antony, and the two went out together.

Joe Dowling had suggested supper, but they had excused themselves and got away without much difficulty. Antony sat on the edge of the bed, chewing his last mouthful of sandwich, and eyeing the glass of milk in his hand with some distaste. Jenny was brushing her hair, and had just completed a somewhat disjointed account of her conversation with Meg Hamilton. Receiving no immediate comment she turned to look at her husband. "Well, what do you think about that?"

"I think it odd that an otherwise perfect wife should be so unreasonable on one subject."

"Antony, I don't believe you've heard a word I said!"

He raised his glass to her. "On the subject of milk, my love, you are definitely unhinged. However—I *have* been listening, so you needn't scowl at me like that. What did you think of the great actress?"

"She took my breath away. Weren't you surprised?"

"I'd certainly expected something a bit more deadly."

"She's rather a dear."

"Very likely. About this knife—"

"Is it very bad, Antony?"

"Not of itself. The trouble is, you see, the police now seem to think Joe went back. If they have any evidence to support that view, it would obviously help their case along to be able to show where the weapon came from."

"But, darling, why? Why should he kill Mr. Winter? Oh, I know what Uncle Nick says about motive, but—"

"The argument is something like this: Joseph Dowling is an actor; actors are queer, unpredictable, and liable to do anything; therefore—! That's logic."

"It's very silly."

"With Bird, say, or Halloran prosecuting, it could be made to sound very far from silly. After all, he had, or believed he had, cause for grievance against Winter. Capital could even be made of the fact that he's playing Macbeth at the moment."

"I don't believe it!"

"I can think of at least three men, offhand—not counting Uncle Nick—who could have the toughest jury believing in a picture of Joe crying, 'Is this a dagger that I see before me,' and rushing off wildly to stick it into anyone he happened to be annoyed with at the moment."

Jenny giggled, and put down the hairbrush. Antony drank the last of the milk, grimaced, and got up to put the glass on the end of the dressing table.

"But he didn't do it, did he? You don't think he killed Mr. Winter?"

"I don't think so. I wouldn't bet on it, though."

Jenny meditated. "Well, I hope he didn't. What are you laughing at?"

Antony had collapsed on to the bed again. "I must say I'd like to see Uncle Nick coping with a client whose idea of pleading 'Not Guilty' would be on the lines of 'Thou canst not say I did it.' And can't you just hear Joe inquiring of the court 'What bloody man is this?' on being confronted with Counsel for the Prosecution?"

"It isn't funny," said Jenny, severely. And began to laugh almost as immoderately as her husband was doing.

CHAPTER 8

THE NEXT MORNING started badly, with a phone call from Sykes requesting that Antony should go round to Scotland Yard to make a detailed and formal statement. He managed to delay the appointment until 11:30, gulped down his breakfast, and went downstairs to find his uncle. His head was ringing with the more magniloquent of the speeches he had heard the night before; but by the time they had finished putting a polish on Monday's case, the deeds and misdeeds of Mr. Isaacs had taken precedence. Of the two, he thought he preferred Macbeth.

Sir Nicholas laughed when he said as much. "That's because you never had to sweat over the defense in his case." And Antony laughed too, at the echo of his last night's thought, and went away to his interview in a better temper than might have been expected.

Sykes was bland and affable. Antony allowed himself to be soothed altogether out of his annoyance. The business of signing the statement did not, after all, take very long, but when it was completed and Antony was about to take his leave, Sykes stopped him.

"As long as you're here, Mr. Maitland, Superintendent Briggs would like to have a word with you." His tone was flat, without hint of apology, and Antony looked at him quickly.

"I must say, I don't see why," he protested. "After all, I've told you all I know. In fact, I've told you three times."

"I know. I'm sorry about it." Again Sykes was choosing his words. "But it needn't take long, Mr. Maitland."

"All right, then, let's get on with it."

Superintendent Briggs's office was comfortable, as such places go. Briggs himself was a heavy man, big-boned, with reddish hair growing now well back from a massive forehead. He greeted Antony pleasantly, with an apology for taking his time, and an almost tender inquiry after his uncle's health and well-being. Antony, for no reason that he could have told, began to feel uneasy.

Sykes was carrying with him the newly-signed statement, and this he handed to his superior officer; retiring thereafter to an unobtrusive position by the window. Briggs waved Antony to a chair and started to read the document, not hurrying himself. Antony sat down and compressed his lips. He was conscious of a rising tide of indignation, and could think of several tart comments on this leisurely approach; but most likely they would be better unsaid. He leaned back and crossed his legs.

At length Briggs finished his perusal. He put down the sheets of foolscap, looked in silence for a moment at the younger man, and then said: "Well, Mr. Maitland?"

Antony contented himself with an inquiring look. After an expectant pause Briggs went on, "There are one or two matters arising out of this statement on which I should like a little further detail."

"Yes?" said Antony.

"You say you arrived at Winter's office at twelve minutes past four o'clock."

"As a matter of accuracy . . . I didn't say that."

Briggs was puzzled. He made a show of looking at the statement, glanced hopefully towards Antony for enlightenment, but as none was forthcoming turned to Inspector Sykes with eyebrows raised.

"Mr. Maitland, sir, disclaimed any knowledge of the precise moment of his arrival. The time was fixed by Miss Harris, who had been keeping an eye on the clock."

"Thank you." His tone had an exaggerated politeness. "In any case, Mr. Maitland, you do not dispute the time?"

"I have no reason to question it."

"And at four-thirty James Winter was found dead?"

"That I can testify to of my own knowledge."

"You are familiar, no doubt, with the private entrance to Mr. Winter's room?"

"I have never used it. I knew it was there, of course."

"On the afternoon in question, you would turn into Bread Court a little after ten minutes past four." He held up a hand to insure a silence that Antony had no intention of breaking. "There is no need to debate the point. I have a witness to the time. But I should like a little more detail. Your statement is not quite complete just here."

"I don't see—"

"Perhaps you would cast your mind back to that afternoon—to the time you turned into Bread Court, let us say."

"I've already done that, you know . . . naturally. It didn't help."

"Then, may I suggest that you give the matter a little further thought." Briggs sat back with the air of one who is prepared to wait all day.

Antony, now thoroughly bewildered, said slowly, "Well, I turned into the court. There were a few people about, I wasn't noticing particularly, you know."

"You were, perhaps, preoccupied." It was not lost upon Antony that the two detectives exchanged glances.

He replied, cautiously, "Not that, either."

"Tell us what you saw."

"A man ahead of me, who paused to look at the brass plates outside Number Three, but evidently didn't find what he wanted: he went on down the court. A tabby cat, cleaning its whiskers on the edge of the pavement. Would you be interested in the cat, Superintendent? And a boy I know, waving from one of the windows across the way—young Harvey, he's Hill's office boy. I waved back, and then I turned into the doorway of Number Seven, and went up to Winter's office." He paused, and looked from one to the other of his companions. "I hope that is sufficiently circumstantial? Are you interested in the man I saw?"

"Extremely interested."

"Well, he was a big chap—at least, that's my impression. Dark clothes, dark hat. I'm very sorry, there's really nothing I could swear to."

"You saw his face?"

"For a moment, when he was studying the brass plates. But—" He hesitated a moment, beginning to see where this

was leading—and it was ironical, he felt, that his concern for
Charles should have led the police to believe he might be
shielding Joseph Dowling. But did that quite account for the
superintendent's attitude, for Sykes's watchful air? "But, as
I said, I wasn't really noticing."

"You didn't recognize the man?"

Antony was aware of a sudden tension in the atmosphere,
and his bewilderment grew. He said, "No, I didn't," and
saw Sykes frown, and Briggs lean back in his chair with the
air of one who now sees his way clear. All of which seemed
quite inexplicable.

Briggs's tone had changed now, become sharper. "You
are acquainted with Joseph Dowling, the actor, I believe?"

"Until yesterday, I only knew him by sight."

"But you did know him by sight?"

"Oh, yes, quite well."

"Then, how is it that you did not recognize him?"

"If you mean that the man I followed was Joe Dowling, I
can only say, you're wrong."

"Am I, Mr. Maitland?" Briggs's tone was almost gentle,
and Antony was again conscious of that surge of irritation.
"Do you remember, I said I had a witness?"

"Are you c-calling me a liar?"

"I am advising you, for your own good, to tell me the
truth."

"You've had my answer; I have nothing to add to it."
Antony clutched vainly at the tattered shreds of his temper.
"If this witness of yours thinks he saw Joe Dowling—"

"He has made a positive identification, Mr. Maitland. I
am telling you this in fairness to yourself. Further, he saw
him turn in at the entrance to the private stair—which also
seems to have escaped your notice!" Briggs produced the
statement with an air of satisfaction. "Now, Mr. Maitland,
the truth, if you please."

"I told you." Antony spoke absently. He was still angry,
but the need to think this out was more urgent than his anger.
He said slowly, "Certainly, I should have expected to notice anybody who turned into that doorway; if that part of
the statement is true, it must have been while I looked across
at young Harvey. Perhaps he was your witness? I suppose I
might have missed what happened."

"Convenient," said Briggs, and there was now no doubt at all about the sneer. "Perhaps you can as easily explain how you came to forget that Joseph Dowling walked down Bread Court in front of you."

"Oh, what's the use! If you believe that you'd believe anything. I couldn't possibly have missed him."

"That, Mr. Maitland, was my point!"

"But, I tell you, he wasn't there."

Briggs smiled, without speaking. Antony glowered at him for a moment, then said abruptly, "There's no p-point in going on with this. Good day to you," and went out quickly, followed by bland words of farewell from the superintendent.

He was halfway to the stairs when he realized that Sykes was behind him, and slackened his pace. Sykes spoke mildly. "Steady on, lad." They halted, facing each other, where the corridor widened at the stairhead. "I know you're angry with the superintendent, but his advice just now was good. Think it over."

"Like hell I will!"

"It isn't just a matter of your statement for our files, you know." Sykes was unruffled. "If it comes to trial, and there's every indication that it will—"

"If it comes to trial, my evidence will be just the same."

"Perhaps you're mistaken. Perhaps you didn't recognize him."

"Of course I should have recognized him. I've known him by sight for years. I tell you, he wasn't there!"

Sykes shook his head sadly. "It's a pity," he sighed. "It's a great pity."

Antony gave an impatient exclamation, and clattered angrily down the stairs. This time the inspector did not follow him.

By the time he had walked home, at about twice the pace which would have been reasonable on so hot a day, Antony fondly imagined that he had his feelings well under control. But he snapped at Gibbs, who was hovering in the hall in order to emphasize the lateness of his arrival, in a way that made that dictatorial old man raise his eyebrows even more in surprise than in disapproval.

It was customary on Saturdays for them to lunch with Sir Nicholas, and he found Jenny and his uncle already in the dining room. The older man took one look at him and poured sherry with a generous hand. "Don't waste time arguing. Drink it and let's get on with our meal." He waited until the dishes were brought in, and then dealt ruthlessly with Gibbs's desire to remain. He went to the sideboard and began dispensing meat and vegetables lavishly, while Jenny sat very still and watched her husband, and Antony sipped his wine and gazed fixedly at a valuable salt cellar, which they all hated and only used because Gibbs was reputed to admire it.

Sir Nicholas made two journeys to the table and then seated himself. He regarded his niece and nephew with some amusement; Jenny was eyeing her plate with marked apprehension, while Antony had picked up his knife and fork and begun to eat, still with an air of abstraction.

"I gather from your somewhat distraught appearance that Scotland Yard had some surprises for you?"

"Well . . . I've been talking to Superintendent Briggs."

"And what transpired?"

Antony grimaced. "He came off with the honors. I lost my temper."

"That," murmured his uncle, "is apparent."

"Don't rub it in, sir." He smiled, without much amusement. "Jenny, love, eat your lunch. There's nothing the matter, except that I'm in a foul mood. Oh, and it seems certain now that Dowling will be arrested; but I'm afraid I've mucked up the case so far as you're concerned, sir."

"If that is all we have to worry us," said his uncle, imperturbably, "let us by all means eat our lunch."

Jenny was suspicious. "You're sure, Antony? That it was nothing personal, I mean."

"Quite sure."

"My affairs, of course," murmured Sir Nicholas to his plate, "are as nothing."

"That's unfair, Uncle Nick. Only of course I don't like Antony having trouble with the police."

"Surely, my dear, you've known him long enough now to be thankful it isn't something worse!"

She laughed at that, and began to eat, though still without

much sign of appetite. Antony related the history of the morning, and avoided his uncle's accusing look. "I shouldn't have lost my temper," he said, at last. "That just made matters worse."

Sir Nicholas pushed back his plate, took a sip of claret, and held up his glass as though to observe the color of the wine. "I don't agree with you there," he said. "The mistake you made was in behaving like a schoolboy when first Sykes talked to you!"

Antony was drawing patterns on the tablecloth with his fork. He was beginning to see now, with distressing clarity, the implications of what had passed at Scotland Yard. It was obvious, too, that his uncle was perfectly alive to the situation; hence—in part—his anger. He said, without looking up, "I'm sorry, sir," and after the silence had lengthened for a little the older man spoke again.

"You said, if my memory serves me, something about 'mucking up my case.' " His voice was still gentle, but he reproduced the phrase with an air of distaste.

"It looks certain that Dowling will be arrested; if he is, you'll be offered the brief. It's the sort of case that interests you—you told me this morning you'd like to accept it."

"Well, where's the difficulty? I intend to accept it."

"But, sir, how can you? If I'm to give evidence." He met his uncle's look squarely now, and his tone was urgent; Sir Nicholas remained maddeningly calm. "I don't know who their witness is, unless it's the boy, Harvey—"

"Not young Harvey," said Sir Nicholas positively.

"No, I suppose not. They probably wouldn't prefer his word to mine. But it must be someone credible enough to make them think I'm lying," said Antony, bitterly. His uncle compressed his lips, but made no comment, and reverted after a while to his quiet tone.

"I think," he said reflectively, "I shall lead Stringer and—perhaps—Horton."

"But, you can't—"

"Why not? You will not, of course, appear in the matter, except as a witness. And if the prosecution tries to discredit you in court," said Sir Nicholas, very softly, "don't forget I also shall have some say in the matter."

"Is it fair to Dowling?"

"Use your head, boy, use your head! I admit you'll come in for some rough handling, and that's just too bad; but what do you imagine I shall be doing while one of the Crown witnesses perjures himself?"

"All the same, sir—"

"There's another thing I must point out to you, since you appear incapable of reasoned thought on the matter. If I refuse the brief who takes it? Is your proof going to look any better to him than it does to the police? And if you're not called, the uncontradicted evidence that Dowling was seen going up Mr. Winter's private stair at ten past four will hang him."

"Yes," said Antony, "I hadn't thought of that."

"So I supposed. There is also the possibility that you could identify the man you *did* see, if you encountered him again."

"I don't think so. You know how it is, sir; I saw him clearly enough to know it wasn't someone with whose appearance I was already familiar, but not for long enough to fix him in my mind. I'm sure I wouldn't know him again."

"Uncle Nick—" Jenny spoke with sudden resolution. "You will be able to get Mr. Dowling off, won't you?"

Sir Nicholas, who had been angry and in his anger had forgotten her presence, looked at her now with compunction. "I'll get him off," he promised (and his use of the colloquialism was a measure of the degree to which he was perturbed). He saw by her expression that she had followed the thought to its conclusion, that she had no illusions as to the seriousness of the point involved; and because he could not say what was in his mind, he said instead, banteringly: "A prophet is not without honor—"

And Jenny laughed back at him; but neither of the two men was deceived by her laughter. The meal continued in almost unbroken silence.

Sir Nicholas was called to the telephone while they were still sitting over their coffee. He returned a few minutes later, frowning, and said without ceremony, "Can you do something for me this afternoon?"

Jenny said, "Yes, of course," but Antony maintained a cautious silence. He was still feeling ruffled, and had hoped for nothing so much as to be able to walk off his irritation when the party broke up.

"That was Miss Hunt. She says Winter's house was broken into last night."

Antony looked up, his attention caught immediately. "That's something we ought to find out about," he said positively.

"It is, indeed. She rang me, of course, as a friend of her cousin, someone she felt she could turn to. I've got to see Casterbridge this afternoon, so I promised—"

"And if you hadn't, it'd be all the same," said Antony; but he spoke without rancor. "Will you come with me, love?"

"Of course, I'd like to."

"That's all you know. You've never met her."

"I didn't know you had."

"Oh, yes, when I was twelve, or thereabouts."

"That doesn't count. You can't possibly know what she's like."

"I remember perfectly. She looks like an undertaker's widow. And I didn't like her; she looked at me."

"I wonder what she thought of you," remarked Sir Nicholas. His ill-humor seemed to have vanished, though Antony wondered uneasily how soon the topic would be reopened between them, without the restraint of Jenny's presence. He decided this was an unfruitful field of contemplation, and began to speculate instead on the identity of the police witness.

In the event, as Jenny afterwards admitted, Antony's recollections of Miss Hunt were more than vindicated; if anything, she had become even more intense with the years. She was a tall, slender woman, dark-haired and of dark complexion, and with an air, even on the most festive of occasions, of a Cassandra. She had been genuinely fond of her cousin, but still his death had supplied her with an excuse for mourning and for a display of dramatics, which she had seized with enthusiasm.

Antony recalled himself to her memory. After eyeing him in silence for a moment she said in a deep voice, "I remember. You came with your father. You were very cheerful."

Antony, feeling rather as though he had been accused, and convicted, of several of the more lurid Old Testament sins, only just stopped himself in time from apologizing for what had evidently been regarded as a lapse of taste. He backed away a little, and thanked Heaven he was married.

Jenny might be shy, but when driven to it she was quite capable of dealing with an awkward situation. She nobly suppressed her desire to giggle at her husband's look of agitation and expressed their condolences simply, but as gracefully as she could.

Miss Hunt turned to her and, taking both her hands, gazed deeply into her eyes. "Ah, you understand," she said at length. "You understand how one feels when a loved one has passed on."

Antony knew a moment's panic that Jenny might reply without thinking that people she knew usually just died. But he needn't have worried, she appeared to be riding the tide quite easily; and indeed was gazing back at her hostess with an almost comparable intensity. This gratified Miss Hunt, but was put down more correctly by Antony to a desire to avoid looking at him and being betrayed into unseemly laughter.

There followed half an hour of almost unrelieved gloom. Miss Hunt disserted at length upon her feelings; at less length upon the sad demise of her couisn. Jenny made sympathetic or otherwise appropriate noises, and at length ventured on a question.

"What happened last night, Miss Hunt? Sir Nicholas asked us—"

"The house was Broken Into! I cannot tell you, my dear, the shock, the repugnance with which that thought fills me—"

It took time, and more tact than Jenny had known she possessed, to elicit the story. The house had been entered during the night through the dining-room window; a general search seemed to have been made—the disorder was particularly noticeable in the study—but nothing seemed to have been taken except some housekeeping money the cook kept in a tea caddy on the kitchen mantelpiece. The police had, of course, been summoned, but seemed to have discovered nothing . . . certainly nothing to make them believe the burglary was in any way connected with the events in Bread Court. "But that," said Miss Hunt dramatically, "I Cannot Believe!"

"But, Miss Hunt, why? We were so fond of Mr. Winter, and we can't think of any reason for such a terrible thing to happen."

"Well you may say so, my dear. But I told that policeman—Sykes, he said his name was, and a very civil-spoken man, I will say that—mark my words, I told him, it was the work of a gang!"

Jenny gave a startled squeak at this unexpected pro-nouncement, but was about to inquire further when her hus-band once more took a hand in the conversation. She perceived he now had himself well under control; a little too well, perhaps, she reflected uneasily a moment later.

"I am very glad you were able to help the police, Miss Hunt. They must have been grateful for the assistance of a lady of your perception." His voice was grave and deferen-tial; he looked like a mute at a funeral.

She turned to him eagerly; and certainly there was noth-ing about him to remind her of earlier lapses into cheerful-ness. "The man was noncommittal, I do not believe he took me seriously. But what else could it have been?" She shook her head in a puzzled way, and for the first time a note of real feeling was to be heard in her voice. "James was—old-fashioned, I suppose you would say; a little severe, perhaps; set in his ways. But he was a good man, nobody could have disliked him enough to— to—"

"To stick a knife in his back?" broke in a voice from the doorway. Miss Hunt uttered a strangled shriek; and, recov-ering herself, said: "Mary! MY DEAR!" in a tone of deep reproach.

The girl in the doorway was in her late twenties; a squar-ish, sturdy figure whose tweed suit made no concessions to the heat. Her features were plain, with the exception of her eyes, which were brown, and really beautiful. She was frowning slightly, and took no notice of Antony's greeting (he was really behaving very nicely now, Jenny felt), but af-ter eyeing him consideringly for some time said abruptly, "You must be Antony Maitland. Charles said you'd been asking too many questions."

Before he could frame any reply to this rather uncomfortable statement, Miss Hunt broke in, saying with some asperity, "Sir Nicholas could not come; it was most courteous of Mr. and Mrs. Maitland to come in his place. Mr. Maitland has certainly not displayed any—any vulgar curiosity."

Mary Winter still appeared put out. She came into the room now, pushing the door behind her with one foot. Miss Hunt muttered introductions in an agitated way, but nobody took any notice of them.

"Oh, I've no doubt the inquisition would proceed tactfully."

"Painless extractions a specialty," murmured Antony. Miss Hunt looked puzzled.

Mary Winter gave him a baleful look, and said, "Don't let me cramp your style. What did you want my cousin to tell you?"

Antony could think of no reply to this, short of open rudeness. He became aware of Jenny at his elbow, and of her voice, with just a trace of tigress-defending-her-young to lend it tartness.

"I'm sorry if our visit gives you offense, Miss Winter. We came to see Miss Hunt, but I'm sure she will excuse us—"

This seemed to Antony the most sensible thing anybody had said for some time. He looked hopefully at his wife, who was now being subjected to the same considering look that had disturbed him a few minutes since. Jenny was now just angry enough to be completely without self-consciousness, and gave back glare for glare.

"I've no quarrel with you. But he," Mary Winter jerked her head in Antony's direction, "should leave the police to do their own dirty work."

"I can assure you, Miss Winter, I am even less popular with the police than I appear to be with you."

She took no notice. "Well, you can tell them one thing. I'm going to marry Charles, it was fixed up months ago, and Uncle was very pleased about it. Wasn't he, Cousin Clarissa?"

"It was indeed my poor cousin's wish that you and Charles should marry." Some of the intensity had returned to Miss Hunt's tone, and Antony wondered briefly if the

Cassandra-role was a refuge. It seemed to him that anyone seeing much of Mary Winter might need one.

"There, you see! So why should he—should either of us want to kill him?"

"I can't imagine." His tone had a quality of blandness, more effective than sarcasm. "Dare I wish you every happiness? I'm sure Charles is very much to be congratulated." Jenny gave him an admonitory nudge, and he turned again to Miss Hunt. "I'm sorry if our visit has distressed you. It was not our intention. But we really should be going now."

"Your visit was most kind. I hope you will both come again."

Jenny said quickly, "Of course we will."

"As to that," remarked Mary Winter, sending a parting shot after them as they went towards the door, "it *is* my house, after all."

Miss Hunt accompanied them to the gate, where she greatly embarrassed them by giving a hand to each, gazing at them soulfully, and saying, "I am indeed sorry you have met with such rudeness."

"Please don't think about it. I'm sure something must have upset her." Jenny knew her words were stupid, and had to admit that her husband's response was more effective.

Antony looked down at his hostess with a sudden, intimate smile and said, "Don't be too cross about it. She was so far right, you know: I shan't sleep tonight if you don't tell me—why a gang?"

"It was what James said." She looked all round before going on, then leaned towards him and spoke in a conspiratorial way. "I don't really know much about it, but a few days before—before he was called, you know—he said there was a lot of black market about. And then he said: 'but I know of one—racket, would it be?—that will soon be put a stop to.' That was all. Perhaps I'm being very silly. But I've heard that gangs sometimes do the most terrible things."

"I think it's a very sensible suggestion, Miss Hunt. I only wish the police were acting on it."

They went down the road to the station with feelings of mingled relief and guilt. It was hotter than ever, though the sun had gone and clouds were piling up; there was that feeling of tension in the air that so often precedes a storm.

"It really has been a most beastly day," said Jenny. "Anyway, we've got the evening to ourselves."

But the day had not yet finished with them. A few yards from the station entrance they walked straight into Charles Prentiss, who eyed Antony with suspicion, greeted Jenny with absent-minded politeness, and then inquired, "What are you doing here, anyway?" in no very gracious tone.

"We've been calling on Miss Hunt. Did you know they've been burgled?" Charles gave a growl that might have signified assent. "She phoned Uncle Nick, but he couldn't come this afternoon." He paused, and added, with deliberate malice, "We also had the pleasure of meeting your betrothed."

"I never," said Charles petulantly, "knew such a damned, inquisitive—"

Antony raised a hand. "Now don't, don't I implore you, say anything you may afterwards regret." He caught Jenny's eye. "Will you be getting the tickets, love? I'll see you in the station."

"Of course. Good-bye, Charles."

As she moved away Antony spoke with vigor. "Look here, I've had about enough of this. You ask my advice—and I bet you didn't take it! I reply with a number of inquiries, certainly; you'd have done the same in my place. However, this apparently enrages you to such an extent that I am now greeted with abuse not only by you (which I should be used to by this time) but by a young woman whom I have never seen before, and at the moment, I don't mind admitting, hope I never see again. All this you will at a later date expect me to excuse on the grounds that you are 'upset.' I shouldn't like to have your conscience, that's all."

"What do you mean, conscience?"

"Haven't you got one? Lucky fellow." He was on the point of departure, but looked back to say, "By the way, I do congratulate you on your engagement. When did you fix it up?"

Charles was still surly, but condescended to reply. "Last Tuesday. She was upset by the news, you know, and it sort of brought things to a head."

Antony was too polite to say what came into his mind. "Well, I must rush now. Give me a ring when you're feeling more amiable." He went into the station leaving Charles, or so he hoped, with a certain amount of food for reflection.

When they got out of the train at London Bridge it was already raining steadily. As they left the station the newsboys' placards greeted them with sensation.

"JOSEPH DOWLING ARRESTED!" they screamed. " 'MACBETH' HELD ON CHARGE OF MURDER."

It was such a story as reporters must dream of.

CHAPTER 9

DENNIS PHONED next morning while they were still sitting over breakfast. Antony spoke to him, and Jenny brought his last cup of coffee and put it down where he could reach it.

"You've heard, I expect. I don't see how anybody could help it."

"I saw the papers."

"Well—what about Sir Nicholas?"

"He told me he'd act if it became necessary."

"What does he think?"

This was not, Antony considered, the time to outline to Dennis the strength of the case against his father. He said, warily, "He hasn't much data yet, you know. As soon as he gets his teeth into it I'll get him to have a talk with you. Meanwhile, are you at a loose end? Why not come round here; we're alone, if that's any inducement."

Dennis laughed, and the sound was hollow and loud in Antony's ear. "There's nothing I'd like better. But I'm not exactly at a loose end."

"Oh?"

"No. I came over to see Mother—I'm in a phone box in the hotel lobby now. She's upstairs, packing. Then I'm to take her home." The prospect did not appear to enthrall him.

"But that's a good thing, isn't it? You said—"

"Never mind what I said. This isn't a reconciliation; she's got the bit between her teeth good and proper. It's all in the line of duty, but the minute Joe's free she'll walk out of the house again!" He paused, apparently to consider the prospect, and added even more despondently, "That is, of course, if—if ever—"

Antony began to sympathize with the other's agitation. He could think of no appropriate reply: to commiserate would be banal, to refrain would be bound to seem callous. He said, "Don't worry. We'll talk when you come," and put down the telephone. He looked at Jenny. "That was Dennis. He'll probably be round later on."

Jenny got up purposefully. "Then we'd better go out now, while we have the chance. We'll probably drown in the puddles, but the park ought to smell nice, after all that rain."

In the event, Dennis was not their first visitor. Meg Hamilton arrived at tea time, and Antony let her in, and thought the smile with which she greeted him a trifle halfhearted. He took her into the living room, and she stood a moment in the doorway, eyeing Jenny doubtfully. "I hope you don't mind my coming, Mrs. Maitland. I want to tell you—"

Antony, motivated more by prudence than hospitality (for he sensed tears in the offing) went away to the kitchen to fetch another cup. When he returned the two girls were sitting together on the sofa, obviously much too engrossed in their conversation to notice whether he was there or not. Meg was saying:

". . . very awkward. I knew why she left him, you see, though of course *they* never told me. Only I didn't know what to do about it. But Dennis said she had gone home, only she hadn't changed her mind really; so I thought it couldn't make it any worse if I went to see her. She's a very fine lady, you know, and I felt like nothing at all when I went in. But then she looked at me as if she were puzzled; I don't know why. So she said: 'This is a great pleasure, Miss Hamilton, but I really don't see why you have come here today.' Something like that. And I said: 'I came because I hoped you'd believe me when I tell you that Mr. Dowling never even looked at me.' She still looked at me a bit haughtily, and didn't answer. So—I never meant to—but I said: 'As for me, how could I be wanting him, when it's his son I'm in love with?' " She looked at Jenny, clearly at a loss. "After that, everything was all right."

"I'm so glad," said Jenny. She sounded, to her husband's accustomed ear, a little out of her depth; but he thought she was doing pretty well in the circumstances.

Meg nodded absently, clearly not attending. "It was a very forward thing to have said to her; but I told her, of course—afterwards—that it wasn't to worry about, he didn't care for me. That would make it all right, I expect." But she sounded a little doubtful. (Antony thought, privately, it was a very good thing she hadn't yet invested in a new coat.)

"I wouldn't worry," said Jenny, "I'm sure she understood. You can forget about it now, and we'll have some tea." Antony was already pouring out. He handed a cup to Meg and smiled at her; she had been crying, he thought, at some point in the afternoon's proceedings.

"Dennis is an idiot," he remarked thoughtlessly, and only realized his tactlessness when he saw Jenny making a face at him. Luckily, however, Meg seemed in no way embarrassed, though a trifle indignant at the suggestion.

"Indeed, he isn't. Why should he ever look twice at me, I'd like to know?"

"Well—" Antony looked at Jenny. "*I* can't tell you, my wife's here."

Meg weighed up the remark for a moment or two, then smiled from one to the other of them and began to drink her tea. Antony provided himself with a pile of sandwiches, and turned his attention to Jenny.

"Let me tell you, my love, this is *not* your cue to start matchmaking."

"Don't play the heavy husband, darling. What will Meg think of you?"

"Well, mind you remember what I said, that's all." He put down his cup and plate on the mantelpiece, and stood looking down at them, his back to the empty grate. Meg regarded him speculatively.

"You haven't brought him up properly," she said to Jenny. "But he looks quite harmless."

"Tyrannical to a degree," said Jenny.

Antony scowled at them, and succeeded in conveying, momentarily, such a likeness to the generally accepted no-tion of a Victorian Father, that Meg was quite startled, and spilled her tea.

"Don't mind him," said Jenny, placidly. "He gets taken that way sometimes."

"Then . . . shouldn't you be on the stage?"

"Oh, no, merely a parlor trick. I could always go on the halls, of course," he added, musingly. "I wonder what Uncle Nick would say."

The mention of Sir Nicholas brought Meg back to matters of importance. "Oh dear, I meant to ask you straightaway about poor Mr. Dowling. What will happen?"

"There'll be a hearing at the Magistrates' Court first—that's not very important; from there he'll be committed for trial. They'll probably try to fit it in during the present sitting, rather than leave it over the vacation."

"But, when the trial comes on. They couldn't find him guilty, could they? I'm sure he didn't do it. He's so full of . . . of turbulence," she added, turning to Jenny, "but he isn't like that really."

"I shouldn't worry too much. It's a long way from charge to verdict, you know."

"I suppose so." Meg sighed; but, seeing that Antony did not wish to be drawn into a discussion at this point, wisely left the subject.

Their number was implemented about half an hour later by the arrival of Dennis Dowling, who brought with him an atmosphere of mingled drama and insanity. Antony thought: "definitely straws in the hair" as soon as he opened the door.

Their visitor appeared to have lost his customary punctiliousness. "Do you know what Meg has been up to?" he inquired, almost before he was inside the door, and almost as explosively as his father might have done. He crossed the room to Jenny's side. "Forgive me for barging in, Mrs. Maitland, but it has been one hell of an afternoon."

"I'm sure it must have been. Sit down and Antony will find you a drink. Or would you like me to make some more tea?"

"Tea is not what he needs," said her husband, firmly. "Leave it to me."

Dennis, meanwhile, had become aware of Meg's presence. "What on earth are you doing here?" he demanded. Jenny considered his attitude dishearteningly brotherly. "I can't move an inch these days without falling over you."

Meg said with some assumption of dignity, "I came to see Mrs. Maitland. I might just as well ask you why you've come."

"That should be obvious. But, seeing you're here . . . to register a protest."

"I don't think that's fair," said Meg. "I only wanted to help. And I'm tired," she added with spirit, "of being treated like . . . like an adventuress."

"Well, all right. I'm sorry about that, but if you knew what I've been through—" He paused, apparently overcome by the recollection, and turned to Jenny again for sympathy. "Lord knows what went on between the pair of them. I know it started with an atmosphere you could have cut with a knife. I left them to it. Then afterwards it was all weeping and wailing, and not a word to be got out of either of them."

"You beast, Dennis," said Meg, dispassionately.

Antony rejoined them with a tray, and spoke over his shoulder to Dennis as he offered the contents to the others. "You have my sympathy. However, as I gather your mother has—er—abandoned her position—"

"Well," said Dennis, calming down a little as he accepted a glass, "I can't imagine what Meg said to her, but I can't complain of the result."

"I should think not, indeed." Meg had the grace to blush, but was still fighting. Jenny intervened.

"How is your mother, anyway?"

"I left her in sackcloth and ashes, preparing to write to Joe. After that she was proposing to go to bed. I wish I could think she'd sleep. This is a damnable business, Maitland. If only—"

They were interrupted by a knock on the outer door, and Antony got up with a faint sigh to answer it. He was beginning to feel like a tollhouse keeper, and eyed his uncle with some severity when he found him outside.

"I heard you had visitors, and wondered if, perhaps, young Dowling was here?"

"Come in," said Antony, resigned.

"I've just had a frantic telephone call from Oates; he's Dowling's solicitor, did you know? Anyway, he's perfectly appalled by all this, wants me to drop everything and hold his hand. I arranged a conference for eight-thirty, and told him to get hold of Stringer—will Jenny forgive me? And I'll have to go to the Magistrates' Court tomorrow morning—it's fairly early, and won't take long. If I'm late you'll have to cope with the Isaacs business. Don't worry, Evans always makes a slow start, I doubt if he'll reach his witnesses before I arrive. Anyway, you know our line."

"I'll do my best. But don't blame me if you find *all* the witnesses having hysterics."

"Don't you dare!" He went ahead of Antony into the living room, where he proceeded to cut Dennis off from the others and drive him across to comparative solitude by the front window, with such skill that his undutiful nephew wondered briefly whether he had some sheep-dog blood in him.

They did not talk for long, however. Dennis looked calmer when he left, taking Meg with him. Antony had not heard what was said, but could only suppose he had found Sir Nicholas's personality soothing; whatever tidings he had chosen to convey could hardly have been of a particularly cheering nature. He had no opportunity to inquire, as his uncle left almost immediately.

Jenny was collecting cups and plates and glasses. "They're both nice, aren't they? I wonder—"

Antony took the tray from her. "Dennis," he said firmly, "is in love with Miss Meadows at the office."

"He may not stay in love with her. I like Meg."

"You'd like Eve Meadows too, if you knew her." Antony rescued an overlooked glass, and made for the kitchen, with Jenny following.

"Is she nice?"

"I don't know. I don't know her well enough to say. I expect you'd find her so."

"I'm not so easily pleased. She sounds a bit—glamorous."

"Well, what's wrong with that?"

Jenny made a scornful noise, and reached for her apron. Antony tied the strings, and inquired, "Did Uncle Nick tell you I'd have to go down to see Oates? Eight-thirty . . . but it shouldn't take long." He added, hopefully, "What's for supper?"

"Darling, you're not hungry already?"

"Well—"

"Then we'll eat first, and I'll wash up when you've gone. Reach me that big basin will you?"

Mr. Oates was a "family" solicitor—the type of man who was more at ease on a golf course than in court. As it happened, criminal cases never came his way; and he was frankly appalled by the sensational nature of the affair in which his most sensational client was now involved. Divorcing Joseph Dowling was one thing; defending him on a murder charge, quite another.

He arrived in Kempenfeldt Square that evening with a bulging brief case and a harassed air. He was accompanied by Derek Stringer, a spare young man with a high forehead and hair already thinning, whose career at the Bar was (like Antony's) considerably shorter than it should have been because of the war years. Fortunately, his disposition was calm, which was more than could be said at this moment of the solicitor. Oates showed a definite tendency to throw the whole thing into Sir Nicholas's lap, and the two younger men watched with some amusement the game of pitch and toss which developed, while the barrister gently but irresistibly placed the onus of the instructions where he felt it belonged. Having eventually established their respective situations to his own satisfaction, however, counsel relented, and generously offered Antony's services in the matter of preparing the case. Mr. Oates, who was by now perspiring freely, accepted with some enthusiasm.

"And now," said Sir Nicholas. "The case against your client."

The solicitor again registered distress. ("Really," said Sir Nicholas later, "*not* a constructive attitude!") "The police appear to think," he began, "that Joseph Dowling, having left Winter's office at—at twelve minutes past four, was it not?—walked to the end of Bread Court, and then turned and went back up the private stair. A clerk in Hill's office saw him return and has identified him.''

"Have they made anything of a test on that point?"

"Apparently the man claims to have seen his face; the question of an identification parade hardly arises, as, of course, my client's appearance is so very well known.''

"I see. Well, my nephew can help us on this point, as I'll explain in a moment. But this matter of the dagger—''

"My dear sir, I do not understand it! A dagger is admittedly missing from the theater, a souvenir presented to him by his—er—his leading lady after the production of *Macbeth* in 1944. Dowling is said to be greatly attached to it, I understand—which perhaps explains why it has not been lost or mislaid before now. But—''

"He was hardly in the habit of carrying it on his person, however?"

"Why, no—it would have been quite unsuitable.''

"But he would not have had time to go back to the theater?" Sir Nicholas was thinking aloud. "They must, therefore, be prepared to maintain premeditation. What do you think of that, Stringer?"

"Not much, " said Derek frankly. "It would be one thing to persuade a jury that Joe did it in a sudden fury. Even the fact that he went away once detracts from that picture, but to maintain he went prepared—''

"Yes, but it would be said that the scene in the office was deliberate, that he left in anger purposely, so that just that line of argument would obtain.''

"Yes, I suppose—''

"Farfetched, sir," said Antony.

"I could make a jury believe it," said Sir Nicholas simply, "Who's leading for the Crown, Oates?"

"Halloran, I am told.''

"Well, then! As I see it, we're up against the inherent improbability of anybody wanting to kill Winter. So when there's a ready-made suspect—breathing fire and slaughter, too—the police are bound to fix on him. The question is, how deeply did Dowling really believe that

Winter was responsible for his wife's refusal to return to him?''

"My dear Harding—I know only that he has said so repeatedly . . . and not only to me!"

"Hm! Well, I have a fair knowledge of what happened, but there are certain points which must be covered by the depositions—" (Oates patted his brief case hopefully, but resigned himself to being questioned when Sir Nicholas waved aside the proffered papers.) "First of all, what did the police find in the room?"

"Nothing out of the ordinary, as I understand it." Sir Nicholas looked despairingly heavenwards; the two younger men exchanged glances, and Stringer said helpfully:

"Fingerprints?"

"It is all written down . . . all most complicated," protested the solicitor.

"Well, at least," said Antony, "the door to the private stair?"

"The office boy's were the only ones in any way clear, and even they were smudged."

"Item," said Stringer, "did Joe wear gloves?"

"I can answer that one," Antony put it. "Miss Harris noticed he had a pair shoved in his pocket."

"Helpful!" snapped his uncle. "What else?"

"If you mean fingerprints," said Oates despairingly, "everybody's. All the office staff."

"Well, I never thought they dusted that office, anyway," said Antony. "The other thing is—and it's probably not helpful either—but, what was J.W. writing when he died?"

"Writing?" said Oates.

"He was writing when Miss Harris went in, which wasn't very long before—"

"There was nothing in the depositions, I assure you."

"Then I'll have to ask Sykes . . ."

There followed a discussion of Antony's evidence which Sir Nicholas, to his nephew's relief, kept short and to the point. After a while the talk became technical, and Antony allowed his attention to wander. He was finding that the legal aspects of this particular case were apt to be swamped by the personalities involved, and was trying to remember what he knew of the clerk in Hill's office, John Armstrong. There was little that could usefully be said, however, and Oates and Stringer departed at last, leaving Sir Nicholas with a look of frustration and a shcaf of notes. He sent his nephew back to his own quarters forthwith; even refraining, with what Antony felt was true nobility, from any last-minute instructions about tomorrow's case.

CHAPTER 10

SIR NICHOLAS was not very late next morning, and by lunchtime the case was well launched. Jenny was waiting for them at their favorite, most convenient restaurant, and explained that she had been shopping, and hoped she might find them there.

"Did you have a successful morning?"

Jenny nodded vigorously. "Meg Hamilton rang up. It was very important, because she wanted to buy a hat."

Sir Nicholas passed her the menu. "I never knew your wife had so strange a sense of values," he remarked to his nephew.

"The point being, sir, that it's probably the first shopping Meg has ever done, in London anyway."

"Oh, I see. That makes a difference." He glanced over his shoulder and added, "I think our waiter's just coming. Have you made up your mind, Jenny?"

"Something with salad, I think."

"Ah, yes, I think you're wise. We'll consult Marco, he always knows. Will that do you, Antony?"

"Not nearly sustaining enough. The mixed grill, I think—if Marco approves, of course; and if he pronounces it substantial."

"I sometimes wonder," remarked Jenny in a considering way, "whether I might not just as well be married to a boa constrictor."

Marco arrived, and was voluble with advice. When they had settled down again Antony turned to his uncle.

"How did it go this morning, sir?"

"Not quite as expected. I had barely a word with Dowling: Oates will take me to see him this evening. He seemed fairly subdued, not unnaturally. I shall be interested to make his further acquaintance.''

"But what went wrong?''

"That was not what I said. The police sprang a surprise, though, by asking for an adjournment to give them time to collect further evidence.''

"They aren't having second thoughts?''

"I certainly did not gain that impression.''

"But—was the Bench willing to play?''

Sir Nicholas looked his disapproval of this casual phrasing. "Nolan was sitting alone; he granted the adjournment—if that is what you mean.''

"But—''

"It was beautifully done—through Halloran, of course. They were very careful, and very proper . . . Superintendent Briggs is a clever man. But certainly the magistrate must have got the impression that Dowling was dangerous, and had been put under immediate restraint in the public interest. In those circumstances the police request for time to prepare their case seemed reasonable—even praiseworthy. And there was nothing I could say that would have helped, at this stage.''

"Did you see Dennis?''

"He came with Oates. Now there's a young fellow who's under a strain, and nothing new about it either, from the look of him. He seems to have taken this divorce business very hard.''

"Yes, he did, though he seemed to think he could handle it, given time—if Meg Hamilton hadn't got in first. But there's more to it than that; think of the life he's been leading since he was articled—office all day, theater in the evening.''

"Hm,'' said Sir Nicholas.

"I don't mean they're a rackety family: leaving aside Joe's tendency to explode, they seem to be rather quiet people. You've only to see the way they treat Meg Hamilton; Dennis has the job of looking after her, and she has obviously no idea of how different the life of a young and very successful actress could be. But Dennis's finals are only a few months off; there was a pile of law books in his father's dressing room, so I rather think that's where he does his studying. It's no wonder he finds it wearing.''

"And if he gets his finals—" said Jenny.

"—which Miss Harris seems to think unlikely,'' interpolated Antony.

"If he does pass, what then?''

"The mixture as before, I expect. And if you have your way, my love—''

"What on earth has Jenny to do with it?'' inquired his uncle.

"She's matchmaking. She wants Dennis to marry Meg.''

"Dear me,'' said Sir Nicholas, returning placidly to his luncheon. "What a tiresome pair you are, to be sure!''

"I don't think I've much chance of succeeding, anyway,'' said Jenny, ignoring this. "Dennis is in love with a girl at the office called Eve Meadows.''

"And she's in love with Charles Prentiss,'' said Antony.

"Who has thrown her over for an heiress,'' added Jenny, taking up the recital with enthusiasm.

Sir Nicholas gave an exclamation indicative of extreme disgust, and unfolded a copy of *The Times*.

Miss Carmichael did not have hysterics, though Antony felt it was touch and go several times. He succeeded eventually, however, in eliciting from her a version of her current evidence that was not especially unfavorable to Mr. Isaacs, and sat down again feeling, on the whole, not dissatisfied. A glance at his uncle had a neutralizing effect on his complacency, but most likely the older man's air of fierce concentration was merely due to the intricacies of the case in general. After a few moments, when the prosecution showed no disposition to re-examine, Sir Nicholas relaxed and said quietly, "All right, I'll carry on. We'd better compare notes tonight, try not to be too late.''

"I won't,'' Antony promised, and departed as unostentatiously as he could.

The offices of Thomas Hill, Solicitor, were at Number 6, Bread Court. Wishing to interview the clerk, John Armstrong, Antony sought first the head of the firm; that genial gentleman was only too glad to oblige him in any way he could, and pressed him to take as much time as he wished over the conversation. "And I fancy," he added, "that you'd better see young Harvey, as well. Talk to him first, if you like, and then see what Armstrong has to say."

Antony was suitably grateful, and expressed his willingness to profit from the advice. Thomas Hill stabbed the bell on his desk three times with a plump forefinger, and in a surprisingly short space of time the junior clerk appeared.

He was smaller and slighter than his opposite number in Mr. Winter's office; altogether more sober, both in appearance and movement, though when he spoke he displayed an eager friendliness with all and sundry which Mr. Armstrong had predicted, more than once, would lead him into trouble.

Mr. Hill gave a short introductory address; Harvey listened solemnly, but beamed at him when he stopped speaking.

"Yes, sir. Of course, sir. I know Mr. Maitland, so I'll be glad to help him if I can."

Mr. Hill waved a hand, as if to say, "Your witness."

"I just want you to tell me about last Tuesday afternoon, Harvey. Do you remember?"

A foolish question! "Of course I remember. What do you want to know?"

"Whether you observed any comings and goings across the court. I know you saw me coming; perhaps I wasn't the only person you noticed."

"I was out early in the afternoon." Harvey was regretful. "I had to go round to the Ideal Homes Building Society for some cash, and they kept me ages; so when I got back Mr. Armstrong was waiting to leave."

"What time was this?"

"It must have been just before three, because I know that's when he was due at Mr. Winter's office; he was getting fussed, for he always likes to be in plenty of time."

"And after that—?"

"Well, Mr. Armstrong went, and there was quite a lot to do, I was busy for a while. I did look out of the window, once or twice, because we were wondering where Mr. Armstrong had got to, he was quite a long time. There was a big man going in, just as he was coming out of Number Seven; they got sort of tangled up in the doorway."

"Did you notice what time that was?"

"About half-past three. At least, I looked at the clock then, and a few minutes later I saw Mr. Armstrong coming."

"And the man who bumped into him; can you describe him at all?" That must have been Joseph Dowling; Miss Harris had said he arrived just after the half-hour.

"Oh, yes. He was the sort of person you notice, you know. I think he was tall, but it's difficult to be sure when you're looking down from a window."

"You saw me walking down the court later. How did he compare with me, for instance? Does that help?"

"Yes, of course, I hadn't thought of that." Harvey frowned for a moment, concentrating. "He would be very nearly as tall as you are, Mr. Maitland. And about three times as wide," he added with a grin.

Antony's answering smile was a trifle absent-minded. "A tall man, heavily built. What else about him?"

"He had a pretty big nose and chin. And I don't think he was a dark man, because his face didn't look as if he had to shave a lot."

"How was he dressed?"

"Just ordinary; like you are, and Mr. Hill."

The two men regarded each other gravely; both seeing as in a distorted mirror, a reflection of his own black jacket and striped trousers. (And, of course, it was unthinkable that Joseph Dowling, visiting in the city, should have done anything else than dressed the part.)

"Hat?" queried Antony after a moment.

"A soft, dark one. Black, I think." Harvey hesitated. "He was dressed like anybody round here, but he didn't look as if he belonged here, either."

"Why was that, I wonder?"

"He looked as if he knew where he was going. I mean— well, for instance, when I saw you, Mr. Maitland, you were strolling along thinking about things; and most of the men you see round here give you that idea. But this man—I said he was big, but moved neatly, somehow; and he wasn't thinking at all, he was just going."

"That's very clear, Harvey. Thank you. What happened next?"

"Well, I told you he bumped into Mr. Armstrong. That was in the doorway of Number Seven. Of course, I didn't know which of the offices he was going to, but Mr. Armstrong stood a moment, and watched him up the stairs, and into the door at the top. Then he came back here—Mr. Armstrong, I mean, and he wasn't half—he wasn't in a very good temper. You see, he didn't like having to wait for Mr. Winter; and then, of course, he doesn't approve of the stage, so he thought it was something rather dreadful, colliding with an actor."

"He recognized him, then?"

"Yes, he told me it was Joseph Dowling I'd seen. I was glad I'd noticed him so particularly, because, of course, I'd heard of him."

"I see. What then?"

"Nothing more for a bit, because he remembered all sorts of things I had to do that I'd forgotten about. So we were all running about. But when we stopped for a cup of tea I was sitting on the desk and looking out of the window. And I saw you coming, and I think I said: 'there's Mr. Maitland'; and I leaned out of the window to wave to you. And Mr. Armstrong came up to look over my shoulder, and said: 'And there's Joseph Dowling, going back to Mr. Winter's office for something he's forgotten.' So I looked, and he was just going into the private door. Then I waved to you, and Mr. Armstrong was muttering something about 'impertinence,' but I think for once he didn't mean me, but because Mr. Dowling was using that way in." Harvey paused for breath, but only for a moment. "Is that what you wanted to know about?"

"Yes, that's very helpful. Now, will you think back very carefully to the time you saw me walking down Bread Court. Did you see Mr. Dowling in front of me?"

"Not until he was going into the door. I was looking at you."

"But you saw him, and recognized him, before he turned into the doorway of Number Seven?"

"Not exactly. I looked when Mr. Armstrong spoke, and just saw his back as he went in."

"Can you swear it was the same man you saw earlier?"

"Well, I'm sure it was, because he was the same build, and had a dark suit, and moved like Mr. Dowling did."

"Can you swear to it?"

"No. No, I couldn't do that. But Mr. Armstrong saw him better than I did."

"Then I'd better ask him about it. Thank you, Harvey, I'm very grateful for your help." As the door closed Antony smiled at the solicitor, who had been sitting patiently throughout the interview, and had, commendably, refrained from interference. "He's an observant boy, Hill, but I wonder if he'd have recognized Dowling if Armstrong had said nothing."

"That, of course, I don't know. But I can assure you, Maitland, Armstrong is a most respectable man, and has been with me for many years."

"He might still be mistaken."

"Possibly. He is very sure of his facts, however. Ah, here he is. Come in, Armstrong, Mr. Maitland wants to ask you a few questions."

John Procter Armstrong was a slight man, of middle height, sharp featured, and with thinning hair that even in its heyday could have warranted no more flattering description than that of mouse-colored. Antony did not feel attracted to him, but told himself with some asperity that this was prejudice, and not to be regarded. He opened proceedings, therefore, with rather more than his customary affability; but his remarks were received with a coolness which he found rather daunting.

The clerk was not, however, unwilling to give his version of the afternoon's events. In the main his statement was neat and precise, in a way that was typical of him.

"It was nearly three o'clock when Harvey came back with the money I needed to attend the completion. I hurried across to Mr. Winter's office, and I must say it was a surprise to be kept waiting so long, he was generally a most punctual gentleman. I can't say I noticed any difference in his manner from what was usual; not knowing him personally, it wasn't to be expected that I should. I left about half-past three, Mrs. Carey stayed with Mr. Winter; she seemed a very pleasant lady, and most respectable. In the street doorway I bumped into Joseph Dowling. I recognized him from pictures I have seen in the press from time to time.''

"Haven't you seen him in the theater?''

"No, Mr. Maitland. Such is not my habit." Armstrong's denial came sharply, and from the glance he gave his employer Antony was pretty sure he would have elaborated the theme if they had been alone. "However, I was in no doubt about it; and, in fact, I understand that Mr. Dowling arrived at Mr. Winter's office almost immediately after I left it. I was a little upset by the encounter; it was certainly not my fault that the collision took place, but his manner was far from civil, and he brushed past me with an oath.''

Antony privately considered it would not have been very difficult to shock Mr. Armstrong, but in deference to the other's feelings clicked his tongue in a grave and sympathetic manner.

Thus encouraged, the clerk continued, "I came back to this office. I saw nothing further that was pertinent to your inquiry until Harvey remarked that you were in Bread Court. I looked out of the window and saw you, and just ahead of you this actor. He turned into the private door, and I noticed it particularly, knowing Mr. Winter's views on the matter.''

"You saw his face before he turned? You can identify him positively?''

"Oh, yes, Mr. Maitland, I can swear it was Mr. Dowling.''

"I see. You can also swear to the time, I believe.''

"I looked at the clock, it was then ten minutes past four. I thought to myself, you see: 'but it's only a few minutes since I saw him going in before.' Then I realized that it was later than I thought.''

"Weren't you suprised to see him going back?''

"Not really. I thought he had forgotten something, and was going back to fetch it.''

"Supposing I told you, Mr. Armstrong, that the defense have a witness who will state categorically that whoever it was you saw going into that door last Tuesday afternoon, it was not Mr. Joseph Dowling." (And why wrap it up, he thought a little wearily as he spoke? It was obvious the clerk must know who the witness was.) ''What would you have to say to that?'' he added.

''I should say, Mr. Maitland,'' said Armstrong, looking at the younger man with a certain amount of malice in his regard, ''I should say he was . . . mistaken.''

CHAPTER 11

WHEN ANTONY left Mr. Hill's office about ten minutes later, he decided that a visit to Mr. Arthur Green could most easily be taken in on his way home; after which he would call it a day, at least so far as interviews went. There was a disagreeable necessity at the back of his mind, a thought only half acknowledged: he'd have to talk to Uncle Nick, and best get it over without delay. There were other witnesses, of course, but their evidence could wait one more day, at least.

Mr. Green had a good address, but the mews property he occupied proved, on inspection, to have about it an air both shabby and makeshift. The double doors were heavily padlocked, and the smaller door, which led to the flat upstairs, presented an uninviting, unpainted exterior, and had neither bell nor knocker. Antony knocked, and waited. He knocked again, rather more loudly, and waited again. At length came the sound of unhurried footsteps on uncarpeted stairs, and the door was opened by a man who was obviously not there in response to his summons but because he was on his way out.

He admitted his name was Green, though with a cautious air, as though the fact might somehow be incriminating. Antony explained his errand, and thought for a moment he would meet with a flat refusal to cooperate; after a pause, however, Green turned and led the way upstairs again, though he did it with a bad grace.

The room to which he took Antony was barely furnished, though what it did contain in the way of chairs and a table, was good stuff, and looked comfortable. This there was no opportunity of testing, as the interview was conducted standing; Green evidently felt that an air of impermanence would get rid of his unwelcome visitor most quickly.

"I'm sorry to trouble you, Mr. Green, but I'm sure you'll appreciate the urgency of the matter."

"I've already been put to a good deal of trouble. It isn't as if there was anything I could say to help you."

"I won't keep you long." Antony was studying the other covertly; a big-boned man, thin, and in hard condition, with black hair, cut very short, and an air of recklessness that was unexpected. "There are just a few things I want to get straight, for the record, you know."

Green eyed him warily, and said, "Get on with it, then," though with no great appearance of resignation.

"Arthur Green: is that your full name?"

"Arthur James—if that's any help to you."

"Thank you. And your occupation, Mr. Green?"

"Put me down as an agent." This was said with a sardonic air; altogether, Antony considered, his attitude was unnecessarily complicated. He essayed an inquiring look, and was rewarded by a little further information. "No special line. I buy whatever comes to hand, and generally there's a little profit to be picked up."

"On the afternoon James Winter died you called to see him at his offices in Bread Court?"

"That's right. He wanted to see me about renewing my lease to this place."

"What time did you get there?"

"My appointment was for two-thirty. I was a little early, I think."

"And your business was concluded satisfactorily, I hope?"

"Oh, quite." Green's laugh had an uneasy sound about it. "It was only a matter of agreeing on a new lease he'd drawn up; he said he'd have it typed out for me to sign."

"And what time did you leave him?"

Green shrugged. "After three o'clock. That's the best I can do, I'm afraid. I just didn't notice."

"About the quarter hour, perhaps? I have been told that was the time you left."

"Near enough. I wasn't watching the clock."

"Well, that's all very clear." Green made a tentative movement towards the door. "Just one other thing, if you don't mind. Did you notice anything unusual in Mr. Winter's manner during your talk with him?"

"I'm hardly in a position to say. I'd never seen him before."

"You must have seen Mr. Prentiss in your previous dealings with the firm?"

"No, I'd never been there before. I took over the premises from the previous tenant; he had to get permission to sublet, and send them my references, and so on. But I never had any personal dealings with them until this business of renewal arose."

"I see," said Antony. "All the same," he persisted, "granted he was a stranger to you, was there anything in Mr. Winter's manner to cause you surprise?"

"He seemed perfectly normal. So far as I could tell."

"Did you notice the door in the corner of the room, which leads to the private stair?"

Green paused to consider; but rather, Antony felt, the implications of the question than the answer he should give. "No," he said at length, "no, I can't say I did."

Antony expressed his gratitude, and took his leave. Green followed him down to the street door, but did not, after all, go out just then. Antony made his way home at a gentle pace, with plenty of food for thought.

When supper was finished Antony announced that he ought to see Sir Nicholas. "Why don't you go to the pictures?" he inquired. "Isn't there anything you'd like to see?"

Jenny looked at him for a moment, then said, "Yes, that's a good idea," and went off without further ado to fetch her coat. They went downstairs together, and Antony found Sir Nicholas still at table, having returned late from his interview with Joseph Dowling.

"Can I sit here and talk to you while you finish?"

"That's a good idea. How did you get on?"

"Not too badly." Antony, who had no wish, this evening, to irritate his uncle, paused a moment to consider before embarking on his recital. "I'll make detailed notes for

Oates later, and just give you the gist now. I've talked to Armstrong; he makes a positive identification, no compromises.''

"Why is he lying?" queried Sir Nicholas.

"That is not apparent. I don't imagine it will be too difficult to throw some doubt on his testimony. Hill lays great stress on his reliability; I daresay he's right as far as his work goes, but I should judge him to be the sort of man who is never wrong. Further, he's a member of one of these hell-fire sects—I'd never even heard the name before—and considers anything at all amusing to be of the devil. When he looked out of the office window and saw me going down the court, he also saw a man just about to turn into the door of the private stair; he had Dowling on the brain, was feeling ruffled by their encounter, and straightaway decided that he was going back for something he had left behind. That's reasonable enough: the second man was dressed in a dark suit and was of comparable figure to Dowling. Along come the police, asking if he's seen anything; oh, yes, he saw Joseph Dowling, the actor. I expect they pressed him pretty closely on the subject, but that's his story, and come hell or high water he's sticking to it. He says he saw Dowling's face but I think that was a later addition. It's not quite the same as deliberate lying; I expect he really thought it was Joe he saw, and he just can't admit, even to himself, that he might have been mistaken.''

"Hm," said Sir Nicholas, meditatively spreading butter on a cheese biscuit. "What about the office boy?"

"He corroborates. He can't swear it was Dowling, only that Armstrong says it was. His evidence might be damaging, for all that; he saw Dowling earlier in the afternoon, and says this man moved like him. He can also trot out, quite pat, several other points of resemblance. Not conclusive, of course.''

"No-o." The older man sounded doubtful. "There is, of course, the possibility that Armstrong's inaccurate evidence has a simpler but more sinister explanation.''

"Yes, there's that. He couldn't have killed Mr. Winter, but he could have unlocked the door. He'd a very good chance of knowing the lie of the land. But that opens so wide a field for speculation I don't think we can go into it now—we've no reason to suspect a conspiracy, after all."

"So I am left with the trusted managing clerk to a reputable solicitor, a clerk who is also a religious maniac and insanely opinionated." Sir Nicholas cut a portion of cheese, and eyed it severely. "Hm," he said again.

"I deliberately refrained from pressing him on the matter, sir. But I'm pretty sure he knows that it's me he's giving the lie to."

"Very likely."

"I've been thinking, if the man I saw really went up the private stair, the time element would be heavily in Joe's favor. But if you throw doubt on one bit of his evidence, who's to believe the rest?"

"Who, indeed? Well, I'll see the proof in due course. But I'll tell you now, I don't like it." Antony looked inquiring, and his uncle went on, "The one subject you must never cross-examine a man about is his religion. It's a million to one it'll recoil on your own head. You can establish his beliefs—preferably on direct examination—if they have a clear relation to your case; but the kind of question I should have to ask in this instance to establish bias . . . never!"

"I see." Antony thought this over for a moment, and found it depressing. He went on briskly. "I made one more visit, to Arthur James Green. He's a queer chap; gentleman by birth, I'd say; man of action; not one of the great brains of the age. He showed too plainly he didn't welcome questions and then answered at unnecessary length."

"Winter's black marketeer?"

"I should think so. Sees himself as a cross between the Saint and Bulldog Drummond, or I miss my guess."

"Could he have been mistaken for Dowling?"

"I think so. They're much of a height. I rang up Miss Harris, and she says he was wearing a dark suit; thought it would create an atmosphere of respectability, I daresay. He's much thinner than Joe is, though."

"I must also mention that he has an alibi, or so Oates tells me. A Mr. Jennings, who called on him at about ten to four, and remained for an hour or so."

" 'Death, where is thy sting?' But perhaps he's a doubtful character, too," said Antony hopefully. "Did Oates know?"

"Would Oates be likely to know? He gave me his address, and no more than that."

"Well, *I* can't do anything about it, that's certain. Witnesses, yes; their alibis, no. But I suppose Oates has someone he can put on to it."

"I doubt it. However, with sufficient prompting he may be induced to oblige."

"There are a number of things to cover, of course."

"So there are. I'll see him again tomorrow." Sir Nicholas sounded depressed at the prospect, and Antony hid an unsympathetic grin.

"How was the Isaacs business going?" he inquired.

"Much as expected. Tomorrow might see it through; perhaps that's being too optimistic, but it won't be very long now. I'll put you in the picture presently."

"First, I'd like to hear how you got on with Joe."

Sir Nicholas smiled. "Words fail me. I found him elated, and busily composing a letter to his wife, for the express purpose of saying 'I told you so.' I can't say he had much information for me; most of my time was spent in trying to explain to him that it is vital he should give his evidence in a reasonable manner when the time comes. As to that, I'm not optimistic. However, it's early days yet."

There was a pause. Antony sipped his coffee, and eyed his uncle. Finally, he put down the cup and said, with an air of resolution, "Uncle Nick, I don't want to worry you, but have you considered that when the case comes up there are several points which the prosecution can make, which will tend to make the jury credit Armstrong's evidence rather than mine?" Sir Nicholas compressed his lips, but said nothing. "I mean—I can't deny being friendly with Dennis; you know better than I do how easy it is to insinuate things. And there's even our relationship . . . I know they can't do it directly, but don't you think they'll bring that in?"

Sir Nicholas got up, and began to walk up and down the room. "Of course they'll bring it in!" His tone was testy. "I can probably stop either point being admitted as evidence, but short of gagging the prosecution I see no way of stopping them from getting them over. Once the implication is made, it will most likely be best to make no objection.''

Antony could think of nothing to say, and sat in silence while his uncle continued his pacing. After a while Sir Nicholas paused, and looking down at his nephew said in a normal tone, as though the subject had only just been raised, ''You're quite right, of course. It's time we spoke frankly together on the subject. I had hoped it might not yet have occurred to you, in which case there seemed no point in our both worrying about it.'' He moved towards the fireplace, and leaned his shoulders against the high, oak mantel. ''I gave you credit, you see, for not wishing to draw back, even when you realized what a rough passage you're likely to have. So far, I have thought of no fewer than seven lines which Halloran can take in cross-examination—none of which it is possible for you to counter. Heaven knows, I wouldn't call you if I had any alternative. But what can I do?''

''It's all right, Uncle Nick. Dowling's got his point of view, after all!''

Sir Nicholas was pursuing his own train of thought. ''I can do a good deal to take the sting out of the two points we've mentioned. If I bring out our relationship in your evidence-in-chief, and also your acquaintance with young Dowling, it is the easiest thing in the world to tell the jury my learned friend would like them to take special note of these facts, and throw a little advance ridicule on his interpretation of them. But when Halloran gets going . . . well, I can't say what line he'll take, but it isn't likely to present you in an amiable light to the jury. We've got to face the fact, unless we can prove outright that Armstrong is lying, it isn't likely to do your career any good.''

''That's what I thought.''

''I'm not too happy about the case, I must admit. They've to choose between your evidence or Armstrong's; but there's also this business of the weapon, which is bad as it stands. And, as I've said before, the sheer unlikelihood of James Winter getting himself killed is against us. We've got to have good grounds for asking the jury to look further for the murderer than a man who had admittedly been bitterly antagonistic to the dead man for some time now. The fact that you'll have an uncomfortable time with Halloran is beside the point; what matters is the impression your evidence will leave—unless we can prove Dowling innocent.''

That was plain speaking, with a vengeance—and no more than he had asked, after all. ''Do you think you can get him off?'' he wondered.

''Is he innocent? You were in some doubt about that yourself, weren't you?''

''Lord, I don't know! If the man Armstrong saw really went in the private door—! What do you think, Uncle Nick?''

The older man eyed him steadily. ''I think he's innocent. That's instinct, I admit, and, as such, I distrust it profoundly. Perhaps I only believe it because it's got to be true.''

Antony got up. He was both glad and sorry that he had voiced his worries: glad because his uncle was a good ally and there was comfort to be had in his strength and confidence; sorry because the issue was clarified now and he found the prospect cold and cheerless. ''There's no use dwelling on it,'' he said, and did not realize how completely his expression gave the lie to his words. He went to the other side of the fireplace, where an electric percolator stood in the hearth. ''Can I warm this coffee up, Uncle Nick? I'd like another cup, and yours has gone cold.''

Sir Nicholas looked down at him as he bent to fiddle with the plug. ''You're a good boy, Antony,'' he remarked; and received in reply, so startled a glance from his nephew that he began to laugh. ''Very well, we'll drown our sorrows in coffee, and then get down to the Isaacs affair again.''

''I had thought,'' said Antony, plugging in the percolator and scrambling to his feet again, ''that you might be feeling slightly aggrieved—after all, if I hadn't got mad when Briggs questioned me—''

''You may console yourself with the reflection that it'd have made not a ha'p'orth of difference,'' said Sir Nicholas, unexpectedly. ''You became involved in this affair when you walked down Bread Court behind a man who was *not* Joseph Dowling.''

''So I did,'' said Antony. ''That hadn't occurred to me.''
Neither of them was feeling particularly cheerful when

they separated for the night. Sir Nicholas set himself determinedly to a study of the case "Rex v. Connor," for which he had developed a profound distaste. Antony went slowly upstairs, and didn't know whether to be glad or sorry when he found Jenny had not yet returned. He considered a drink, but decided against it: no harm, though, in preparing for her coming. He set out glasses and rummaged in the larder until he came across a tin containing a large fruit cake that looked as if it might be ready for cutting.

As he returned to the living room with this trophy the telephone rang. He had an impulse to ignore it, but was overtaken by a horrid image of Jenny, run over by a bus, and snatched off the receiver in alarm. The voice of Charles Prentiss greeted him, saying in aggrieved tones, "I've been trying to get you all evening."

Antony restrained another, and stronger, impulse to ring off. He said, "I've been out," and his voice was deceptively mild.

"Well, I thought—" Charles sounded to be in difficulties. He said, at last, in a rush. "I hoped you could meet Mary, properly. You and Jenny, of course. The other day, we were both upset, not ourselves; I'm sure you'll understand."

"I think so." Antony was in no mood, this evening, to be conciliatory. "Jenny, however, has far too nice a mind to put the same construction as I did on your behavior."

"I say, that's a bit thick."

"Well, think it over. As for meeting, I'll get Jenny to write to Miss Winter and fix something; when I'm not quite so rushed as I am now."

"That'll be fine, then."

"By the way, Charles, did you take my advice? You never told me."

"Advice?"

"To tell the police where you were on Tuesday afternoon."

"No, I didn't. I knew there was no need, and I was right, wasn't I? They've cleared it up, now."

"They've made an arrest, certainly."

"Well, then!"

"Unfortunately, from some points of view, I'd give you odds that Dowling didn't do it."

"Here!" said Prentiss, in agitated tones. "Say that again." Antony obliged. "Anyway, what makes you think that?"

"Uncle Nick is defending. I've got inside information." Prentiss sounded relieved. "You mean he's pleading 'not guilty'?"

"I mean just what I said: I don't think he did it."

"Now, look here, Antony, if you're thinking of using information I gave you in confidence to bolster up this defense of yours—"

"Calm yourself, Charles; whatever I think I won't say anything without proof." This was hardly fair, perhaps. But no more, he felt, than the other deserved. Olive branch, indeed! "By the way, shall I ask Jenny to write to Mary Winter?"

"Oh, go to hell!" said Charles, exasperated, and the line went abruptly dead. Antony grinned to himself, and was sufficiently cheered by the conversation to put on quite a good show when Jenny came in; not good enough, of course, to leave her in any doubt as to the real state of his spirits . . . but he wasn't to know that.

CHAPTER 12

IT RAINED again during the night; and next morning was dull, but fine, and fresher than of late. The hearing of the Isaacs case dragged through long hours in court, without reaching a conclusion, and was adjourned when the afternoon was far advanced by a judge who showed unmistakable signs of impatience with the arguments on both sides.

Antony, watching his chance to cross the Strand, changed his mind suddenly. "I'm going down to Putney, Uncle Nick, and on to Wimbledon, if there's time. It'd save time if I see Sykes on the way."

"That sounds rather a full program. Won't any of it wait?"

"Well—!" said Antony. "Sykes will probably be out, anyway, but I may as well try. Will you be free if Jenny comes down? I'm neglecting her shamefully."

"I'm always free if Jenny wants me. You know that, Antony."

"Yes, sir, I know."

In the event, his luck was in, and he encountered Inspector Sykes stumping up Whitehall towards the bus stop. The detective stopped without sign of impatience, and exchanged greetings affably. "Were you looking for me, Mr. Maitland?"

"It isn't urgent, if you're going home."

"No hurry, I'm early tonight. Shall we go back to my office?"

"Well, I could do with some tea. Is there somewhere?"

"I'll show you," Sykes offered.

Their destination was down six stone steps from street

level; a darkish room, but clean, and pleasantly filled with a smell of home baking. Antony, who had been expecting a teashop, looked round with appreciation. "I was lucky to meet you, Inspector." He broke off to place his order; Sykes was obviously a familiar of the place and it seemed likely that their wishes would get detailed attention. "Well, how are things with you? Are you happy about the way your case is going?"

Sykes made no direct reply. "I understand Mr. Dowling's solicitors have briefed Sir Nicholas Harding for the defense?"

"Yes, that's right."

"Then, I suppose, Mr. Maitland, your evidence will not be called?"

Antony frowned a little. "On the contrary, Inspector. My uncle will tell you he has taken the case because he is the only man in London who would be willing to produce my testimony."

"I don't understand you, Mr. Maitland." Sykes seemed perturbed. "Have you . . . has Sir Nicholas considered the consequences?"

"I assure you, Inspector, my uncle misses very little." They were interrupted by the arrival of their tea. When they were alone again he went on. "As for me. I've considered little else during the last few days."

"Well, then—"

"All the consideration in the world won't alter facts."

"No, Mr. Maitland." Sykes's tone was flat, but his companion turned on him with sudden impatience.

"Do you think I'm fool enough to risk my career, just for a whim?"

"I think you have great faith in your uncle's powers of persuasion," said Sykes, dryly.

"I s-see." Antony tightened his lips. "But I don't understand," he said angrily a moment later, "why you should give credence to Armstrong's evidence in preference to mine."

"That's not quite fair, Mr. Maitland. There are other facts in our case, you know."

"Oh, what's the use?" Antony was exasperated, and concentrated for a while on the toast he had ordered. Sykes watched him in silence and sipped his tea. After a while he said, in his usual placid way:

"It's only right I should tell you, Mr. Maitland, I was just as anxious to see you as you say you were to see me."

Antony pushed aside his plate, and cocked an inquiring eyebrow. "Sounds sinister," he remarked.

"The superintendent wanted to find out whether the defense would, in fact, be calling you. If not, the prosecution would have issued a subpoena."

"I don't get that." Antony looked at him in bewilderment. "You mean, Briggs is so sure I'm lying he thinks I can be tripped up in court, even on direct examination?" Sykes stirred his tea industriously, not looking up. "Well, I never did," said Antony mildly, after a moment. "I'm surprised the D.P.P.'s office agreed."

Sykes raised his eyes briefly. "Superintendent Briggs is very sure of his facts."

"He must be!" He brooded a moment, then smiled at his companion. Having been betrayed once into showing his temper, he did not mean to be caught the same way twice. "Nay, Inspector, you're making me feel proper gloomy," he remarked.

"That's a pity. If you're satisfied with the position, Mr. Maitland, it's not for me to complain."

"I don't believe," said Antony, shrewdly, "you're particularly happy about the case yourself."

"The evidence is very clear."

"Well, that's what I wanted to talk to you about. There seem to be certain omissions in what you have made available to the defense." Sykes looked inquiring, and he added quickly, "As you're about to point out, I haven't been briefed. But I'm devilling for my uncle, as usual."

"I see. But these omissions, now—"

"Very minor. Just for the record, though, what was J.W. writing when he died?"

There was a silence. Sykes was drawing on the tablecloth with the handle of his teaspoon, but after a while he looked up and said slowly, "Now, there's a point, Mr. Maitland. He wasn't writing anything that I saw. There were plenty of papers on his desk—documents, and so forth—and in front

of him just the green blotting pad, and nothing even the most
painstaking of detectives could make of that!''

''But Miss Harris said—''

''She said he was writing when she went in with his tea.
There weren't any letters in his 'out' basket, so it couldn't
have been that.''

''Well, Inspector?''

''Well, Mr. Maitland? I don't honestly think it signifies,
do you?''

Antony grinned. ''Speaking without prejudice, Inspector
. . . no. But I wouldn't forget it, if I were you.''

''I'll bear it in mind,'' said Sykes. He sounded amused.

''The other thing is: did you find the draft lease of the
mews property Arthur Green rents?''

''Not on Mr. Winter's desk, anyway, that I do remember.''

''Never mind, I'll ask Miss Harris. Most likely he gave it
to her.''

''A fine assembly of irrelevant matter,'' said Sykes,
absent-mindedly pouring what was left of the tea into his
own cup.

''Then you won't like my next question. What did you
make of Miss Hunt's burglary?''

''Now on that, Mr. Maitland, I must decline comment. It
can have no possible bearing—''

''What'll you bet my uncle gets it admitted?''

''I've no sporting blood, Mr. Maitland.''

''Well, at least you can tell me, do you know who did
it?''

''As it happens—no.'' He looked up, to signal to the wait-
ress, but added less austerely, ''Believe me, there's nothing
to help you there.''

''Probably not,'' said Antony.

Sykes got to his feet, and stood for a moment looking
down at his companion. ''If you should happen to change
your mind, Mr. Maitland, about your statement, you
know—''

''For heaven's sake, don't start that bee buzzing again,''
interrupted Antony, crossly. ''Do I look like the kind of
idiot—''

''You don't look like any kind of idiot,'' said Sykes

bluntly. "Nor do you look like a man who would contemplate perjury with equanimity." (This was a well-intentioned attempt, Antony realized, to put a proposed course of action squarely to someone who might not quite have realized what he was doing. His temper was lost irretrievably, now; and, as his uncle might have done, he spoke very gently.)

"You mistake me, Inspector. Aren't you familiar with the villain of fiction, who hides his perfidy under a smiling mask? Or do you prefer your villains old-fashioned and wholehearted in their wickedness?" Sykes was momentarily startled by the impression that he had strayed into a theatrical melodrama of the sort no longer fashionable, but the effect passed, and the pair left the café to part on the pavement outside. Antony's farewells were quietly spoken, his message to the superintendent unexceptionable—though the detective was well aware that it was neither well-intentioned, nor would it be well received. But in Sykes's mind, as he went, were his colleague's remarks: "Acting as innocent as you please . . . but I saw him in action one night." Decidedly, he thought, there was more to Antony Maitland than met the eye. He reflected further, that though you might make him lose his temper he did not simultaneously lose his head; in fact, he wasn't giving away anything he didn't want to, even in a rage, as he had been when Briggs questioned him. "Well, now—" said the inspector, to himself, as he took up a position in the queue for his homeward bus.

Antony, meanwhile, having set off rapidly in the wrong direction, had retraced his steps and was on his way to Putney. He phoned from the station when he got there, was greeted with something like enthusiasm by Stanley Prentiss, and having an hour to wait before the time named for their interview went out to find himself a meal.

There are two definite sections in Putney, above and below the Upper Richmond Road. In the former of these the neighborhood grows gradually more select as you climb towards the heath—where the atmosphere is so rarefield that ordinary mortals are scarcely able to breathe. Antony, his supper over (and best, he felt, forgotten), took a bus to the top of the High Street, and set off up the hill. After no more misdirections and false starts than are customary on such occasions he found himself on what he mentally termed "the third parallel," and a few moments later was walking up a short path towards a small, well-built modern house. The garden, he noted in passing, was neat enough but suggested rather the occasional professional attention of a jobbing gardener than the personal enthusiasm of its owner.

The door was opened to him by a blonde, well-groomed young woman; while she certainly looked hard-boiled, she showed no obvious signs of the oddity Charles had mentioned. She seemed to be expecting him, and waved aside his careful explanation of his presence. As she went back down the hall she pushed open a door on the right and called casually, "Darling, it's Tony Maitland," and then departed towards the rear of the house, smiling over her shoulder at the visitor in an evident endeavor to take the sting out of this unceremonious treatment.

Antony (on whose ears the unaccustomed diminution of his name grated unpleasantly) took this as sufficient invitation to enter, and reached the door just as his host was heaving himself out of a deep armchair. Stanley Prentiss was taller than his cousin, and had, if truth were told, changed a good deal since last Antony saw him; as men so often do between the ages of fifteen and thirty. His hair was wiry and as unruly as Charles's, but his expression was infinitely more placid and easygoing. Like his wife, he paid no heed at all to Antony's explanation, waved his visitor towards the other armchair (from whose depths he felt he might never emerge alive), and was obviously determined that the occasion should be a social one. The room was rather more heavily furnished than its size warranted; either it had been filled from some former home, or from postwar, unrewarding visits to secondhand stores.

"Nice to see you again, Maitland. Muriel's got the coffee on. Seen anything of Charles lately?"

"Last week. Now about Mr. Winter," said Antony, firmly.

"Oh, yes, bad business that. Nothing I can tell you, though. I hardly knew the old boy."

"No, I realize that. It's only a matter of form. About the afternoon in question—"

"I went to Bread Court straight after lunch, got there

about two. They took me in to J.W., I hadn't known Charles was away."

"And did he seem as usual? Was his manner in any way peculiar?"

Prentiss laughed. "There was some sort of a flap going on in the office. I'd gone in to sign my will—did you know that?—and they seemed to have mislaid it. Finally, I think they must have typed it again, because it appeared in sections; J.W. was in and out of the room, and seemed pretty peeved, but I should think that quite normal in the circumstances."

"The door to the private stair—you know it, of course?"

"Well, I've come out that way from seeing Charles; the door from the corridor, you know, not the one from J.W.'s room. As a matter of fact, I'd never been in his room before. I was at the office once or twice after Aunt Amelia died, and I saw the old man then, but it was in Charles's room."

"Well, I'm trying to find out the time that door was unlatched. I don't suppose you had any occasion to try it, but you might have seen Winter do so—"

"I'm sorry I can't help you there. I never noticed the door, and I certainly should if he'd gone to it."

"Yes, I suppose so." Antony grinned at him. "I think I'm wasting your time, don't you? But unfortunately, it's got to be done."

Stanley Prentiss waved aside the apology. "Think nothing of it. If you want the rest, I was there until about two-twenty; at least, I didn't notice particularly, but I know I was back in my office at twenty-five to three, because I had an appointment at two-thirty and was a little late for it."

"That's the lot, then, except—you know, I don't remember what your business is."

"You may set me down as a wholesaler. Fancy goods. Junk, I expect you'd call it."

Antony, who found the room, though overfurnished, commendably free from ornament, disclaimed politely, but the other added, "Well, I would, anyway," in a decided tone. And, warming to his theme, disserted for a while, and with some humor, on the horrors of a trade which brought him into constant association with garish disembodied heads and squads of flat, flying ducks; to say nothing of "cute" cherubs in colored nightgowns, and pot rabbits, more numerous than the sands of the desert, of varying degrees of frightfulness.

Muriel came in with a tray while he was still speaking, and remarked brightly as she handed Antony his coffee, "Not much longer of that, anyway."

"You're thinking of making a change?"

"Well, there's no need to *slave*, now that Granny's left us so comfortable, you know. So if you know anyone who wants to buy a *salon*—a beauty parlor, you know—there's mine in the market right now."

"I'm afraid I don't, not just at the moment," said Antony, rather as though this negative state of affairs were abnormal. "Don't you think you may miss having something to do?" he added.

"Not me," said Muriel, and her tone was emphatic. "Nice change, and about time, too. Of course, I expect Stan will want to do something. We might go into the country." Antony, who could visualize neither his host nor his hostess in such a setting, murmured something. Prentiss, who had been ready enough to talk himself but seemed to find his wife's chatter embarrassing, got up with a sudden, quick movement.

"Brandy?" he said. "Or a liqueur?" He waved his hand towards a venerable piece of furniture, which Antony put down, vaguely, as a whatnot, and guessed—quite correctly—to have assumed in its old age the function of a wine cupboard. "What'll you take?"

Antony settled for brandy, and did not find the suggestion unwelcome after the supper he had endured. Stanley said as he reseated himself, "I haven't seen Charles since I went in about the will. Taking my instructions, he called it, but he and J.W. had it all decided between them."

"Silly, I call it," said Muriel. "All this fuss! When there only are two of us."

Prentiss looked at her. Antony, who found her a trying young woman, was surprised to see that his look was one of simple affection. "Darling," he said, "it would make it easier for you—"

"Well, I don't see why you're all so down on intestacy," said his wife irrepressibly (producing the last word with

some triumph, as one she had heard frequently of late).
"Look what it's done for us!"

"Well, all right." Stanley's look at his guest was one of
amused apology. "But I was going to ask you, Maitland,
how this affects Charles."

"I believe the police tried his temper," said Antony, will-
fully misunderstanding.

"I meant, from a business point of view."

"I really don't know. He didn't tell me . . . but, by the
way, do you know he's engaged?"

"Not that Mary Winter?" said Muriel. "She's a horrid
girl, and I'm sure she'll be bossy."

"I've only met her once," said Antony. "But that's the
one." Stanley said nothing, he seemed at once to have withdrawn from the conversation. Antony added, "Do you
know her well?" and was surprised that this simple question
seemed to confuse both the man and the girl.

"No . . . yes. Well, Stan did. She was sure she'd have
one of them," she went on, spitefully. "But she's welcome
to Charles." She looked at her husband, and her expression
softened. "I couldn't stand him. Too stuck up, " she said.

"Charles is all right," said Stanley, indulgently. And
succeeded this time in steering the conversation to less con-
troversial channels.

Mrs. Carey lived in Wimbledon, so it wasn't too inconve-
nient to visit her after he left the Prentisses' house. Her tip-
ple was tea; fragrant China tea from cups of a rather fearful
fragility. Antony sipped and listened quietly to a quantity of
gentle chatter, reminiscences of dear Mr. Winter, and restrained lamentations over the manner of his death. Outside
the summer twilight deepened, but though by now he was
desperately tired he was also possessed of a scruple, which
kept him attentive even while it aggravated him. He might
hear something useful, but it seemed very unlikely that he
would do so.

There was a large photograph, occupying what was obviously the place of honor on top of the piano. Antony eyed it
as he listened: the likeness of a man in his late twenties, with
fair, curly hair and a thin, handsome face. After a while his
hostess noticed the direction of his glance, and accepted ea-

gerly the opportunity it offered to turn to a subject that
pleased her.

"That is Paul, my son. Of course, that was taken some
time ago, at the beginning of the war, just before he joined
up." Antony murmured something that he hoped would
sound interested and encouraging. "He was in the air force,
a pilot."

"I hope—" began Antony cautiously, not quite sure
whether the past tense referred to Paul Carey, or to his wartime occupation.

"Oh, yes, he came through quite safely. Though I sometimes think," she added, more with the air of one who
speaks to herself than of one who confides, incomprehensi-
bly, in a stranger, "that all that made him—well, restless."

"A lot of people find it difficult to settle down after so
much excitement and danger."

"Yes, that's how it is." She sounded quite eager. "Mr.
Winter thought—of course, he was a dear man, but he *was*
old-fashioned, and I don't think he understood the difficulties a young man has, making his way in the world at the
present time. And with a family, too; well, just the one
daughter, but a girl of her age needs so many things."

Antony, feeling unequal to comment on this interesting
subject, stirred his tea and said nothing. After a moment
Mrs. Carey smiled at him. "You spoke as though you understand, Mr. Maitland. I expect you were in one of the
forces, too?"

"Army," said Antony. And added, to soften the abrupt-
ness of the statement, "A staff job, very dull."

"Oh, I see." She sounded disappointed. "But I seem to
remember Mr. Winter telling me—"

"He must have been thinking of someone else," said Antony idiotically.

"No, I remember your name quite well, because I used to
have a very dear friend called Maitland. And he said you'd
been wounded," she added, eyeing him accusingly, as
though he were somehow to blame for concealing the evidence of this interesting fact.

Antony sat very still. He was tired, and his shoulder was
painful, and she was an old lady, he mustn't be rude to her;
but he was damned if he was going to indulge either her or

himself with reminiscences. Perhaps she noticed the strain he was under; in any event she dropped the subject and asked instead, with a rather uncertain smile, "Can I give you some more tea?"

"I think not, thank you." He put down the cup, and fished in his pocket for a pencil. "If you can just tell me about last Tuesday afternoon, I won't worry you any further."

"Well," said Mrs. Carey, and paused for a moment. "I think I can tell you quite clearly, because the man from the police asked me so many questions. And then he asked me to sign my statement, and there it was: everything I'd said, but all put into order as neat as you please!"

Antony smiled at her. She really was rather a dear, and old ladies, he supposed, were naturally curious. "That's much what will happen to it this time. Only when the solicitor has finished with it, and sent it on to counsel, it will be called a proof, not a statement."

"Well," she said again. Then, suddenly determined, commenced briskly, "My appointment with Mr. Winter was for three o'clock, but I like to take my time, you know, so I left early and got there at about ten to the hour. Miss Harris took me to the waiting room and stayed and talked for a few minutes, but I think she was busy, and she went away quite soon. Just before the hour a little man came in, I found afterwards he was the clerk from the other solicitors. Miss Harris came in again to apologize. Mr. Winter had someone with him who was keeping him longer than he had expected; it was unusual for him, but he was a very busy man, so I didn't mind waiting. I thought Mr.—" She paused a moment, then brought out the name "Armstrong" with an air of triumph. "I thought Mr. Armstrong was rather fidgety, but that doesn't really do any good, does it? Anyway, after a while Mr. Winter was free. I do not," she added, with some firmness, "recall the time. The business was quite simple and didn't take long. After Mr. Armstrong left I stayed talking to Mr. Winter for a while, and when I left I looked straightaway for somewhere to have tea, and found a nice little place, and when I got there it was four o'clock." She took a deep breath and beamed at Antony. "There!" she said.

"Thank you, that's very clear indeed. There are just two points—"

"Yes?"

"Was Mr. Winter's manner just as usual?"

"I think it was. He seemed a little thoughtful, perhaps, but you see, he didn't like me selling anything—any property, I mean, so I just put it down to his being a little disapproving."

"And you didn't notice anything while you were there that seems to you worthy of comment?"

"Nothing at all. I've thought about it very carefully, especially since Inspector Sykes was here."

"Did you know the door to the private stair?"

"I knew there was another way out; my husband told me, many years ago. But there are two doors in the corner of the room, and I don't know which one it is."

"You had no occasion, then, to observe whether it was locked or unlocked at the time you were with Mr. Winter?"

"No. No, I hadn't."

"Then, just one other thing. During the time he was there did Mr. Armstrong have any opportunity of approaching the door unobserved? Could he have unlatched it without anybody noticing it?"

"Oh, no, I'm sure—" She paused, considering: this was something her interview with the police had not touched on. "Well, perhaps," she said, doubtfully. "When I was signing, and Mr. Winter was leaning across the desk to show me where to do it, and Miss Harris was watching me, I expect, as she was there to witness my signature; I suppose he could have done it then."

"And that's the lot! I'm very grateful to you, Mrs. Carey; you've been put to a lot of bother, I'm afraid, one way and another." He got up, and she looked at him in a troubled way.

"This Mr. Armstrong . . . I wouldn't want to get anybody into trouble."

"Don't worry, you haven't done that. If you'd told me he couldn't possibly have approached the door, that would have settled the matter. As it is, the question is still open."

"I wouldn't like to have felt you were jumping to conclusions." She pushed the tea table aside, and got to her feet with just a little difficulty. "But I'm sure you are a most sensible young man!"

Antony went home a little stunned by what he felt was a completely undeserved tribute.

CHAPTER 13

THE ISAACS CASE was ended in good time before the midday recess, and Sir Nicholas looked bland when they met Jenny for lunch, a fact which she immediately remarked on.

"Is your case finished, Uncle Nick? Did you win?"

"Our client got three years."

"Then I don't see what you've got to look so—so smug about."

Sir Nicholas smiled at her. "You see, my dear, he deserved seven," he explained, gently.

Jenny did not appear to find this very satisfactory, but allowed herself to be distracted to a study of the menu. Sir Nicholas turned to his nephew.

"Have you plans for this afternoon?"

"If you don't need me, I propose to persecute Miss Meadows. I feel just in the mood," he added, viciously.

"An excellent scheme," approved the older man. Jenny, who usually would have plunged headfirst into so inviting a topic, looked from one to the other of them, and made no comment.

She left them when the meal was over, and the two men strolled back to chambers together. Antony, finding it was already past two o'clock, left his uncle at Temple Bar. Sir Nicholas had an appointment with Mrs. Dowling and seemed to be expecting an unrewarding afternoon. "It is impossible for me to give her any very cheerful tidings," he said.

"Poor woman," said Antony, with sympathy. "Don't flatten her altogether."

"I shall endeavor," replied his uncle, on his dignity, "to

give her a fair picture of the position on the evidence as we at present know it.''

Antony could think of no reply to this repressive remark, and departed in the direction of Bread Court.

Miss Harris seemed to have forgiven him, and offered the use of her room for his projected interview with Miss Meadows. Antony was duly grateful, and Willett, who seemed strangely subdued today, was dispatched to fetch her. Miss Harris, having thus given the affair her blessing, picked up a ledger and departed for the general office.

Eve Meadows was as neat and imperturbable as ever, but he had an impression that she was thinner, and certainly there were shadows under her eyes. She greeted him coolly, and crossed the room to sit at the typing desk under the window, swinging the chair round to face him. Antony perched on his favorite high stool and looked down at her amiably. After a few moments her foot began to tap.

"Well, Mr. Maitland? I understood there was some way I could help you.''

"You could, Miss Meadows, I'm sure you could. The question is, will you?''

She said, stiffly, "Have you any reason to doubt it? Have I refused to answer any questions?''

"Well, you know, to put it mildly, I don't think you've been quite frank—with me, or with the police.''

"You've no right at all to say that.''

"Perhaps I hadn't, until my uncle was briefed by Joseph Dowling's solicitors. That changes things, doesn't it? Murder's a serious charge, Miss Meadows. Besides, I don't think he's guilty—do you?''

"How should I know?'' Her tone was sulky now. "Anyway, I can't help you, or him.''

"No?'' said Antony. And waited. After a moment she broke the silence, speaking rapidly now.

"If it's about my thinking for a minute I saw Charles Prentiss, I've told you before I made a mistake. The police believe me, anyway they never mentioned it again. Why should you keep dragging it up?''

"That's simply answered,'' said Antony, and his tone was as insolent as he could make it. "I think you're lying.''

She flounced to her feet, the perfect picture, he reflected with some admiration, of injured innocence. Her voice was shaking with anger. "How dare you!" she said, and Antony laughed.

"Is that the best you can manage? How unoriginal! Let me remind you: you were so sure at the time you'd seen Charles that you went through into his room and looked for him."

"Well, he wasn't there!"

"What time would that be?"

"I don't know. I didn't notice. Ten minutes after we came in, perhaps more."

"And what did you do then?"

"I just looked, and saw he wasn't there, and came out and shut the door again."

"I see."

"And that's all I can tell you; so I may as well go now."

Antony let her get halfway to the door before he spoke. "I ought to tell you, Miss Meadows, the defense will call you as a witness if Joseph Dowling comes to trial."

She stopped, and turned slowly to face him. She was very pale, so that the make-up she used with such discretion and effect looked garish; and when she spoke her voice was very low. "But—why?"

Antony slid off his stool. He said, in a more gentle tone than he had previously used to her, "Is it so very dreadful? A man's life is in danger—if you'll forgive a rather florid phrase. Surely you wouldn't wish to refuse your evidence."

"Yes, yes I would! Why should I care about him?" Her voice was rising again, and Antony eyed her uneasily. "You're trying to drag Charles into this, just to help your beastly case; and he didn't have anything to do with it."

"Take it easy. And try to get this into your thick head," said Antony, ungallantly. "I know quite well Charles was here that afternoon, and don't especially want your confirmation of that fact. I believe him to have left immediately after four o'clock."

"But it was—" She broke off, and shut her mouth with a snap.

"What, Miss Meadows? It was later than that when you saw him, do you mean? Then he was in his room, perhaps?"

She shook her head, positively. He thought the gleam in her eye was one of relief.

"Then you went farther, into the corridor, maybe you looked down the private stair?" He was speaking slowly, watching her, and there was no mistaking her look of panic. "Thank you, Miss Meadows. You've been very helpful. I won't trouble you any more just now."

"But . . . but you're only guessing. *That* won't help you."

"Don't you think so? You may not realize it, but a really first-class counsel could turn you inside out in about two minutes—in court, I mean, no holds barred. Wouldn't it be better to tell me about it now? I should take a good deal of convincing that Charles Prentiss murdered anybody; whatever you saw must be capable of some other construction, and might be helpful if you give us a chance to examine it in detail."

She hesitated. "I—no, I don't believe you. You're trying to trick me. I won't listen to you any more." She turned again, but before she could reach the door it opened and Dennis Dowling came in.

He was carrying his hat, and looked astonished to see them. "I was looking for Miss Harris. Have I interrupted something?" He eyed the girl more closely. "Eve, what's upset you? What's been happening?"

She jerked her head—the first inelegant gesture, Antony reflected, that he had seen her make. "It's him! He's asking questions and questions, and he won't believe a word I say. And he's trying to bully me."

Dennis looked from one to the other of them, bewildered. "That sounds very unlikely. I'm sure you've got it wrong. Hasn't she?" he appealed to Antony.

"Well, no. I wouldn't say that."

"Then I think—" began Dennis. Antony interrupted him without ceremony.

"Hold on a minute. I'm here on behalf of a client; your father, Dennis."

He looked puzzled. "I don't understand. Can you help us, Eve?"

"No, no, no!" Her tone grew more shrill on each word. "He wants me to help him prove Charles Prentiss did it. He says your father's innocent; I don't know about that, I don't care either. I won't say anything to hurt Charles.''

She made for the door, and Antony watched her go with some relief; Miss Harris would probably deal with incipient hysteria more capably than he could. He turned to look at Dennis, who was still staring at the door, his face expressionless; he had taken off his glasses and was fiddling with them nervously. After a moment he said, ''Well, that's that,'' and put on the glasses again. But he still did not look at Antony. ''Do you really think Prentiss killed Mr. Winter?'' His tone was mildly curious.

''I don't. She appears to.''

''So I gathered. I don't think,'' said Dennis carefully, ''I'm being especially influenced by personal considerations—I mean, because it's my father she refuses to help. Anyone in the same position would be entitled to expect it.''

''I may be wrong. I've no way of knowing unless she'll talk to me. If she does in fact know anything, it may not be helpful at all.''

Dennis shook his head. ''It isn't that, so much. She doesn't care,'' he said. ''Why should she, after all?'' He went out, and a moment later the main door of the office closed with a slam.

Antony hesitated, and then followed him into the corridor, which he crossed, and went into the general office. Miss Bell was there, frowning over some shorthand notes, and Willett, seated before a rather dog-eared ledger, was counting over the contents of a small cashbox with every appearance of despair. They both appeared to feel some relief at the interruption.

''Hello, Mr. Maitland. We thought you'd just gone.''

''That was Dowling, he came in for a moment.''

Miss Bell eyed him severely. ''What have you been doing to poor Eve?'' she inquired.

''Well—'' said Antony, taking heart, however, from the fact that her tone was less forbidding than her expression. ''Some people just don't like answering questions, you know.''

Miss Bell nodded wisely, appearing to gain more information from this rather vague remark than its author would have believed possible. ''Well, they won't be back yet;

Miss Harris took her to tea across the way. Sensible, really, she won't have hysterics there." Her tone was unsympathetic. Antony reflected that working at close quarters with a grand passion, and an unrequited one at that, must be a trying experience.

Willett said impatiently, "Never mind all that." He appealed to Antony. "Girls are mostly silly, aren't they? This is important. Can you add up?"

"Indifferently. What's the trouble?"

"It's the stamp money," said Miss Bell. "Really, how you can bother Mr. Maitland with anything like that—"

"But I'm seven and threepence out!" Willett's tone was tragic.

"Up or down?" inquired Antony practically.

"Down, of course. And if I don't find it by Friday he'll say I've been embezzling."

"Don't be so silly."

"Well, I wouldn't put it past him."

"Him?" said Antony.

They both spoke together. Miss Bell said, "Mr. Prentiss," and Willett, disdaining a direct reply: "I've got the sack!"

Antony had got no further than a vague murmur of commiseration when Miss Bell interrupted him. "It was all your own fault," she scolded. "You ought to know better than talk about your employer."

"Well, I thought he was out." Willett sounded sulky. "And, anyway, it was true."

"That only makes it worse. Doesn't it, Mr. Maitland?"

Antony declined to be drawn into discussion of this interesting point. "What was this slander, anyway?" he asked.

"I only said—well, I know I shouldn't have, Miss Bell, so you needn't look at me like that—I only said something like, he shouldn't let his *affaires* overlap; and—and about marrying for money, you know."

"And then the door opened." Miss Bell gestured dramatically. "I could have died!"

"He didn't *say* anything, only afterwards he told me I could go at the end of the week, so of course I knew why."

"Well, altogether I'm not surprised."

"No, I know." Willett was resigned. "But it doesn't help

at all to have people continually saying: It's all your own fault.''

Miss Bell said suddenly, "Go and fill the kettle, we may as well have some tea, even if the others are out. And—where's my purse?—go down to Stone's and get some of their buns, will you? We may be late tonight.''

She turned to Antony as the door closed behind the boy. "That'll keep him for a while. I want to tell you something. At least," she added, suddenly doubtful, "I think I do.''

Antony smiled encouragingly, and hoped for the best. After a moment she went on. "It's about Mr. Prentiss. I didn't mean to say anything, only I got thinking about poor Mr. Dowling, and then Eve has been so—so tiresome, and that made me wonder, you know.''

"What did you wonder?''

"Well, you see, first Mr. Prentiss seemed to be interested in Eve. Ever since she came here. Then he cooled off, and he was being attentive to Mary Winter. Well—I'm not trying to be catty, truly, Mr. Maitland—but have you seen her? I mean, she isn't a patch on Eve, not for looks, or anything. Only, she didn't have any money of her own. Not then.'' She paused, apparently for consideration of what she had just said. "I sound worse than Willett, don't I? I'm not trying to provide anybody with a motive. It's just that I'm sure Mr. Prentiss really was in the office that afternoon, and that would explain it.''

"I'm afraid I'm being very dense," said Antony, politely. "But I'm not at all clear what you're driving at.''

"It was Matthew Winter's deed box, that's Mary's father. He didn't leave anything much, and what there was was used for her education, I think, but our Mr. Winter had a copy of his will filed there when he made it. Well, that deed box was in Mr. Prentiss's room; there were about half a dozen of them moved in there because the waiting room got so there was hardly room to sit down. So I think perhaps that was what he came for that afternoon—to have a look into it, before he took the plunge. Because it wasn't until after that he said about being engaged to her.''

"I see.''

"There'd be nothing really wrong about that. Only rather—rather calculating. But I can see he wouldn't want to say he'd been here if it meant explaining what he had been doing.''

"No, I see that." Antony got up. "Well, Miss Bell, that's very interesting, and I wouldn't be at all surprised if you've put your finger on what happened. All the same, as it's all pure conjecture—''

"I know. I'm not likely to mention it to anybody else. Only Eve has been so queer, she'd make anybody think things—I mean, that there was more in his coming in that afternoon than there really was.''

"Yes. I'm grateful. I'm wanting a word with Charles. Is he in?''

"I haven't heard him going out, and there's nobody with him, either. Do you want me to ring through?''

"No, I'll announce myself. By the way," he stopped on his way to the door, "tell young Willett to go and see Mr. Mallory in chambers. If he approves of him I daresay we can find him something to do. But tell him to be on his best behavior.''

"I will." Miss Bell's smile was suddenly warm and friendly. "That'll be a weight off my mind, anyway. He's an awful little beast, of course, but he doesn't really mean any harm.''

"Oh, it's you again," said Charles Prentiss, sourly. "What do you want now?''

"A little straight talk with you.''

"I'm busy. Is it important?" His tone was ungracious, and he shuffled impatiently among the papers on his desk.

"Very—to you. You need my help badly, and I'm trying to give it you.''

"Ha!" said Prentiss, in a disbelieving way. But he laid down his pen, which Antony interpreted as a sign to proceed.

"The position is this: Eve Meadows, for her own good reasons, refuses to admit to me that she really did see you in the office the afternoon Mr. Winter was killed. I want you to persuade her to talk to me.''

"I'm not very likely to do that. All things considered.''

"That's a pity. Look, Charles, I'm honestly not trying to double-cross you, whatever ideas that young woman of yours may have put into your head. What time did you leave the office that day?''

Prentiss considered before he replied, grudgingly, ''Just after Eve saw me. Just after four o'clock.''

''And did you come back again, even for a moment? You might have forgotten something.''

''I went straight out and got a bus to London Bridge. I went to see Mary.''

''Charles, is that true?''

The other frowned quickly, but seeing Antony's look of earnestness said with surprising mildness, ''Yes, quite true.''

''Then, for your own sake, do as I ask. Miss Meadows went into your room to look for you, but that was nearer a quarter past four. I'm as sure as one can be of anything that she saw somebody or something at that time; she admitted as much, though only by implication. She must think it has something to do with you, or she wouldn't be so upset, but if you had gone by then that can't be the case. Well, I'd like the chance to question her in detail; there may be something to find out, something she has put a wrong construction on.''

''Yes.'' Charles sounded doubtful. ''Well, that's all very specious, Antony; but I don't quite see what good it's going to do me.''

''Then I'll be blunt with you. As things are now, Uncle Nick proposes to call both you and Miss Meadows as witnesses. I don't know how you'll make out, but in case you haven't realized it, she's badly upset—very near breaking point. I don't think there's any doubt she'd spill everything within two minutes—what she knows, and what she thinks she knows. There'll be no chance then of getting past it to the truth of the matter. I leave it to your imagination how it will sound.''

''That's—very like blackmail, Antony.'' His voice was still unwontedly quiet.

''If you like. Hard words break no bones, they certainly don't alter facts.''

''No. And if I do as you ask you'll keep me out of this; and Eve, of course.''

''I make no promises. I see no reason why either of you

BLOODY INSTRUCTIONS   139

should be brought into it; only if Miss Meadows proves to
have any useful evidence shall we call her, of course—but
then there'd be no awkward questions from Uncle Nick.''

"So I suppose. Well, I don't seem to have much option,
do I?"

Antony got up. "Think it over. I'll look you up, in a day
or so." He paused, but Charles was looking down at his
hand which was clenched on the desk before him. "Believe
me, I've given you good advice."

"All right, all right, I'll talk to her." That was said impatiently, much more what Antony had expected, but he went
on, again with the strange, unexpected quietness he had
shown throughout the interview. "But it's awkward. You
don't know how awkward it is."

"I can guess. Well, I'll be seeing you, Charles. Good-
bye for now."

Charles looked up, said, "Good-bye" absently, and returned again to the contemplation of his hands.

CHAPTER 14

DEREK STRINGER dined with Sir Nicholas that evening, and Antony joined them in the study about nine o'clock. Oates seemed to have been galvanized into some sort of activity, and some fresh papers had arrived to swell the growing mass of documentation; these included the typed copies of Antony's reports, so far as they had been submitted. Derek was reading the account of his meeting with Stanley and Muriel Prentiss, and seemed to be getting some amusement out of it.

"Some people have all the luck," he remarked. "Now, my aunts all dote on me, but none of 'em has a bean!"

Antony took up his favorite position, with one shoulder leaning against the high mantel. "How was Mrs. Joe?" he asked his uncle.

"Unhelpful," said Sir Nicholas briefly. "How did you get on?"

"It wasn't a particularly enjoyable afternoon, but it may turn out to have been useful."

"Well?"

"I've told you, haven't I, that Miss Meadows is normally noted for her calmness. She chose to go all temperamental, and nearly threw a fit of hysterics—"

"This tendency of yours—"

"Yes, well, I meant to be rude to her, and I was."

"With what result?"

"I didn't get anywhere with her, I'm sorry to say. Then I had a talk with Charles. You know what he's like—I expected he'd be breaking up the furniture after the first two minutes. Instead he received me with a sort of gentle resignation which was quite unnerving."

"I've never seen Charles either gentle or resigned. It must have been quite an experience."

Antony grinned. "At a guess, he was facing the fact that sooner or later he'll have to have a heart to heart with Eve Meadows, and he doesn't know what kind of a scene she'll put on."

"You feel it's better to get her to talk willingly?" Stringer put the question tentatively. "I mean, I should think she'd make a pretty good job of obscuring the issue . . . from what you've told me."

"As it happens, I want the truth," said Sir Nicholas shortly.

"Yes . . . well—" said Derek, a little taken aback.

"He means," Antony explained, "an acquittal for lack of evidence would be better than nothing from Joe's point of view; but it won't help me. That's what we think, anyway; I don't know if you agree."

Stringer took his time to consider this. "I think you're right," he said at last. "Human nature being pretty illogical, at best."

"And if that point is settled to your satisfaction," said Sir Nicholas, who was growing impatient, "perhaps we could hear if anything else transpired at Bread Court."

"I talked to Miss Bell; she thinks Charles won't admit he went into the office that afternoon because he wanted to look up Mary Winter's expectations. Which is reasonable. She doesn't realize it might be regarded as providing him with a motive. I had a brief word with Miss Harris, after I left Charles; she was never in J.W.'s room again after the discovery—not until after the police had finished with it—and so she doesn't know anything about what he was writing. So I asked about Green's lease, but she said whatever Mr. Winter had done with it, he hadn't given it to her. Then she got puzzled because she couldn't remember the draft at all, so she went and looked up the old lease and found it didn't expire for another two years!"

"Green said he went to see Winter about renewing it?"

"He said, to be exact," said Derek, referring to one of the papers on his knee, " 'it was a matter of agreeing on a new lease he'd drawn up; he said he'd have it typed out for me to sign.' "

"But it isn't really helpful, because we knew already he was up to something—"

"No, I like it," Sir Nicholas decided. "The more people who are going about telling lies, the better."

Neither of the younger men showed any sign of being shocked by this rather amoral statement. Derek nodded his agreement, and Antony asked, "What about his alibi?"

"Mr. Jennings is a tobacconist, with a shabby little shop in a back street in Hackney. Which might mean anything, or nothing."

"There must be many innocent people living in Hackney" said Sir Nicholas meditatively.

"Yes, sir, no doubt. Oates's chap also found a chauffeur—" Stringer waved a hand towards the desk, where the statement might presumably be found. "He lives over the garage he uses, nearly opposite Green's place. A pleasant, talkative little chap, I gather, with a good deal of time on his hands as he drives for an old lady who doesn't go out very much. *He* says Green has no apparent occupation, and his visitors look a rum lot. That part's pretty vague, but what I think may be useful is this: the double garage under Green's flat is apparently used as a store by a firm of furniture removers. Their vans call constantly, but never load and unload in the street; the van is always driven into the garage and the doors shut again. There is also a certain amount of activity at night, he doesn't know if that's the same people, of course. The name on the vans is RESTFUL REMOVALS LIMITED, and and address in Fulham." Derek paused for breath. "What about that?"

"It makes it pretty certain we're right about Green's activities. From what Miss Hunt said, it would seem that Mr. Winter had become aware of them in some way. In which case, their interview was certainly not so uneventful as has been represented."

"It puts him right in the picture, doesn't it? As far as motive is concerned, I mean."

"It does. Can we use it, sir?"

"Like a curate's egg," said Sir Nicholas, "it is good in parts. However, we must remember that too much confusion might be as bad as too little."

"Well, all we can do is worry away at the people who

could have done it," said Antony reasonably. "And in this case the motive may be present, too."

"That also applies to Charles Prentiss."

"Yes, but don't start going round in circles. We've finished with him for the moment. The next on the list is cousin Stan, who could—I suppose?—but I don't see why he should have wanted to. And there was nothing fishy about his business with J.W. that afternoon."

"As a matter of fact, the only motives we know about are Joe Dowling's and Green's."

"Yes, but there are still several people for the 'opportunity' list. Eve Meadows could have done it, and opened the door by way of a diversion; the same applies to Miss Harris, and of course to Dennis."

"But, why—"

"I don't know! I like Dennis, and I hope he didn't; but you've got to admit he's way ahead of the field when it comes to opportunity."

"And if you must waste your time with idle speculation," said Sir Nicholas, re-entering the conversation with a certain amount of acid in his tone, "you'd better add that Armstrong, Mrs. Carey, and young Willett could, any of them, have opened the door."

"I won't even consider a conspiracy," remarked Antony. "It would make things much too complicated."

"It's complicated enough already, to listen to you," retorted his uncle. "I've been waiting for you to tell me about the leading lady's evidence. You said you were going to see her."

"Well, I did. But you won't like it particularly."

"My likes and dislikes could not very well be more irrelevant," said Sir Nicholas, coldly.

Derek exchanged a look with the younger of his companions; but, finding his host's eyes fixed on him accusingly, said in a hurry, "That's Stella Farraday, isn't it? I've seen her in some Ibsen—shocking stuff!—and as Rosalind, of all things. But not as Lady Macbeth."

"She was extremely appealing as Rosalind," said Sir Nicholas unexpectedly. "I am speaking now of a prewar performance—before your time. She had a good leg; it isn't every woman who looks well in tights," he added reminiscently.

"Well, I daresay her legs are still good; I didn't notice," said Antony, with a maddening assumption of virtue. "Though for all the good her evidence did me, I might just as well have had some fun out of the interview," he added gloomily.

"What did she tell you?" Sir Nicholas had obviously returned to the present day, and was in no mood for trifling.

"A young soldier gave her a dagger—I wonder what he thought she'd do with it? She doesn't like knives, but thought it would be a suitable gift for Joe when they were playing together in 1944. The police had shown her the weapon that killed J.W. She had to say it was similar, but she didn't remember well enough to be certain either way. And that was all, except that she was quite sure Joe would never—"

"Useful!" snapped Sir Nicholas. "You appear to have utilized to the fullest extent today your genius for wasting time!"

"Well, we've nearly three weeks," said Derek, who was quite inured to this skirmishing, and indeed had developed a certain facility in diversionary tactics. "Oates says they should reach the case by the middle of July."

"Then we'd best return to the statements. One never knows, one of them may contain A Fact." Counsel did not sound hopeful. "But we can't reach a decision as to the line to take until we've heard what this Meadows girl has to say."

Antony, whose spirits had momentarily lightened, under the stimulus of sparring with his uncle, returned to the depths again. He did not feel that a defense based on Eve Meadows's evidence had much chance of success.

It was, therefore, as a consequence of this discussion that he decided next morning to see Arthur Green again. Having nothing more urgent on his desk than an opinion, which should in any event have been delivered two weeks before, and which the interested parties weren't going to appreciate, anyway—so that it was, perhaps, a kindness to postpone their receipt of it?—he made his way at about eleven o'clock to Camden Mews. He wondered vaguely as he went what reason he could offer for the visit. Or did it matter so much? He could trust the inspiration of the moment, and no harm done.

His first knock went unanswered, but there was such a noise of humping and bumping from within that it seemed likely that perseverance would be rewarded. He knocked again, loudly this time. The bumping was for a moment louder than ever, then abruptly ceased. He heard steps on the stairs, and a window over the door slammed up.

"Who—?" said Green, sticking his head out. "Oh, it's you again," he added. "I'm busy just now."

Antony stepped back to look up at him more easily. Green was in shirt sleeves, and looked hot and harassed. Now that the nearer sounds had stopped he could hear that there was also some activity going on behind the garage doors.

"I'm sorry to disturb you, Mr. Green. I won't keep you long."

"You won't keep me at all," said the other, rudely, and withdrew his head.

"I hope," said Antony, "that you've remembered to leave the police your new address."

"What the hell do you mean?" He spoke angrily, but his head had reappeared, and he made no further move towards shutting the window.

"Just what I say. Don't you think you'd better let me come in for a few minutes?"

"Well, I can't." Green was sulky now. "The sofa's stuck on the stairs." He glared at his visitor, who looked back at him mildly, but had obviously no intention of leaving. "All right," he added, after a moment. "I'll come down—if I can."

Negotiating the sofa evidently took a few minutes, and Green was more flushed than ever by the time he opened the street door. "Come in, if you must," he said. "I can't take you upstairs."

"This will do nicely." Antony entered, and looked up the staircase with interest. The offending piece of furniture was bulky indeed, and pretty hopelessly wedged; a small, sturdy man, also in shirt sleeves, was standing below it on the staircase, considering ways and means.

"What you want here," he remarked, including the new-comer in the conversation in a friendly way, "is a bit of science."

"Science be blowed," said Green. "Go and help the others for five minutes. I'll call when I need you." He opened a door at the side of the narrow hall, standing so as to obscure Antony's view of what was on the other side. He managed, however, to gain an impression of activity, and remarked, as the small man slipped through, "Are they a good firm?"

"Who?"

"Restful Removers. You don't look, if you'll forgive my being personal, as if they lived up to their name."

"Look here," said Green, sitting down on the third step and taking out cigarettes, "have you been watching this place?"

"No. I wouldn't have time, even if I wanted to."

"Then . . . I don't understand what you're after."

"And I thought I explained so clearly, when I was here before."

"It didn't cover the facts my friend." Green was cooling down now, and seemed to have recovered his temper. "How did you know I was moving before I opened the door? And how did you know the name of the firm?"

"I put myself in your place," said Antony, promptly. "In your place I'd be moving. And having heard of your frequent dealings with Restful Removers . . . that, I admit, was a guess."

"Are you from the police?"

"I am not." Antony was tart. "In the interests of my client however—"

"Oh, skip it!" Green interrupted. "I know nothing about your blasted case."

"In that event, you have my sympathies. But you didn't answer my question: have you told the police what your new address will be?"

Green eyed him speculatively. "No, I haven't," he said after a while. "What about it?"

"I can hardly connive at the disappearance of a possible witness."

"Then you mean to go to the police?"

"Not necessarily. If you can convince me that you do in fact know nothing of Mr. Winter's death I shall no longer have any interest in your movements."

"How can I do that? Anyway, what's to stop me shutting your mouth?" He jerked his head towards the door that led to the garage.

Antony grinned at him. "That would hardly convince me of your innocence. But I somehow feel such a course would be distasteful—if not to you, at least to your present associates."

Green flicked ash from his cigarette, and he too smiled. "I wouldn't be too sure of that," he said, with genuine amusement. "What makes you think so?"

"From what I've seen of you, added to what I have seen in the papers—"

"Here!" said Green, startled. "What have the papers got about me?"

"Reports of your various activities. Oh, anonymously, I assure you, but it wasn't very difficult to put two and two together. And when I had done so," Antony added, impressively, "I found they added up to the portrait of a silly ass."

Green regarded him, but apparently without resentment. "You're a queer customer," he remarked. "What's your racket?"

"In this case, I want the truth."

"I tell you, I can't help you."

"That's a pity." He sounded resigned, and the other man looked apprehensive.

"What do you mean to do?"

"I told you I couldn't let a possible witness disappear. And *I* can't undertake to keep an eye on you to find out where you're going—'

"The police aren't interested in me." This was said defiantly, but he sounded uncertain.

"They might be induced to take an interest," Antony pointed out gently.

"I've a very good mind," said Green angrily, "to call your bluff."

"Please yourself." He sounded indifferent.

Green lighted another cigarette; he was obviously suffering from indecision, and after a moment said gruffly, "What do you want?"

"I'm not particular. An alibi, say; that would be just the thing. I've heard about Mr. Jennings, of course; somehow I don't take to him." He looked down at his companion encouragingly. "But before we go on with that, what did you and Mr. Winter talk about for so long?"

"Business. You know that already."

"Ah, yes, the terms for renewing your lease."

"That's right."

"A complicated document, I presume . . . if it was going to take two years to prepare."

"Damn you," said Green, unemotionally.

"And now you've decided to leave after all. It seems a pity to have gone to so much trouble—"

"Now what are you getting at?"

"I wish I knew. Well, if you won't tell me what you talked about, at least tell me what you did when you left Mr. Winter; three-fifteen we agreed that was, didn't we?"

"I came back here."

"Any witnesses?"

Green jerked his head again in the direction of the garage. "Three of them. And Jennings. Any good?"

"On the face of it, no."

"But I don't see what good it would do you. After all, Joe Dowling did it, didn't he?"

"My dear sir!" Antony was scandalized. "My client!"

"That's all guff, isn't it? I mean, they always plead 'not guilty,' but it doesn't really mean anything."

"Have it your own way. We don't really seem to be getting anywhere, do we?"

"Well, I don't know," said Green, sulkily, "where you want to get."

"I told you, but if you can't help me I'll be off now."

"What are you going to do? Go to the police?"

"As a matter of fact, no. I'm going to see that you're served with a subpoena right away, to attend the Magistrates' Court on Monday. After that, you can skip if you like, but you'll really be on the run. Have you ever tried it? It's no fun at all."

Green looked at him for a long moment. Strangely

enough, he seemed to feel no special resentment. After a while he laughed. ''It looks as if I'd better see about having the sofa taken upstairs again,'' he said.

Antony left him to his domestic arrangements, and went back to chambers. He felt momentarily elated, having found the visit illuminating; but what was the use of that, he thought angrily, after a feverish half-hour spent in trying to get his impressions down on paper . . . what the hell was the use of it when there wasn't any proof?

CHAPTER 15

IT SEEMED wisest not to press Charles's cooperation too closely, and Antony delayed his further visit to Bread Court until Friday afternoon. Later he was to regret that he had exercised so much patience.

An air of gloom hung over the offices in Number Seven when he arrived there. He was conscious of it the moment he pushed open the door of the general office: Dennis was very quiet, and had every appearance of being deep in his work—nobody could have said he looked cheerful; Miss Bell seemed out of temper, though she did make some effort to disguise this in honor of his visit; even Miss Harris seemed preoccupied; and if Willett bounced gently—alone among them unaffected—this was so normal that everyone took it for granted. Antony asked after Miss Meadows.

"She isn't here today," said Miss Harris.

"She isn't coming back," said Willett.

"She's left; she left last night," said Miss Bell.

Dennis said nothing, but ruffled the pages of a fat book on his desk in a way that dissociated him from the discussion, while indicating that he was giving it enough of his attention to be polite.

"Well," said Antony, taken aback. "I didn't know she was thinking of leaving."

"It was the best thing," said Miss Bell, glancing briefly at Miss Harris, and apparently throwing caution to the winds. "She'd never get over it, seeing him every day." She brooded a moment, and added firmly, "And even if she was rather silly, I still think he treated her very badly."

Miss Harris coughed, and said, "Really, Daisy!" in a

deprecating way. Antony gathered that she concurred with
the sentiments, though she did not feel it proper that they
should be given expression. "I'm sure Eve's affairs are no
business of ours, and if she has got a better job to go to—"

Miss Bell gave an irritated exclamation and slammed the
carriage of her typewriter back to the beginning of the line.
She glared for a moment at the letter she was typing and began to hunt unsystematically among the papers on her desk.
"Men!" she said.

"If you want the eraser," remarked Willett, helpfully,
"it's down there."

"Well, of course it is," she snapped, and began hauling
on the long piece of red tape that attached the eraser to her
typewriter. Then she looked up and smiled. "I'm just too
cross to think," she remarked apologetically, "and you
must admit, Miss Harris, it is Too Bad."

"Well," said the other, with caution, "at least, to do Mr.
Prentiss justice, I think leaving was her idea."

"I daresay it was. The Situation was Impossible," said
Miss Bell, still speaking in capital letters. "And *that* wasn't
her fault."

At this point Dennis Dowling got up and strolled out of
the room with an absent-minded air that deceived nobody—
not even Willett. The two women exchanged glances.

"Oh, dear, and this used to be such a happy office. I can't
think what's come over everybody."

"Never mind, Miss Harris, things will settle down again,
you'll see."

"Well, perhaps they may. But everything will be
different—only you and me, and Mr. Prentiss. I'm sure Mr.
Dowling won't stay when he has taken his final, though,
goodness knows," she added, with the air of one who has to
have something to worry about, "whether he'll pass. And
even Willett is leaving."

"Well, that's no loss," said Miss Bell, briskly. Willett
made a face at her, but apparently without resentment, and
turned back to Antony.

"I say, Mr. Maitland, I went to see Mr. Mallory at
lunchtime yesterday. He's a—" Judging from his sudden
pause and look of embarrassment, Antony conjectured that
frankness and policy were struggling for precedence. After a

moment he coughed and started again. "He was very kind and said he'd give me a month's trial, but I'd better take my holiday first and start in a fortnight. Do you think it'll be all right, Mr. Maitland? Or shall I get thrown out when the month's up?"

"Perhaps not, if you watch your step. I'm issuing no guarantee. Is Charles in, Miss Harris? I'd better have a word with him if he is."

Prentiss was in, but his greeting was not cordial. He looked as though he had slept in his clothes and hadn't brushed his hair for a week. Antony sat on the edge of the desk and took no notice of the look of irritation that greeted this piece of casual behavior.

"Well, Charles?" he asked.

"If you mean, have I talked to Eve?—yes, I have."

"That's good."

"Oh, is it? A fine time she gave me! For one thing, she practically went off into raving hysterics at the mere mention of your name—don't laugh, damn you, it wasn't a little bit funny."

Antony obligingly removed his grin. (He was not, himself, feeling particularly cheerful, but the picture his companion's words conjured up was irresistible.) "What was the upshot?" he inquired.

"She'll talk now, if you want. I had the devil of a job persuading her I'd left long before quarter past four, and a still worse one making her believe that you believed me. I hope to goodness that's true, Antony."

"It's true enough. What—no, I'll wait and see what she says. I've changed my mind about seeing her myself, though. It seems to me to be a job for Uncle Nick. What about arranging it? I hear she's left the office."

"Yes, she seemed—er—to feel it was best. She's on the phone."

"Then get on to her, and ask her to come and see Uncle Nick this evening."

Charles reached for the telephone, but protested as he did so. "She may not find it convenient—"

"The very least she can do," said Antony inexorably, "after all the trouble she's caused."

In the event, however, it did not prove quite so simple. As

Charles spoke the look of strain on his face deepened. He turned from the phone at last, with a shrug. "I spoke to her landlady—she's gone away for the weekend—the old girl doesn't know where."

"Well, that's just too bad. Will you arrange something as soon as she's back?"

"If you like." Prentiss sounded ungracious.

"I think it's up to you, you know."

"Oh, all right! If I must."

"Thank you, Charles. I'll stop worrying you now, and let you get on with your work."

"Work? Can't concentrate at all. By the way, I'm being married next week."

Antony paused on his way to the door. "I wish you joy."

"Wednesday afternoon. Quiet affair, in the circumstances. Just Stan, as best man, and Mary has a friend coming to back her up. Saves having to ask that wife of his—Muriel, you know. Ghastly woman!"

"I think, you know—"

"Yes, he's completely besotted about her. No accounting for tastes. But he saw my point, all right—Mary still in mourning, can't make it a *party!*"

"No, indeed!" said Antony. And kept his amusement well enough to himself.

"Mary will be selling the Purley House," Charles went on; now he had started, he seemed quite unable to stop talking. "Cousin Clarissa's going to a hotel; suit her down to the ground, I should think. And Mary's already got ideas about making my flat really comfortable."

"I'm sure she has." He tried not to put undue emphasis on his words, but he could imagine no subject upon which Mary Winter would not have ideas, and definite ones at that. He expressed, however, such sentiments as were courteous, and left a few minutes later in meditative mood. As he turned out of Bread Court he wondered whether anything would be gained by seeing John Armstrong again, but decided against turning back. It was unlikely to be a profitable visit, and might even do more harm than good.

He found Sir Nicholas still in chambers, and stood in his favorite place by the window while counsel and his clerk wrestled with a timetable that showed every indication of getting out of hand. He turned as Mallory left the room, and came back to sit on the corner of the desk.

"I've just come from Bread Court, sir. Eve Meadows is away for the weekend. However, Charles says he has convinced her that he left the office by four o'clock, so she's willing to talk. So he says. Your witness I think, don't you, sir?"

"Don't tell me," said Sir Nicholas, much moved, "that I am at last to be presented with some evidence."

"Well, we don't know what she'll say, after all."

"Never mind about that. The wretched girl must know something, or why is she making so much fuss?"

"She's left her job," said Antony irrelevantly. Sir Nicholas gave him a sharp look. "I only wondered—I mean, Jenny is sure to ask—"

"I understand from Mallory that I am already employing one discarded member of Charles Prentiss's staff," remarked the older man dryly. "Let me be quite plain with you, Antony; in no circumstances will I consider taking a woman into my chambers in any capacity whatever."

"I didn't mean that," said his nephew, hastily. "Particularly Eve Meadows, she might fall in love with you." Sir Nicholas scowled at him. "All the same, sir, she might be in rather a mess—"

"Good heavens, boy, you must see I can't do anything about it. If I find she needs a job I'll put her in touch with Bellerby, he's always bemoaning the inefficiency of his typists; and you needn't worry," he added. "He's a married man and has, I should say, a strong instinct of self-preservation!"

After that, things settled back into something approaching normal routine. The police put their case briefly in the Magistrates' Court, Sir Nicholas held his fire, and Joe Dowling was committed for trial. The newspapers were happy, if nobody else. The Connor brief was dissected, discussed, and argued; the case, after the customary delays, arrived in court, and their client departed unostentatiously from his usual haunts for the space of some six months. Sir Nicholas reduced Jenny to a state of simmering fury by a bitter denunciation of his nephew's part in the affair; but at least this took her mind from other things. Antony, though with his own role as witness uncomfortably present in his mind, was by now genuinely more concerned on Joe Dowling's behalf with the outcome of the trial. But Jenny could achieve no such objectivity, and though she tried to hide her worry it was always with them.

It was nearly a fortnight before Eve Meadows put in an appearance, and the interview was not an easy one. She looked wary, and Sir Nicholas's carefully prepared introduction seemed only to add to the general air of suspicion with which she had surrounded herself. It was over an hour before she left, and Antony—banished to his own room for the duration of her visit—was back in his uncle's office almost before she was out of it.

"Well, sir?"

"Quite an interesting interview," said Sir Nicholas, who hated to be rushed.

"Was it any good? Did she talk? Did she know anything?"

"Calm yourself. No wonder you scared the girl if you snapped at her like that."

Antony sat down. "Pax," he said. "Please tell me, sir."

Sir Nicholas relented. "The beginning of her statement you know. When she came in at four o'clock she saw Charles Prentiss at the turn of the corridor; it was only after Mr. Winter's death was discovered that she thought it better to say instead that she might have been mistaken. She heard, of course, Dowling's voice, and guessed why Dennis immediately took himself off to the strongroom. She joined Miss Bell and Willett, and had some tea with them. They both said they hadn't seen Prentiss, and that made her curious. She started to set out her abstract, but after a while she thought she might as well see if he was in his room, so she went through by the door that leads there direct from the general office."

"Does she know what time that was?"

"Nearly a quarter past four. The room was empty, but she could tell he had been there. The chair at the desk was pushed back, and there was still a faint smell of cigarette smoke. Also, some of the deed boxes were disarranged; she noticed because she had had cause to go to one of them only that morning, and had replaced them quite tidily. Your friend, Miss Bell, was probably right, by the way; Matthew Winter's box, which was halfway down the pile that morning, was now on top.''

"Had Eve drawn the same inference?"

"I think she had. Obviously, she has been under no illusion as to Prentiss's feelings for her for quite a time now. Her final decision to leave the office is certainly a sensible one, though made at some inconvenience to herself; I understand (as you surmised) that she is dependent on what she earns.''

"Damn Charles!"

"Certainly, if you feel it would do any good. You have lured me, however, from the main issue. She then went out of Prentiss's room by the other door, and opened the door that leads from the corridor on to the private stair.''

Sir Nicholas paused, and looked down at the notes he had been making. ''It was at this point that the interview became difficult,'' he said. ''Up till now she had been tolerably calm, though not at all forthcoming; she answered my questions, but didn't volunteer a thing. I asked her what she had seen. She became violently agitated, but said at last that someone had just been leaving by the street door. Had she recognized him? She had only seen his shoulder and one arm, she said; but she was obviously equivocating, because after a moment she began to cry. She said: 'I thought it was Charles; I was sure it must be him; who else could it have been?' I pointed out that Charles said he left the office just after four o'clock; after a while she dried her eyes, and said in rather a dreary tone: 'He said I should talk to you. He said I must have thought I saw him, because I expected to.' ''

"I daresay he was right, at that. Was that all?"

"Not quite. She talked more freely after that. She said she had called out 'Charles,' and the man at the bottom of the stairs had stopped for a moment, and half-opened the door again so that she caught a glimpse of his head, only in silhouette, and only for a moment. Then the door closed. She still took it for granted it was Prentiss, and wasn't really surprised.''

"Could she give any description?"

"Not much to the point. I tried height first. That was no good, because looking down she couldn't tell. Build, she hadn't seen clearly enough. Clothes, she didn't know, she hadn't noticed; no, certainly not an overcoat, a jacket, not loose like a sports coat, and made of a dark, smooth material. I rang up Charles then—luckily he didn't go in for an extended honeymoon—he was wearing a sports jacket that afternoon, he said; we could probably prove it by reference to Miss Hunt, who saw him when he went to see Mary Winter. I thought that might cheer her, but she seemed quite apathetic. We went back to the question of build, but it wasn't any use, she just didn't know. And she only got a glimpse of his head; and she's not quite sure, but she doesn't think he was bald!"

"But she must know that. No, really, Uncle Nick, I call that the limit!"

"It was the best I could do," said Sir Nicholas. He had picked up a pencil, and was drawing on the back of his notes.

"Can you trust her in court?"

"As much as one ever can. But I wouldn't like to say what her evidence will sound like by the time Halloran has finished with it. He'll let the first part ride, of course—I mean, I can't see him being interested in whether Charles had been to the office or not—but he's bound to attack the description of the man she saw."

"Well, that's that, then," said Antony, after a moment.

Sir Nicholas was still busy with his sketch. "I'll do what I can with it," he told his nephew, not looking up.

The trial, of course, was much longer in being reached than had been estimated. The production of *Macbeth* had limped on for a few days with an understudy after the principal actor's arrest; but Meg Hamilton was resting now, and a frequent visitor in Kempenfeldt Square. She had seen little of Dennis, she said; he had been served with a subpoena by the prosecution, which seemed to have both surprised and upset him. It transpired that the Crown was calling all the visitors to the office, and all the members of the staff except Eve Meadows. "That gives us a line, at least," said Sir Nicholas, and summoned Derek Stringer for a conference.

Indeed, they spent more and more time together, these two, while the older man growled his way through the preparation of his case, and the younger showed commendable patience with the vagaries of his leader.

Antony, meanwhile, not directly concerned and up to his ears in other work, was making something of a name for himself for plain speaking in court, and for delivering unpalatable opinions in a forthright way which delighted solicitors (who felt they couldn't be blamed), and disconcerted their clients (who, however, having paid good money for advice, did not feel capable of ignoring it). He kept away from the conferences, after the first few days, except when they called on him for something in connection with his own evidence, and tried to ignore the fact that his uncle was silent about their prospects, and Stringer was looking preoccupied.

It couldn't last, of course, this interlude. The days went by with all their customary dispatch; the weather was hot, and gray, and inclined to thunder, but gave at least a convenient excuse for tempers that were frayed by waiting. And so, on a Monday evening, the third week in July, their period of inactivity was over; Mr. Justice Carruthers had worked his way steadily through his list and would hear on the morrow the Crown's case against Joseph Dowling.

CHAPTER 16

THERE WAS EXCITEMENT among the ladies and gentlemen of the press. That, perhaps, was inevitable. Antony was conscious of the stir of it in the crowded courtroom, long before the prisoner appeared, long before the judge made his entrance. All through the preliminaries, essential but unexciting, he was aware of the sense of expectation . . . in the assembled reporters, in the public gallery (whose crowd would later be described as "fashionable"); it would be in the corridors, too, in the room where the witnesses waited— where he should be himself if Uncle Nick hadn't made such a point of his presence. He looked at Joseph Dowling and became aware of bitterness; the vultures were gathered, and the kill couldn't come too quickly for them. A moment later, some amusement tinged his thoughts: the accused man wore his gray lounge suit with an air that brought the phrase "customary suits of sober black" most vividly into Antony's mind, though he was behaving—for the moment at least— with extreme decorum.

Mr. Justice Carruthers was a small man, with a face like an intelligent bloodhound. He received Sir Nicholas's request that one of the witnesses might remain in court with equanimity, looked for a moment with open curiosity at the young man concerned, and then turned courteously to counsel for the Crown to ask his views.

Bruce Halloran, Q.C., was leading for the prosecution, and appeared with two juniors: a stout, middle-aged man named Potter and a silent youth named Horton, who was believed (on what grounds nobody knew) to be a dark horse. Halloran got to his feet and surveyed the defense counsel with leisurely amusement. He was a big man, a little too heavy to be considered good-looking and so dark of countenance as to make his wig and bands appear quite dazzling by contrast. Stringer gave Antony an encouraging grin and murmured, behind his hand, "I thought my wig was white—"

Halloran, who could not possibly have heard the words, turned his amused glance upon the two younger men, and said slowly, "I should not wish to disoblige my learned friend, but this request is—surely?—a little unusual."

Sir Nicholas smiled. "It may be easier for my friend to—er—to follow his inclination not to disoblige me," he said, "if I explain that he will be giving nothing away by agreeing to my request. Maitland has been intimately concerned in this affair ever since I myself was briefed, and but for the accident of his being a witness would have been associated with the conduct of the defense, in addition to my learned junior." He inclined his head briefly in the direction of Stringer and turned to his opponent with a look of inquiry.

"My friend leaves me without an argument." Halloran turned to the judge. "I have no objection to the defense's request."

"I have no doubt you have a good reason for this application, Sir Nicholas?"

"I have, m'lud." He gave no sign that he would prefer not to be called upon to produce it. (What could he say, after all? "Perhaps as a result of his work during the war, my nephew has developed an instinct for investigation which I have come to trust. It is unlikely that anything further will emerge from the evidence, but my case is so weak I can afford to take no chances.") Fortunately the judge, after one doubtful look had inclined his head.

"If Mr. Halloran agrees, I can have no objection."

Sir Nicholas sat down again, and the business of the day went on. The progress of a trial has often been described as tedious, and Antony had plenty of opportunity for reflection during the hours that followed. He had seen Halloran before in court, but today, of course, he observed him closely; and the more he watched him, the less he liked his own prospects. Here was a formidable opponent indeed; for himself, he would as soon have sat down to supper with a man-eating tiger!

Meanwhile, Halloran had briefly made his opening remarks: nothing sensational, a plain statement of facts—as interpreted by the police. There was a point when Joe Dowling was heard to mutter, only too audibly: "Away with him, away with him, he speaks Latin"—counsel had referred to a prima-facie case. Sir Nicholas made no sign that he had heard, but his nephew, observing a little later that he had drawn on the back of his brief a barrister in wig and gown, lying dead with a lily in his hand, deduced correctly that he was thankful his client had avoided the more familiar, and even more apposite, quotation: "First thing we do, let's kill all the lawyers."

Halloran proceeded to unfold his case with an air of leisured calm that must certainly have impressed the jury. Antony, surveying the little group of citizens with a more personal interest than usual, tried to decide which of them—if any—was likely to believe his story. There was a thin-faced man who reminded him of one of his schoolmasters, and to whom he took an instant dislike; it seemed probable that this would be reciprocated. On the other hand, there was a stout, motherly body, who obviously had at least ten children, on whom he felt he could rely for sympathetic attention. (The lady in question was single, a professor at London University, and held men in general, and lawyers in particular, in aversion, but that is beside the point.)

Miss Bell . . . Inspector Frazer . . . an architect to swear to a plan of the offices. Sir Nicholas awoke briefly at this point from a fit of apparent abstraction to show enough interest in the two doors at the top of the private stair to make it quite evident he regarded both of them as being of importance. Medical evidence . . . nothing startling there . . . the knife put in as an exhibit. Charles Prentiss, to speak of what little he knew about Joseph Dowling's dealings with his partner; Sir Nicholas speaking suddenly, quietly—with the briefest of glances at the judge, "M'lud, my friend is leading his witness." No cross-examination here . . . Charles left the stand with a look of relief which Antony would have found comical if he had been in a mood to be amused. That was before lunch.

Afterwards came Miss Harris—questions as to the organization of the office, the events of the afternoon when James Winter was killed there. Stringer was on his feet as Halloran sat down. "The private door to Mr. Winter's office, Miss Harris?" and proceeded with gentle persistence to obtain from her a list of the people who would have had the opportunity of unlatching the door—assuming it to have been latched, as usual, at lunchtime. Halloran, who knew perfectly well that to prove others besides Dowling to have had opportunity of unlatching the door made it neither more nor less likely that the actor had done it, maintained for some time his air of quiet amusement.

After a while, however, it became evident that Stringer's persistence puzzled him, and presently he was moved to protest. "M'lud . . . this is outside the witness's knowledge. She was not present—"

"Very true. I withdraw the question." Stringer's haste was almost convincing. "Miss Harris—you know that Mr. Stanley Prentiss was alone in the office, on at least once occasion?"

"Yes, because of the muddle about his will. Mr. Winter came out to see if Miss Bell had finished. I met him in the corridor."

"Quite so. And, as counsel for the Crown has so reasonably pointed out, you were not present during the interview with Mr. Arthur Green, and only in the room a few minutes while Mrs. Carey and Mr. Armstrong were there."

"That is true."

"So you cannot be certain that Mr. Winter did not, in fact, leave his office during that time? For one reason, or another? It seems likely, does it not, that he may have done so?"

They returned then to Miss Harris's last talk with her employer. Halloran was objecting again (and with sufficient reason, Antony considered), "Neatly done," said Sir Nicholas, with approval, as his junior resumed his seat.

The question of the door was to be elaborated during Willett's evidence, during which, too, there was another exchange between Sir Nicholas and Bruce Halloran on the subject of "leading." Antony thought the prosecution came off slightly the better, but counsel for the defense had made his point and seemed well enough satisfied. Halloran had established that the door was locked at two o'clock; what happened after was anyone's guess, as far as Antony could see.

Arthur Green arrived at the witness stand with a look of defiance that barely concealed his nervousness. He had nothing, of course, to fear from the prosecution (who were concerned to show the routine nature of James Winter's business that afternoon); Sir Nicholas's cross-examination was another matter, and seemed to take Halloran by surprise. Antony saw his expression as he turned to say something in a low voice to Potter, and he did not look pleased. Sir Nicholas, however, having tangled the threads to his own satisfaction, let the witness go, smiled sweetly at the opponent, and resumed his seat.

Stanley Prentiss followed; he seemed puzzled to find himself giving evidence, but reasonably philosophical, and neither counsel detained him long. Mrs. Carey made an even briefer appearance. Halloran, Antony felt, should regard her with affection, as being exactly to specification!

The next witness caused a stir in the court, quite out of proportion to the value of her evidence. This was Stella Farraday, who had played opposite Joe Dowling in the *Macbeth* production in 1944. She gave her evidence reluctantly; yes, she had given him a dagger as a souvenir of the production. Some young soldier had given it to her . . . he was a commando, she thought, but she did not remember his name. She herself had a horror of knives, but it had seemed a suitable gift in view of the play they were doing. No, she couldn't identify the knife produced, but she couldn't say either (though only too obviously she would have liked to) that it wasn't the same one. Sir Nicholas wrote "dynamite" on the pad in front of him, and declined to cross-examine.

Adams, the stage manager, followed, and his evidence was similarly vague and consequently difficult to attack. Sir Nicholas asked him a few questions, feeling his way, but as he had declined to swear to the dagger—"all I do say is, it is like, very like"—there wasn't really very much to be done.

Inspector Sykes's evidence was, in the main, an elaboration on the theme of Halloran's opening address. Potter took him through it, with no opening for an objection by the defense; at the end Sir Nicholas had two questions to ask.

"You would not maintain, Inspector, that Joseph Dowling was the only person who could possibly have unlatched the private door?"

Well—there was only one answer to that one, of course. "No, I could make no such assertion."

"About the weapon, Inspector. Would you suggest there was anything unique about the dagger that killed James Winter?"

"Far from it. It was of a type commonly referred to as a fighting knife, issued to Special Service troops."

"Issued by the thousand, Inspector?"

"Very probably, sir. I have no means of knowing."

And at that point the court adjourned for the day. Sir Nicholas took Stringer back to chambers with him, and Antony went home to supper and took Jenny to the pictures. They chose a Western which was long and uncomplicated and strangely soothing—because black was black, and white was white, and nobody even dreamed of suggesting that ever they should meet.

They were off to a brisk start next morning, with Dennis Dowling's evidence. Halloran took him relentlessly through his reluctant corroboration of Stella Farraday's testimony, without any interruptions from the defense counsel. Dennis made, on the whole, a better showing than Antony had expected. Like the other witnesses he could make no positive identification of the dagger, but it was inevitable that his natural reluctance to make even the smallest of admissions should sound like an evasiveness born of guilty knowledge; and Sir Nicholas felt that any intervention on his part could only make a bad business worse. He cross-examined briefly, and rather with the air of one who re-examined his own witness. Dennis was free to leave the witness stand, which he did rather clumsily, and had to be twice directed to the bench behind counsels' table where the witnesses were accommodated after their evidence had been given.

Young Harvey did not get very much attention, either from defense or prosecution. Antony had the impression that Halloran was much more interested in what he might say on cross-examination than in anything he himself might elicit from his testimony, while Sir Nicholas was far too wily to be lured into asking ill-advised questions, even when invited to do so in the most handsome way by a display of apparent ineptitude on the part of his opponent.

So then there was Armstrong; and there was no doubt in his manner, and no doubt of the conviction which his evidence carried. Sir Nicholas varied his tactics here, intervening every few questions with protests—justified or not; but Halloran was a seasoned campaigner, and thrived on their exchanges, while as for the witness he was very sure in his self-approbation and seemed quite unshakable.

As for the cross-examination, Sir Nicholas proceeded with circumspection. He kept off the contentious subject of religious beliefs, but at the same time succeeded (by some devious means of his own) in provoking an outburst of dislike for actors, actresses, and the theater in general, which made Halloran visibly uncomfortable—and brought on a spate of objections even more frequent and vehement than those with which the defense had enlivened the examination-in-chief. On the identification, though, Armstrong was unshakable. Antony (knowing him to be wrong) could still believe that by now he was fully convinced of the truth of what he was saying. How could you make the court doubt a man who had no doubts of himself? Sir Nicholas, however, showed no signs of perturbation as he came to his last question.

"Mr. Armstrong, would you say you have never made a mistake?"

"Not often, sir, I assure you. And in this instance there was no room for error—I saw the accused man's face quite clearly."

Sir Nicholas sat down with a swirl of his gown that was somehow contemptuous. Antony took a look at Joseph Dowling, sitting quietly enough in his place. Earlier he had thought how worn the actor looked; now, surprisingly, all trace of fatigue had left him; he was alert and listening with fascinated interest. But it was not the evidence that was claiming his attention, it was the man who was giving it: a man who was a stranger to him, and almost beyond the comprehension of his generous, tempestuous mind. At that moment, more than ever before, Antony felt himself very much in sympathy with the prisoner. An awkward man, as he himself had boasted, but sincere in the interest he had in his fellow men . . . which in itself had led directly to his considerable stage success. An awkward man . . . a violent man . . . but nearly always likable, and never dull.

Halloran, with a glance at his opponent that was not very far from smugness, declined the opportunity of re-examining. And rested his case, at this highly satisfactory point.

The judge glanced across at Sir Nicholas with a look of courteous inquiry. Being a man of mournful cast of countenance, it would have been hard to say he was enjoying himself, but his eyes were bright with interest, and Antony was pretty sure he wasn't missing a point. Counsel for the defense was on his feet.

"M'lud, at the commencement of this trial my client made to the court a statement of 'not guilty' which now I must substantiate . . ." Antony listened with half his attention. Time was getting on now, and the prosecution's case seemed only too firmly established. And what could they do to refute it, after all? He glanced across at Sykes and wondered what he was making of the evidence. The inspector's expression was as serene as ever, but Briggs, beside him, was mopping his forehead. Well, it was hot enough, worse even than yesterday. He looked again at his uncle; he could not see his face, but instead watched his hands which, with their studied, tranquil gestures, were—as much as his voice—part of the impression of quiet confidence he was striving to convey.

". . . at first I thought I should not call upon Joseph Dowling today; that to do so would be to give undue weight to the accusations against him, and to the strength of the prosecution's case which (I shall show you) can be refuted without his help. But then I considered that it is the right of every man to speak in his own defense . . ." Well, that was all very pretty, and perhaps it might impress the jury. There were dangers which were all too apparent in putting so volatile a man as Joe Dowling on the witness stand; the trouble was, the danger of keeping him off it might be even worse.

In the event, it was unpleasant even beyond expectation. Dowling's story was soon told, and it was when Halloran rose to take up the questioning that Antony found himself sweating in sympathy with the accused man. Dowling seemed bewildered, and it was some time before he realized that the actor was troubled by something that to him went deeper even than the fear of what would follow if the verdict went against him; every statement he made was subject to the same silent criticism: "After all, the man's an actor!" His very plausibility told against him, and though he retained a degree of dignity his answers became wilder, and less considered.

The luncheon adjournment came and went, and the afternoon was far advanced before Bruce Halloran signified that he had come to the end of his questions. His "thank you" to his victim had an irony which Dowling's answering bow parodied and underlined; even Antony, prejudiced as he was in the prisoner's favor, could not help but wonder, momentarily, whether he might not see this action duplicated one day on the stage. He was brought up sharply by the thought that this might well be Dowling's last performance.

As time went on, Sir Nicholas's air of bland satisfaction had grown slightly more pronounced; and as his nephew got up to take his place as a witness it was with the far from encouraging feeling that the older man was getting rattled.

Sir Nicholas was far too old a hand, of course, for this to appear in his manner. He took his nephew through the preliminaries with practiced speed, brought out their relationship—both in their private and professional life—with just the right degree of emphasis, and allowed himself one malicious glance at his adversary, which conveyed clearly enough his purpose in this particular line of questioning. He then left Antony alone to make his statement; added at the end the minimum of queries necessary to underline the main points; waved an inviting hand in the direction of the opposing counsel; and sat down with an air of confidence which his nephew admired but did not feel capable, just then, of emulating.

In this, he wronged himself. Bruce Halloran, rising to

cross-examine, found himself facing a calm young man, who met his gaze squarely, with untroubled eyes. Counsel for the prosecution was himself at this moment in a state of acute bewilderment; until he had heard Antony's evidence he had not believed it possible that it would be of so unequivocal a nature. Briggs's interpretation of the position he had put down as the result of one of those queer antipathies to which the best of men are subject. Believing his own witness, he had not felt that the defense's evidence on this point could be other than vague. Now it seemed that he must reconsider his opinion; perhaps, even, Briggs might be in the right of it. There was, besides, the fact that the witness had some acquaintance with the people concerned. It seemed there was something to uncover here, and an adversary, perhaps, not unworthy of his best endeavors. There was no lack of intelligence in young Maitland's face, and a steadfast look was no guarantee of guilelessness. He turned to his task with something like enthusiasm.

"You are on oath, Mr. Maitland."

It wasn't the statement that shook Antony, nor the tone in which it was made, but the prefix to his name, from anyone else the commonest courtesy, from a fellow barrister set him at once outside the ranks of his profession. Halloran was addressing him as a stranger, an outsider. He answered with something of a snap, "I am aware of it!"

"And you have heard . . . indeed, owing to your somewhat unorthodox connection with this case through your position in my friend's chambers, you were already familiar with, the evidence of the Crown's witness, John Procter Armstrong?"

"I have heard it, and knew of it beforehand."

"Yet you give him the lie." Halloran's voice was gentle, and Sir Nicholas was on his feet almost before he had finished speaking.

"M'lud, I object. My learned friend is well aware that his statement is not proper cross-examination."

"I will withdraw." Halloran bowed his apologies, without waiting for an official direction. "Mr. Maitland, the court has heard the evidence of John Armstrong, and it has heard your evidence. How do you account for the discrepancy?"

"It is not my business to explain it."

"But you feel—of course, you must feel—that we should accept your testimony in preference to that of the previous witness?"

Antony's lips tightened. From the corner of his eye he saw his uncle's hands close suddenly to crush the paper he was holding. There was no answer he could make except one that would lead to the point that counsel wished to make, the point of direct conflict. He said, "I do feel that," and was conscious, as he spoke, that he was only delaying the inevitable.

"As a corollary, then, you wish us to believe that you speak the truth, while the Crown's witness is lying?"

Sir Nicholas looked up, but there was no point, Antony felt, in further evasion.

"I know his evidence to be untrue. He himself may be . . . mistaken." (Who had said that? Armstrong himself? "I thank thee, Jew, for teaching me that word.")

"Ah!" It was Halloran's characteristic note of triumph. "But you said, did you not, in the course of direct examination, that there was no possibility of a mistake about your evidence?"

"That is so. I cannot speak to Mr. Armstrong's observations, however, of my own knowledge."

"But he, too, has said there is no possibility he is wrong. Do you think he was . . . mistaken about that, too?" His voice was quietly scornful.

Antony was silent, seeing his uncle on his feet again. Sir Nicholas said, with an air of studied detachment, "The court may perhaps feel that this is not a matter upon which questions can properly be put to the witness."

Again Halloran retreated without argument. He said conversationally, "You are, I believe, a friend of Mr. Dennis Dowling, the son of the accused?"

Antony was ready for this one. "I have been acquainted with him for some time, and we have become better acquainted while this case has been in preparation."

"Because of your position in your uncle's chambers?" (Damn the fellow . . . perhaps, after all, it would have been better—)

"Partly because of that." (As soon as he spoke he knew

that was the wrong answer; here it came, and he had asked for it.)

"And partly, no doubt, because of a natural sympathy with a friend in trouble." Halloran was bland. (And what could you say to that?)

He looked full at counsel, and answered deliberately. "May I remind you, sir, of your own statement a few minutes ago? I am on oath. My 'natural sympathies' don't tempt me to perjury."

Halloran looked up at the judge, but Carruthers's expression was noncommittal, and he let pass the opportunity for comment. Instead he remarked, "No, as you have already implied, we are rather to believe that Mr. Armstrong is lying." His tone held a query, but Antony made no answer, and after a moment he went on. "Come now, Mr. Maitland, that isn't a very difficult question, surely."

"You made a statement, sir. I hesitated to contradict you; his lordship might think me lacking in courtesy."

"Then perhaps you will answer me this." It was perhaps a mistake to attempt to take a rise out of so experienced an adversary as Halloran. He was on his mettle now, and the witness could expect no quarter. "If you are telling the truth, Armstrong is lying. Do you admit the logic on that?"

"It all depends," said Antony, with the air of one who has given careful consideration to an interesting question. "It all depends what you mean by lying. I say he is not telling the truth. I have not accused him of deliberate falsehood."

"That sounds very fine, to be sure," said Halloran, with something like a sneer. "I'm afraid these distinctions are too subtle for me."

"Then I must hope," Antony spoke with sudden asperity, "that the jury has a better understanding."

That brought Mr. Justice Carruthers to life. He leaned forward a little, the better to catch the witness's eye. "I find that remark impertinent, Mr. Maitland; I think I may say, in both senses of the word."

"I apologize, my lord."

"Perhaps you will also withdraw your remark."

"As your lordship pleases." Sir Nicholas might have been seen to give a suspicious look at his nephew, but the judge evidently found nothing to quarrel with in this rejoinder.

"Then, I think, Mr. Halloran, you may proceed."

Counsel for the prosecution bowed, and turned back to the witness. He did not seem to be in a hurry to speak, but eyed Antony in silence for a while before saying, "Let us return, then, to the afternoon in question. A man walked down Bread Court in front of you; you admit that, I believe?"

"I have stated so . . . on oath."

"Ah, precisely! You saw him clearly?"

"Clearly enough. But I didn't specially *observe* him."

"This passion for fine distinctions! Will you describe this man?"

"A big man. At least, that is my impression."

"Stout?" Halloran's gaze, moving from the witness's face to the silent figure in the dock, left no doubt as to the trend of his thoughts. A demon of perversity possessed himself of Antony's mind.

"If you wish for a comparison, not quite so stout as yourself, sir."

Halloran coughed. He said amiably, "That's very helpful, Mr. Maitland," but there was a gleam in his eye that might have been amusement, and equally well might have been anger. "And can you not add something to this . . . masterly description?"

"No more than I have told the court. He wore a hat, and a dark suit."

"And yet you have stated . . . categorically . . . emphatically . . . that this man was not the prisoner?"

"That is so."

"It is difficult to see upon what you base your opinion."

"May I explain, then? Mr. Dowling is a neighbor; to put it in familiar terms, he lives just round the corner from my uncle's house—which has been my home for almost twenty years. I know him, therefore, very well by sight. And he is not—I think you will admit—a man it is easy to overlook."

"And you say you did not know the man you saw."

"I did not."

"You would recognize him again, perhaps?"

"No, I don't think so."

Bruce Halloran looked round the crowded court; he seemed to be asking for sympathy. "You must forgive me, Mr. Maitland," he said. "I find this very difficult to understand."

"Do you, sir? It's really quite simple—"

"Is it indeed? You were too preoccupied to notice anything about this man, to be able to describe him at all. Yet you are willing to swear—"

"I have sworn it was not a man I already knew well by sight," said Antony. And added, turning suddenly towards the jury box; "You'll find it's quite reasonable, if you think about it."

Before Halloran could voice his protest the judge had intervened. "Mr. Maitland, you mustn't address the jury."

"No, my lord."

"Just confine yourself to answering the questions. Yes, Mr. Halloran—"

"To return to this man, Mr. Maitland, do you admit that he went into the door at the bottom of Mr. Winter's private stair?"

"I hate that word 'admit,' " said Antony, plaintively. Bruce Halloran showed his teeth, momentarily, in a smile that held nothing of humor.

"Shall I re-form the question?" he asked.

"I shouldn't bother. I said, you know, that I didn't see where he went. But I don't quarrel with Mr. Armstrong's evidence on that point; he may well be right." He smiled, suddenly. "I hope you'll be satisfied with that 'admission,' sir."

"I'm afraid *not*, Mr. Maitland. However, let us turn to the question of your researches into this matter. I understand—"

That brought Sir Nicholas to his feet again, this time in a hurry. "I protest, m'lud! This is a matter with which the court is not concerned."

The judge's inquiring gaze traveled back to Bruce Halloran. "Can the prosecution justify the question?"

"In the peculiar circumstances, m'lud—"

"Irrelevant!" snapped Sir Nicholas. "There is nothing

odd in Maitland helping me in the preparation of a case."
He turned towards the judge with an expressive gesture.
"M'lud, I must ask you—"

"I think I must sustain this objection, Mr. Halloran,"
said Carruthers. "I do not feel it would be proper for me to
allow you to follow this line of questioning."

Sir Nicholas sat down again. Halloran said with an air of
great amiability, "Then perhaps I may return to this question of truth and falsehood, upon which we find it so difficult to reach an agreement." He looked at Antony for a
moment, and then turned a little, so that his remarks had the
effect of being addressed to the court, rather than to the witness. "Let me set out the situation . . .

"On the one hand we have a man of mature years, a man
who has held a responsible position for a long time, a man of
deep religious convictions. Above all, a man completely un-
acquainted with any of the protagonists in this unhappy affair. I am speaking of the Crown's witness, John Procter
Armstrong." He paused, for effect. Antony opened his
mouth to comment, caught his uncle's eye and thought better of it. Halloran went on. "We have heard a great deal
from the present witness about the difference between 'lies'
and 'deliberate falsehoods.' I do not think we need concern
ourselves overmuch with these distinctions. On the other
hand, therefore, we have a young man, intimately acquainted with the son of the accused; a young man who, I
understand, spent (most praiseworthily, I am sure) nearly
seven years of his life in the army, where great pains were
no doubt taken to instill into him a single-mindedness of
purpose, a disregard of anything but the objective in mind.
Could it be thought wonderful, or indeed very reprehensi-
ble, if such a young man—believing in the innocence of his
friend's father—should decide that the end justified the
means, and take his own course to secure an acquittal?"
Halloran had been making a jury speech, but nobody
seemed to notice it except Sir Nicholas, and he held his
peace.

Counsel for the Crown turned back to Antony to ask his
final question. "Which of these two people, Mr. Maitland,
do you think the court is most likely to consider has—shall
we say?—prevaricated in giving evidence?"

Antony looked at him for a moment, and he was very angry. He knew it was damnably clever; and he knew, in the face of this, just how much chance he had of being believed—knew, too (though he must not think of it now), how great an effect the argument, if it gained credence, would have on his own career. He said, scornfully, "Oh, c-come off it, Halloran! You d-don't really believe all this—this eyewash, yourself, you know!" He saw counsel's look of astonishment (Halloran could not have been more surprised had a pet lamb suddenly snarled at him), and then turned his eyes towards Sir Nicholas, whose expression was more than usually austere. He looked down at his hands, and found that he was clutching the rail in front of him, and deliberately relaxed his grip. And he missed altogether the sudden relaxation of his uncle's expression, and the quick, amused glance which passed between him and the prosecuting counsel. Somebody laughed at the back of the court and stopped again abruptly. There was an appreciable pause before Carruthers spoke, and when he did Antony—still contemplating his hands—heard the severity in his voice and did not see the laughter that had transformed his rather solemn countenance.

"The court will accept your apology, Mr. Maitland."

Antony looked up at that. He said, "Thank you, sir," and left it there—though he was well aware that this was not precisely what the judge had meant.

There was a further, slightly uncomfortable, silence before Bruce Halloran said briskly, "Do you recall the question, Mr. Maitland, or shall I repeat it?"

"Your question concerned probabilities, I think." It was hard to tell whether his tone was weary, or merely bored by the reiteration. "I cannot answer for what others may, or may not, believe."

"So we make no progress. You have called Mr. Armstrong a liar by implication, but you seem very anxious not to repeat that accusation in plain language." He stopped for a moment and eyed the witness appraisingly, but said at last, in the manner of one who washes his hands of a hopeless affair, "Very well, then, since you are still reluctant we must leave it at that. The court will draw its own conclusions." He sat down abruptly.

Antony glanced across at his uncle, and received a shake of the head to his unspoken inquiry. He bowed to the judge, and made his way back to his place. Carruthers glanced at the clock, and said briskly, "The court will adjourn . . ."

CHAPTER 17

IT TOOK Dennis Dowling some little time to extricate himself from the crowds in and around the Old Bailey, but when he had done so he made the best speed he could to Sir Nicholas's chambers in the Inner Temple. He found Sir Nicholas and Derek Stringer seated at the desk, with the proof of Eve Meadows's statement between them; they had been arguing halfheartedly about possibilities, but Antony, who stood in his favorite place by the window, had not spoken since they returned from court. He was trying, a little desperately, to bring some sort of order to the turmoil of his thoughts, but so far he had had no success at all.

Dennis was agitated, and past caring that this should be evident. He said, with an odd concession to politeness, "I'm sorry to disturb you." And then, as though he could no longer contain himself, "It was pretty bad, wasn't it?"

"Pretty bad," said Sir Nicholas. Stringer got up, and pushed a chair towards the newcomer.

Antony turned from the window, and said abruptly, "I'm sorry, Dennis."

"I never thought, you see," said Dennis, "that they mightn't believe you."

Sir Nicholas sat back in his chair, and picked up a pencil. "I have never attempted to minimize to you the strength of the case against your father," he said.

"No, I know. I know what you said. And I've been worried, of course. Only I didn't realize until today—"

Sir Nicholas looked at Stringer and waved a hand in the direction of the corner cupboard. "Brandy, I think," he said. Derek got up obediently. "And you musn't think, even now," he went on, turning back to Dennis, "that the verdict is a foregone conclusion."

Antony settled his shoulder against the end of the bookcase. "You're not saying you think they believed me?" he inquired; his voice sounded strangely detached, as compared with his look of strain.

"No, I don't think so. Halloran is not the man to lose a hand when he holds all the trumps. All the same, I think you played your cards well enough to make the jury feel some doubts as to Dowling's guilt."

"Do you indeed?" said Antony; and his tone was disbelieving.

"And you must remember," Sir Nicholas continued, addressing himself to the newcomer, "from your father's point of view, a reasonable doubt is all we need." His eyes moved, until they met his nephew's carefully expressionless look. "We'll pull through somehow," he added, deliberately.

Whatever Antony had expected from his uncle it had not been sympathy, however indirectly expressed. Something in the nature of blistering comment; and on the whole, he thought he would have found it less disconcerting. "You can give me some of that brandy, if you like," he said to Derek, who grinned at him and obliged.

Dennis meanwhile had taken the proffered chair, and had regained sufficient control to apologize again for his intrusion. "I expect you're busy," he said, and looked curiously at the papers on the desk. Sir Nicholas shook his head.

"Not at this stage. It isn't as if there'd been any unexpected developments today."

"I see." He drank a little of the brandy, and added carefully: "But tomorrow . . . what's going to happen?"

"Eve Meadows's evidence. The jury may believe her, after all."

"And then we . . . just wait." He put down the glass, and said violently, "I shouldn't have come, I know that. There's nothing to be done or said." He looked again at Antony, who did not meet his eyes. "And I should be sorry, we've caused you enough trouble, between us. Only I don't seem to be able to think of anything but Joe. And my mother—she's just about reached the end.''

Antony looked at him then. ''I'm sorry,'' he said again.

''You needn't be. You've done your best, after all.''

Antony stiffened. Once before, in a moment of failure, he had been tossed those words for comfort; and then, as now, they had seemed the final insult, the ultimate condemnation. He said, through his teeth, ''I suppose you had to throw that up at me.''

''I don't understand.'' Dennis was genuinely bewildered.

''I know who killed James Winter,'' said Antony, slowly. ''I can't prove it; I don't even know why. That's the best I could do. I should have left it alone!'' He knew as he spoke that he was wrong, and he turned on his heel and looked out of the window unseeingly. And he remembered—was it foolish to remember?—that Jenny had once said to him, ''it isn't failing that matters; it's trying and trying and never giving up.'' They had both been young then; the words were childish, perhaps, but for all that they contained a truth which he knew he must never deny.

Behind him Sir Nicholas was drawing on his blotter, Derek had gone back to the cupboard, and was helping himself to brandy, and Dennis was talking at random. ''I know how you feel. I keep thinking, myself, about that afternoon, you know. After all, I was practically on the spot, and I wonder . . . if I'd not spent so long looking for that wretched schedule . . . if I'd left the strongroom sooner, I might have heard something—''

Antony unhitched his shoulder from the bookcase and turned back to the room again. ''That schedule,'' he said, and something in his tone made his uncle glance sharply in his direction. ''The list of the contents of Amelia Prentiss's deed box,'' he added thoughtfully. ''Tell me about it,'' he demanded.

''But it wasn't there!'' Dennis seemed to find the request unreasonable, and his voice rose protestingly.

''Well, what was there then?'' He added impatiently, as the other seemed to be turning the query over slowly in his mind, ''Damn you, Dennis! Think!''

''There were the deeds, of course, the ones I was looking

for, I mean. And several other bundles of title deeds; she had quite a bit of property. And some leases. There were some share certificates, too, I can't remember exactly—"

"You needn't. Go on!" His tone was peremptory, and Dennis glanced at him uneasily.

"There was one very odd-looking document—her parents' marriage settlement. I noticed it particularly, it was beautifully engrossed. And the application for letters of administration. And her birth and death certificates. And her passport, very out-of-date." He was speaking slowly, and now he looked round with an air of bewilderment. "But I don't see—"

"And was that all?"

"Yes, that was all. Except—"

"Except what?"

"There was a cover—one of those pocket-sort-of-things that insurance policies come in sometimes. I remember it because it looked amateurish, and I remember wondering why Mr. Winter—"

"What did it contain?"

"Well, nothing, that's what I was telling you. It had held her will, but of course that wasn't there any longer—"

"You incredible idiot!" said Antony, angrily. "Don't you know that Amelia Prentiss died intestate?"

"Steady!" said Sir Nicholas. "After all, the will may have been destroyed before she died."

"Do you think so, sir? *I* think it all fits too neatly for there not to be a pattern. After all, the schedule was missing."

"We made another one," said Dennis, helpfully. "Miss Harris said she thought J.W. must have taken it, he asked for that deed box the day before he died. But it never turned up among his things."

"We can get possession of the wrapper, I suppose," said Sir Nicholas. He shook his head at his nephew. "But even so, it won't be proof, you know."

"I know, sir. But at least, this tells us *why*. And that gives you a line, doesn't it? Something to work on." His tone was less positive than his words, and his uncle smiled at him.

"Very well. We aren't finished yet. Tell me, Antony, what do you suggest?"

But Antony was retreating to the window again. "Your pigeon, sir. Yours and Stringer's. Don't you think?"

The newspapers next morning were boisterous; and while prudently refraining from comment were able, nonetheless, to make much of the "conflict of evidence" and the "clash between defense witness and opposing counsel." Antony accompanied his uncle to court with a grim look about his mouth; and after a while Sir Nicholas took his arm—an unaccustomed gesture.

"It is of little use to say 'don't worry,' " he remarked. "But if it is any comfort to you, at least we'll go down fighting." Antony grinned at him and tried to shut out the nagging echo of Halloran's words that was sounding in his brain. His uncle's phrase substituted itself; a fighting chance, he thought, isn't a very good one.

Eve Meadows seemed self-possessed that morning, and took the oath in a clear voice. Sir Nicholas gave her her head, and though there was one tricky moment when it seemed she was going to jib at mentioning her visit to Charles Prentiss's office and the subsequent investigations which took her to the head of the private stair, on the whole she told her story well enough. There was not, at any time, any danger of her saying too much. Sir Nicholas directed a look of triumph in the direction of his opponent, which was not altogether assumed, and prepared to elaborate.

"We should like to hear a little more about the man you saw, Miss Meadows. You saw, you said, very little of him?"

"At first, only his arm and shoulder. Then, when I called out, he moved and I saw his head—the silhouette of his head—for a moment."

"And—this is a question to which the prosecution is going to ask you to pay particular attention, Miss Meadows—are you quite certain about the time you mentioned?"

"I saw him at four-fifteen. And I'm quite sure about it . . . not more than a minute, either way."

"When you called out, what did you say?"

She hesitated there, and looked around her with the first signs of panic she had shown that morning. "Charles," she said at last, but her voice was almost a whisper. Mr. Justice Carruthers leaned forward.

"Your witness really must speak up, Sir Nicholas. The court cannot hear her."

Eve looked up. "I said 'Charles!' " she repeated.

"You thought, in fact, that it was Mr. Charles Prentiss?"

"Yes . . . yes, I thought that." She paused again, and added more firmly, "You see, Mr. Winter didn't like people to use that stairway; only, of course, Mr. Prentiss being his partner—"

"The assumption was quite natural. Well, now, Miss Meadows, supposing I tell you that I know—and can prove if necessary—that Charles Prentiss, on the day in question, was wearing a sports jacket and a shirt with a soft collar. If I tell you that, and add that the jacket was made of a light-colored tweed, could that have been what you saw?"

"No, it couldn't. Not possibly."

"A dark material, you said?"

"Yes."

"Then let us see if we can assist your memory. My client now—will you please look at the prisoner, Miss Meadows—would you say it could have been him you saw?" (And heaven send, thought Antony, she doesn't agree with him, just to be done with it!)

He need not have worried. Eve took her time, but she shook her head decisively. "Not possibly," she said again.

"Mr. Dowling is a well-known figure; you think, perhaps, you would have known him?"

("Do *you* not think m'lud," said Halloran, with an illusory air of diffidence, "that my friend is leading his witness?" The judge turned his melancholy regard on Sir Nicholas, who inclined his head and rephrased his question without argument.)

"Can you give a reason for your opinion, Miss Meadows?"

She was studying Joseph Dowling doubtfully, and the actor looked back at her gravely. It seemed to Antony that his expression was one of interest, perhaps even of sympathy; or was it merely that Eve Meadows was an exceptionally good-looking young woman? She said, at last, "The man I saw wasn't bald."

Halloran got up again, at his most friendly. "M'lud—"

"Something is worrying you, Mr. Halloran?"

"Irregular, m'lud," he said, and waved a languid hand to include both defense counsel and the witness.

Carruthers was puzzled. "I find Sir Nicholas in order," he said. "He has, after all, given his witness every opportunity of identifying the prisoner."

"But m'lud—"

"No, Mr. Halloran." Counsel sat down again, and Sir Nicholas took a moment to grin derisively in his direction.

"Then we may proceed," he stated. "Now, Miss Meadows—still on the subject of the man you saw at four-fifteen on the afternoon of James Winter's death—let us take this exercise a stage further. I should explain, m'lud, to forestall the objection which my learned friend has doubtless on the tip of his tongue, that I am following the Crown's own line of argument: that the murderer was either someone in the office, or someone who visited the office after two o'clock that afternoon."

"I think we understand that, Sir Nicholas." Carruthers glanced at the jury, rather as though he were daring them to disagree. Antony, following his look, found himself unable to decide the degree of accuracy of the judge's statement.

"There are now present," said Sir Nicholas, "several of the persons who visited James Winter on the afternoon of his death." He paused, and looked around him; but it was evident that he, at least, had little faith in the jury's understanding, for he went on, "The prosecution has very ably made the point—"

"M'lud!" Halloran was plaintive. "I must protest at this . . . this sneering—"

"Sneering?" Defense counsel seemed shocked by the suggestion. "I assure you, m'lud, I have the greatest admiration for the way my learned friend has handled his most unpromising material. "

"Nevertheless, Sir Nicholas—"

"I shall be most happy to withdraw anything which might distress my friend. But surely he cannot object to my emphasizing a point which he himself has made."

"The court will accept the point, Sir Nicholas; but—I think, don't you?—without embellishment."

"By all means, m'lud. I merely wish to remind the jury of the evidence of the Crown's witness: that the door from James Winter's room onto the private stair was locked at 2 P.M., and that (accepting also the fact that the murdered man himself was unlikely to have unlocked it) there were a limited number of people who could have done so." He paused invitingly, but Halloran was silent. He had now assumed a look of weary boredom, but Antony thought he was puzzled. "But I will hasten to my point," said Sir Nicholas. And suddenly, as he spoke, there was tension in the court, and an odd sort of hush, as though every one of the company, from the judge on the bench to the most crowded spectator in the farthest corner, was holding his breath.

Counsel went on, as though unaware of the suspense he had himself induced. "Would you stand up, Mr. Green, so that this lady can see you." Back where the witnesses sat, Arthur Green came to his feet; if little of his customary jauntiness had remained when he left the witness stand the previous day, now there was nothing. He was undeniably nervous, and though he tried to meet Eve Meadows's look squarely he did not succeed in conveying anything but a rather uneasy defiance. "Miss Meadows," said Sir Nicholas, "could this be the man you saw?"

"Oh, no." She was in no doubt about her answer; and Green's look of relief would have been, at any other time, laughable.

"Why?" insisted Sir Nicholas.

"Well, I think . . . of course, I know now . . . it's his hair that is different."

"Could you explain that for us?"

"I . . . I mean, the other man's hair wasn't so dark—at least, I don't think so. And it wasn't so smooth as . . . as Green's."

"You are quite sure about that. You are thinking, no doubt, of the silhouette you saw."

"Yes, I am."

"The other man had—shall we say?—thick, wiry hair." The girl closed her eyes and took a firm grip on the rail in front of her. "Like Charles Prentiss's hair, for instance?" he added, gently.

Eve opened her eyes at that, and she looked at the prisoner again before she replied. When she turned back to Sir Nicholas again her eyes were reproachful, and she said grudgingly, "Well, I suppose so."

"But we have decided it could not have been Mr. Charles Prentiss whom you saw. Will you look then at the gentleman next to Mr. Green (you may sit down now, Mr. Green, I am grateful for your help): the gentleman at the end of the row." Stanley Prentiss came slowly to his feet. "I am sorry to trouble you," apologized Sir Nicholas, "But for the purpose of our experiment . . . could that be the man you saw?"

Eve was silent for a long moment. She looked bewildered now, and troubled. "He's taller than Charles," she said doubtfully. "But he's very like—"

"You were looking down" Counsel reminded her. "It would be difficult to judge height."

"Yes . . . it could be . . . but—" She turned back to Sir Nicholas with an air of helplessness. Stanley Prentiss stood like a statue. "Why should it have been him?" she asked, and her tone held an appeal. Antony realized suddenly she had never believed it had been anyone but Charles that she saw . . . that she didn't believe it now! He thought uneasily, this is the end, there is nothing more we can do: we have brought them to this point, and perhaps the jury will feel a doubt, but there is no certainty . . . nothing like proof.

Sir Nicholas was saying blandly, "I am not concerned with reasons—"Well, that sounded well, but it meant that they were beaten. Stanley's tension was relaxing again—not a nice position, but why should he worry, the innocent victim of a rather shabby trick? Halloran was on his feet; the judge's eyes moved inquiringly from the defense to the prosecuting counsel. And Eve Meadows threw out her hands suddenly, in a gesture that was strangely appealing.

"Sir Nicholas—" she said.

"Yes, Miss Meadows?"

"What should I do? I can't—" She stopped, and looked again at Joseph Dowling. A moment stretched endlessly while they regarded each other. Antony thought, bewildered, he's *sorry* for her! And Eve said, in a voice that was no more than a whisper, yet clearly audible because of the stillness of the room: "I thought nothing mattered. But they'll find him guilty . . . and I know he didn't do it!"

Halloran's mouth stayed open on a protest that was never uttered. Sir Nicholas said gently, "What do you know?" And perhaps only his nephew, in all the crowded court, heard the brittle tone in his voice and knew him to be shaken.

Eve looked across briefly to where Charles was sitting, as though she were asking for his understanding. Stanley, still on his feet, was ignored now as though he had not been, a moment before, the focus of the court's attention. Antony watched his uncle's hands tighten, and heard the sharp sound as the pencil he was holding snapped between his fingers. Sir Nicholas still presented an inscrutable face to the court, and he maintained his composure as the witness turned back to him and said, a little wildly, "I knew it was Charles I saw—even when you said you believed him. Not just seeing him, it was so brief a glimpse, I could have been mistaken. But there was the paper, there on the stairs; and I don't see who else could have dropped it."

"What paper?" queried the judge with sudden impatience. His voice was loud in the silent room. Eve turned to him and spread her hands in the same odd gesture she had used before, as though disclaiming responsibility for what she was about to say.

"It was a list of deeds, my lord," she said. "But it had come out of Amelia Prentiss's deed box, and I don't see who else would have been interested in that."

Sir Nicholas drew a deep breath. "You were not familiar with the disposition of Mrs. Prentiss's estate, Miss Meadows?" he asked. And as the girl shook her head he added, turning to the judge, "If my friend does not wish to cross-examine, m'lud, I shall ask your permission to recall one of the prosecution witnesses, Charles Prentiss, who can inform the court on this matter."

Stanley Prentiss sat down again slowly, and clasped his hands between his knees, and fixed his eyes on the dusty floor of the courtroom. Carruthers turned his melancholy regard on counsel for the Crown.

"Do *you* understand what all this is about, Mr. Halloran?" he queried, plaintively.

CHAPTER 18

IT WAS TWO days later when Derek Stringer, admitted to the Kempenfeldt Square house by Gibbs just after dinner, was greeted with the information that Sir Nicholas was not at home, "but I think Mr. Maitland is in the study, sir."

He found Antony just replacing the books he had been consulting. "Did you know, they've arrested Stanley Prentiss?" he demanded.

"Sykes rang up," said Antony. He went over to the desk and began to pile together the papers he had been annotating. He did not look at his companion, but added after a moment, "He kept his nerve, it seems; but that was a ghastly business in court!"

"Ghastly!" agreed Derek. He sounded enthusiastic, and the other man looked up and grinned at him. His own feeling of compunction was irrational, no doubt, but the closing scenes of Joseph Dowling's trial remained only too vividly in his mind. There had been no dramatics, of course; Halloran had nodded his agreement of the defense counsel's request, and Charles—white as a sheet now, and tense-looking—had stumbled his way back to the witness box to give the evidence that would damn his cousin. Through it all, Stanley Prentiss had sat quietly, almost stolidly; only Antony, catching his eye at one point, had seen there comprehension and the beginnings of fear. As Charles finished, Sir Nicholas had looked up inquiringly at the judge, and there had been a brief adjournment. "I knew what he was up to, of course," said Derek. "But I wonder what the jury made of it all."

"Lord knows," said Antony. "They were being offered

an alternative, a man on the private stair at the material time, who might not have been Joe Dowling. Then Eve gave us something further: a motive for someone who could have been on the scene, and whose appearance, moreover, didn't outrage her recollections of the man she saw.''

"What did Sykes have to say?'' asked Derek. He had perched himself on the arm of one of the chairs, and Antony left the desk now and came over to the empty hearth.

"Nothing much. Just—their inquiries had proceeded to a stage where the public prosecutor felt an arrest would be justified. *You* know!''

"Yes, I see. Did Briggs send his love?''

"I gather not. Sykes himself was faintly reproachful; he now seems to feel I knew something all along that would have kept them from making a mistake.''

"Well, I've wondered myself,'' said Stringer frankly, "just how you knew.''

"Nothing very clever,'' said Antony. He sounded impatient. "Willett's evidence left us with two possible groups of people: staff and afternoon visitors. Armstrong's story, as corroborated by young Harvey, gave us a man who went in by the private door at about eight minutes past four, which seemed like a visitor, or Charles Prentiss returning. But my own observations ruled out anyone I knew well by sight: Charles or Joe Dowling, but not Stanley Prentiss whom I hadn't seen since he was about fifteen and I was still younger. He was still a possibility, and so—of course—was Green.''

"But you ruled him out, finally. Why?''

"I thought about his motive, which seemed obvious at first sight—that Winter had found out he was up to something. But my impression was very strong that his own answer to that situation would have been flight, not violence. So if he had resorted to strong measures I felt it was possibly because of pressure from his associates, which in turn seemed to suggest that they found the Camden Mews premises convenient and didn't want to give them up.''

"Yes, but I still don't see—''

"I told you when I visited him the second time he was moving. But at that point the inquiries couldn't have worried him unduly, and Joe was under arrest. It seemed unlikely that he would have yielded to pressure in the matter of killing J.W., and then defied his associates by doing the very thing they wished to prevent.''

''But you still didn't have a motive for Stanley Prentiss,'' Derek pointed out.

''Don't be so reasonable. He had, after all, some previous connection with the firm, and with J.W. It seemed more probable—''

''Yes, I suppose so. That chap Green, though: I wish I knew what he and Winter had to say to each other.''

Antony grinned. His mood seemed to have lightened now, and he embarked on this part of his story with obvious enjoyment. ''I can tell you, as it happens. I was a bit intrigued myself, so I went to see him yesterday.''

''Did you, though?''

''Yes, Jenny was furious. She said: 'After all, you *knew* he was a gang.' But I wanted to know—''

''But what on earth did you say to him?'' Derek demanded. ''I understand you are a black marketeer, and have been engaged in hijacking stolen goods from your even-more-reprehensible colleagues?''

''More or less. He's a queer chap, I can't help liking him. When he saw I wasn't proposing to take a high moral tone he was frank enough. Apparently Winter happened to be passing when somebody had left the garage doors ajar. I expect he only gave a second look because he knew the address, and then he looked again because he thought Green was doing something or other contrary to the conditions of the lease. And then he went away and thought about it, and sent the message that he wanted to see him.''

''What was he going to do?''

''Give him twenty-four hours' start, and then tell the police.''

''Why on earth—?''

''He said he knew Green's father, was sorry to see a son of his—you know the sort of rot.''

''But of all the coincidences!''

''You haven't seen the full beauty of it yet. If I'd known there was even this rather tenuous connection between them, it would have invalidated the whole of the argument that led me to Stanley Prentiss.''

"So it would!" said Derek, and began to laugh.

"I must say," remarked Antony, "I'm a little shaken by J.W.'s attitude. I thought he had more respect for law and order."

"What about you? Are you going to give the police a tip about this fellow?"

"I am not."

"Antisocial behavior, Maitland!"

"Ha!" said Antony.

"Isn't he even proposing to move now?"

"Well, I don't think so." He had the grace to sound a trifle apologetic. "I did suggest he might give up his present occupation, but he didn't think much of the idea."

"You shock me," said Derek, placidly.

"Then you'd better come upstairs and talk to Jenny." He unhitched his shoulder from the mantel. "This is a social call, I hope; I mean, you don't want Uncle Nick?"

"Not at the moment."

"And just as well. He is not, I must admit, at his most amiable just now."

"I should have thought—"

"But perhaps you didn't see the paper that hailed him as 'the greatest advocate of the age.' He's been like a bear with a sore head ever since!"

Derek grinned. "I can imagine," he said, with feeling.

They were on their way upstairs when they heard Gibbs cross the hall to open the front door. Antony said, "Go on up, there's a good chap," when he heard Dennis Dowling's voice, and leaned over the bannisters to call to the newcomer. Derek went on obediently up the stairs.

Dennis was inclined to be deprecating, but his apologies were brushed firmly aside. "I'm glad you came. Meg's here, I think—at least, she was an hour ago."

"Then I expect they're still talking," said Dennis, ungallantly. He followed Antony up the stairs, but paused on the landing. "I wanted to tell you . . . Joe's dagger turned up again."

"No! Where was it?"

"At the bottom of a trunk his dresser swears hasn't been unpacked for at least six months. And a fine time we've had convincing him it's just one of those things, and not part of a dark scheme for his undoing.''

"I gather he finds himself in form again."

Dennis grinned reluctantly. "Never better. Though he says the papers have disserted at such length upon his innocence the last few days that if there's much more he'll begin to doubt his ability to play the villain. They're reopening on Monday, did Meg tell you?"

"I'm glad to hear it."

"Well, so am I. Joe tends to be even more troublesome when he's resting—and that's saying something." He began to move towards the door, but Antony stopped him with a gesture.

"There's one thing I wanted to tell you—about Eve Meadows—"

"What about her?" Dennis's tone was flat; Antony wondered if he could really be as disinterested as he sounded.

"She did her best to help your father when it came to the point. In the circumstances, I shouldn't think too much about her former attitude."

"What circumstances?" said Dennis, deliberately uncooperative.

"She's in love with Charles," said Antony, annoyed. "She thought her evidence would incriminate him."

"And he's married to Mary Winter. Poor Eve."

"I don't doubt she'll survive." Antony's tone was tart, and the other man smiled at him.

"Was that what you wanted to tell me?"

"Not exactly. I thought you might like to know she's starting work in Bellerby's office next week." He cocked an inquiring eye. "Interested?"

"Not particularly. No . . . really!" he added, seeing Antony's skeptical look.

Meg was still there, and Derek had already made himself at home. Antony had by now become used to the alteration in the girl's appearance. She was no longer out-of-date, and the effect was startling, but only to one who knew her. A stranger would see only a quietly dressed girl whose clothes seemed so right as to be almost unnoticeable. What *was* surprising was that Dennis seemed unaware of the transformation. He greeted Jenny with his usual politeness, and Meg with the offhand manner that characterized his attitude towards her.

"You seem to be living here these days. However, you won't be idle much longer, that's one good thing."

"Well, and if I've been idle, what about you?" Meg retorted. "Not that you know a thing about it, for I haven't seen you for weeks." She paused, and then added with her grandest air, "I hope now you'll be able to give your mind to your studies again."

Dennis accepted whisky. "Have a heart, Meg," he said. "I'm nowhere near ready for the exam; it hardly seems worth while going on, really."

"That," said Jenny, "is a very defeatist attitude." Antony recognized one of his uncle's dicta, but Dennis was startled, and began to look quite hunted.

"Miss Harris has taken to shaking her head and muttering to herself every time she sees me," he remarked, gloomily.

"I shouldn't worry too much about that. She always expects the worst; every articled clerk they've had since I remember has been foredoomed to failure, in her estimation. And most of them got through."

Dennis, however, declined to be cheered about his prospects. Meg said, "There's one thing I *do* want to know about Mr. Winter," and neatly conveyed the impression that she wasn't really the least bit curious, but felt it was time the subject was changed.

Antony, feeling Jenny's eye rather anxiously upon him, asked—with quite reasonable amiability, "What is it?"

"Well, it was just—I don't quite understand about the motive. Mr. Stringer had just told us—" Derek and Jenny both began to talk at once.

"Stanley got the money because they thought there wasn't a will—" said Jenny; and, "Mrs. Prentiss hadn't really died intestate—" said Derek. They both stopped, and looked at each other, and Antony took up the tale.

"It's mostly surmise, of course. The only fact we've got is that Amelia Prentiss did make a will—according to the endorsement on the pocket that was found in the deed box, she made it in 1930. At that time, Miss Harris tells me, her affairs were looked after by old Mr. Curtis, and he mentioned to her frequently the necessity for making proper arrangements. I imagine her as a stubborn old lady, not wanting to take his advice but too sensible not to see it was good. So she went out to the post office and got a form, and never said a word about what she had done.''

"Horrible!" said Dennis, suddenly. The others looked at him, but he seemed to be expressing a perfectly serious opinion. The solicitor-side of his nature, Antony thought, must temporarily have come uppermost.

"It seems she was in the habit of keeping all kinds of things in the deed box, so she put the will in among a bundle of old documents and I expect she just forgot that she'd never told anybody about it.''

"I expect at first," said Jenny, "she enjoyed the feeling she'd been too clever for him. And then she forgot afterwards—''

"Probably. However it was, Mr. Curtis retired, and passed on the information to J.W. that the old lady hadn't made a will, and I expect J.W. spoke to her about it, too, and she never contradicted him. So when she died they applied for letters of administration, and that was that—Stanley got the whole works. And they needed the money, and his wife in particular was happy to think of all the things they could do with it. He was fond of his wife . . . poor devil!" he added. And was silent.

Meg said, in a small voice, "It's so dreadful for her. What will she do?''

"What can she do? I expect she has some family," said Antony. He did not find the thought agreeable, and it was not one he had any wish to see fixed in his wife's mind. "But about what happened at the office—I had a talk with Miss Harris, and she says J.W. was dealing with the estate, and she knew the details, and so did Miss Bell; but neither you, Dennis, nor Eve Meadows had anything to do with it. Except that—one day when Miss Bell was away with a cold—Eve typed the schedule of the contents of the deed box; but she, of course, didn't realize there was anything odd about there being a will there. So the list was put away, and nobody ever looked at it until the question of selling some property came up; and that, of course, was *after* the letters of administration had been granted.''

"It seems a bit careless . . . not to have made sure," said Jenny doubtfully.

"Not really. I expect J.W. was quite sure, and had all the steps he must take clear in his own mind even before the old lady died. And then—well, it's anybody's guess what happened. He may just have looked in the deed box because the house was being sold—"

"I think," interrupted Dennis, "from what Miss Harris said today he must have had some reason for asking for it when he did. I mean, the question of selling hadn't got to the stage where the deeds were needed."

"There was one thing Sykes said that I think might be the answer. He said: 'Old Mrs. Prentiss had kept a diary for years.' So perhaps he glanced through one or two of them, and chanced upon the entry for the day she made her will."

"It's the sort of thing she'd be bound to record," said Derek reflectively.

"Yes, and that would account for Miss Hunt's burglary," said Jenny. "I mean, Stanley must have taken the will away after . . . after Mr. Winter was dead, you know; and he didn't notice the schedule was with it, and that's why he dropped it. But if something had been said about the diary, he might have thought it was at the Purley house."

"I'd have thought he'd have looked at his grandmother's house first."

"I expect he did; after all, he'd every reason for going over there—it belonged to him."

"J.W. wouldn't have left it there," said Dennis. "I expect he took it home with him and put it away somewhere safe."

"Sykes didn't say, but I expect so too. Anyway, that's how it was: J.W. got wind of the will, and found it in the deed box. He'd want to break it to Stanley before he told anybody else; besides, if I know him, he felt put out at the mistake having been made. But having once got it off his chest, he was most likely making notes of what had to be done in that matter—" He let the sentence trail, and got up in a determined manner. "And that's enough of that, my children. Who's ready for another drink?"

"There is still one thing," said Dennis. "What will happen now . . . about Amelia Prentiss's estate, I mean?"

"Nothing, I should say. What do you think, Derek? After all, nobody will ever know what her will said."

"But you can't profit by a crime," objected Meg. "I'm sure I read that somewhere."

"No, but Stanley isn't accused of Amelia's death," Derek pointed out. "That's what you meant, isn't it?"

"That's what I meant," said Antony. "So perhaps—"

"Poor Muriel," sighed Jenny.

They left the subject after that, to Antony's relief, and the talk returned to the affairs of Joseph Dowling and the new run of *Macbeth*. After a while Dennis got up to take his leave. "Come along, Meg. I'll take you home."

"I'll get my hat," said Meg docilely.

Dennis looked round vaguely, obviously expecting the old blue beret to be thrown down on a chair somewhere handy. But Meg marched out decidedly, and was gone for several minutes. He scrambled to his feet again as she returned, and then for the first time that evening really looked at her. "Angels and ministers of grace," he exclaimed. "Where *did* you get that hat?"

"At Simonette's," said Jenny, maddeningly literal. "Meg should never go anywhere else," she added idiotically. "Simonette understands her."

"Well . . . well . . . well," said Dennis. He looked her up and down, from the engagingly simple little hat to the sheer stockings and plain well-cut court shoes. "Well!" he said again. His gaze came back to the hat. "Who told you it was fashionable to wear dog-daisies?" he inquired disagreeably.

"How ignorant," said Meg, with her nose in the air. "They're marguerites."

"Same thing, I'm afraid," Antony told her; and Derek interposed with an air of enlightenment, "A trade mark, Miss Hamilton? It's a charming idea—and looks charming, too."

Meg smiled at him warmly, and said, "They're nice, aren't they? Jenny thought it, of course."

"I might have known!" Dennis exploded suddenly. "As if Meg weren't enough of a handful already," he added, bitterly.

After that they went away. Antony, surveying his wife

over the empty glasses, shook his head sadly. "You'll come
to a bad end, my girl, if you go on like this."

"I only went shopping with her," said Jenny, on the de-
fensive. "Somebody had to."

"Very likely. But you know as well as I do, love, that you
had the possible effect on Dennis in mind all the time."

"Well, at least he saw her today. I bet he's never done
that before."

"Dennis has enough troubles, without you trying to en-
tangle him with an actress."

"But she's nice, Antony. Don't you like her? And she
needs someone to look after her."

"I can see the poor chap had better give up all idea of a
career of his own. Joe Dowling and Meg look like being a
full-time job between them."

"Well, I think so."

"And don't you realize he's only just stopped being in
love with Eve Meadows? That is, if he has stopped," he
added, uncertainly.

Jenny was firm. "The sooner he gets over her the better.
He needs another interest, and you can't say," she added,
with a wicked look, "I've not done my best to give him
one."

"Hopeless," said Antony.

"And I was thinking . . . about Eve," said Jenny. She
eyed their guest consideringly. "We might introduce Derek
to her," she added.

"Now that's an excellent idea," said Antony. "Especially as she seems to fancy legal types."

Derek declined to be drawn. He raised his glass to his
hostess with a look of affection. "It's no good . . . all the
nicest girls were married years ago. But what's this about
young Dowling's 'troubles'? I should have thought—"

They were still explaining the Dowling ménage to him—
in chorus—when Sir Nicholas arrived, resplendent in evening dress and looking (as Jenny did not hesitate to inform
him, severely) distinctly sleek and well fed.

"I've been dining with Bruce Halloran," said Sir Nicholas, sinking into his favorite corner of the sofa and eyeing
them benevolently.

"Have you, sir?" Antony sounded cautious. He had

known some qualms since the trial ended. His uncle seemed to have mellowed now, but there was no telling how Halloran might have taken what had occurred.

"It was a most fortunate occurrence," said Sir Nicholas. "Mrs. Stokes had gone out—why was she out on a Friday evening, Jenny?"

"It was the last night of *Hearts and Flowers* at the Odeon, Uncle Nick."

"Then that is explained. But I was telling you, I had just declared my independence by instructing Gibbs to give a particularly revolting blancmange to the cat, and the atmosphere was frigid, when Halloran telephoned. His invitation was most welcome." He turned to Derek. "Does your landlady feed you well, Stringer?" he inquired.

"Reasonably well, sir."

"I can never understand," went on Sir Nicholas, waving away the decanter, "how a woman who generally cooks like an angel can perpetrate such horrors when called upon to leave me a cold collation. I hope you never give your husband blancmange, my dear."

"Never," said Jenny. "It's the first rule in the book."

"You reassure me. Now, there was something else—" He looked at his nephew. "Ah, yes, my conversation with Halloran." He seemed to be recalling it with gentle amusement. Antony was both uneasy and exasperated, but refrained from the questioning which he knew would only delay still further whatever disclosure his uncle might be about to make. "He has accepted a brief, he tells me, from Barton and Glossop," Sir Nicholas went on. "On behalf of a man named Hallett who is accused of arson, and whose defense promises to be an intricate affair."

"That's the fire at Reading, isn't it?" said Stringer, interested at once in this inside information.

"In Reading, in Carlisle, in Glasgow, in Middlesbrough, and—I believe—in Lincoln," corrected Sir Nicholas, "An ubiquitous gentleman, you'll perceive."

"What fun!" said Jenny. "At least—if nobody was killed."

"You seem to have rather a macabre taste in amusement, my dear, which I had not hitherto suspected. Nobody was killed."

"Never mind that, sir. What is all this: just general gossip from the bar—or is there a catch somewhere?"

"No catch," said his uncle. His tone was gently regretful. "Halloran—who really seems to be of a most magnanimous disposition—has indicated to Barton that he would welcome the chance of having you as his junior. Mallory may expect a call from their clerk tomorrow."

Derek whistled, and said, "What a bit of luck!"

Jenny said, "But that's *good,* isn't it, Uncle Nick?"

Antony, for once in his life, said nothing at all.

Sir Nicholas looked from one to the other of the three young people. "I thought you'd be surprised," he remarked, with satisfaction.